SPANISH PESOS

**Center Point
Large Print**

Also by William Colt MacDonald
and available from Center Point Large Print:

The Battle at Three-Cross
Master of the Mesa
Ranger Man
The Singing Scorpion
Powdersmoke Justice
Thunderbird Trail

**This Large Print Book carries the
Seal of Approval of N.A.V.H.**

SPANISH PESOS

William Colt MacDonald

CENTER POINT LARGE PRINT
THORNDIKE, MAINE

This Center Point Large Print edition
is published in the year 2012 by arrangement with
Golden West Literary Agency.

The text of this Large Print edition is unabridged.
In other aspects, this book may vary
from the original edition.
Printed in the United States of America
on permanent paper.
Set in 16-point Times New Roman type.

ISBN: 978-1-61173-336-5

Library of Congress Cataloging-in-Publication Data

MacDonald, William Colt, 1891–1968.
Spanish pesos / William Colt MacDonald. — Large print ed.
p. cm. — (Center Point large print edition)
ISBN 978-1-61173-336-5 (library binding : alk. paper)
1. Large type books. I. Title.
PS3525.A2122S68 2012
813′.52—dc23
                                            2011043460

I. THREAT OR CHALLENGE?

A MAN MAY SENSE DANGER before actually coming to grips with it, and still plunge recklessly on, heedless of the inner, intangible warning that may have caused the hair at the back of his neck to bristle, or sent tiny quivers of chill uncertainty coursing the length of his spine, disregarding that subtle extra sense which sometimes admonishes its owner to tread cautiously. Some men are built like that, their entire being so constituted that the slightest warning immediately takes on the form of a direct challenge, and they are no more able to resist the danger they inevitably attract, than a cowthief is able to resist the rustling of another man's beef stock.

Such a man was Andy Farlow, sometime bronc peeler, cowhand, miner of sorts; at present, a roving cowpuncher occupied with a rambling search for strange places and new trails and the ever-present urge to learn what lay beyond each morning's horizon. As though forecast by destiny, the hoofs of his wandering pony had brought him to Ensenajo, a Mexican settlement located some short distance below the international border line. Thirst had prompted the halt at Ensenajo; succeeding events prolonged the visit.

Andy Farlow sensed trouble almost as soon as he sighted the small *cantina*, situated a short

5

distance along the street from the spot at which he had swung down from his Heiser saddle. Loud voices from the interior of that squat adobe building reached his ears as he was leaving his pony at the nearest hitch-rack. Sounds carried far through the drowsy lull that enveloped Ensenajo, and were, during the *siesta* hour, distinctly unusual. Andy pricked up his ears and strode on. It didn't occur to him to seek another *cantina*; besides, there wasn't another *cantina* in Ensenajo.

Brown hills, which by sundown would turn to purple, surrounded the dusty pocket in which the town was located. Wood-cutters' trails crossed and criss-crossed those hills with their sparsely dotted brush and scrubby mesquite. The square, 'dobe buildings of the town itself were set down helter-skelter, and looked as though some gigantic hand, having employed them as dice, had ceased playing after one, final, careless throw. Mostly, the few inhabitants of Ensenajo were indoors, or dozing in the shadows between buildings. There was scarcely any sign of movement along the single winding street, excepting for the scratching of a scrawny hen that picked hopefully in the wagon-ruts and the stamping and switching of four horses beside Andy's at the hitch-rack.

Andy Farlow didn't care for this town of Ensenajo, but he was thirsty. There didn't seem to be any sign of water for his pony, either. That would have to be remedied later. Andy clumped his high heels along the warped twin planks that served as a sidewalk and approached the *cantina*. The voices from inside were sounding louder now, were being raised in some sort of altercation. The door of the saloon stood wide open. Myriad flies buzzed in the blistering sunshine before Andy's face as he strode across the rough board platform that fronted the entrance to the place. Not an inviting *cantina*, surely. Still, Andy Farlow was thirsty.

The angry voices inside the saloon ceased abruptly as Andy rocked through the doorway. Once inside, he paused a moment to accustom his eyes to the dim interior, after the sun-glare of the street. Gradually, he picked out four men seated at a wooden-topped table in one corner, a squat brown bottle and glasses before them. Andy switched his gaze to the other side of the room and discovered a short bar of unplaned pine, presided over by a round-faced, greasy-featured half-breed who grunted an unintelligible greeting.

Andy replied with a short nod and moved across the floor to the bar, his spurs clanking on the pine flooring. He felt the eyes of the four men at the table boring into his back. Again, Andy sensed there was trouble afoot. Oh, well, it was no affair of his. He'd get a drink and ride on to a more inviting town. These local troubles were the business of the local citizenry. And yet, even while such thoughts were coursing Andy's mind, he couldn't overcome the feeling of impending evil.

Here he was, a stranger in a strange town, knowing, so far as he knew, not one single person among its inhabitants. He had no interest in the town of Ensenajo, save that of procuring a drink. On the surface, there didn't seem to be a chance that Andy could become embroiled in any difficulties that might arise. On the other hand, Andy had experienced a "hunch" that spelled danger in any man's language—and it was Andy Farlow's habit to heed his hunches. Unconsciously, he shrugged his shoulders, as the half-breed behind the bar asked, "What to drink *señor*?"

"First, water—lots of it."

The bartender set out a none-too-clean tumbler half filled with muddy colored water. Andy downed this and a second one besides.

"My horse could do with a mite of *agua*," Andy suggested.

The barkeep shook his head. "For the *caballo* I have not of the water, *señor*." An air of finality attended the words.

Patiently, Andy explained that his pony had traveled since sun-up across hot, parched country. The barkeep sympathized with the horse in garbled Spanish and English, but remained adamant. Water for horses was not to be had at his *cantina*. From that point he entered into a series of directions having to do with the location of a water hole, not ten miles distant, from which all water for Ensenajo was drawn. But the directions were too involved.

Andy finally gave up. "We'll let it ride," he said wearily. "If you'll prime me with one more glass of water, I'll be about ready for some bourbon."

The third glass of water was placed on the bar, but the bartender shook his head. "Whiskee, I do not have, *señor*. Can give *tequila*—ver' fine *tequila*. Also, I have of *pulque* and *aguaridente*—"

He broke off, noting that Andy was eyeing the brown bottle on the table occupied by the four men. At the same time, the four men were staring at Andy. Andy turned back to the bar to hear the barkeep's explanations:

"My last bottle, *señor*." He chuckled fatly. "They have buy out my stock—no?"

"Bought the whole bottle, eh?" Andy nodded, then shrugged his shoulders. "It don't really matter. I'll try your *tequila*." He spun a half dollar on the bar.

The half-breed made the change, then set out a bottle, small tumbler, a salt cellar and withered slice of orange. Andy drank the *tequila* Mexican fashion: first, the pinch of salt on his tongue; then the shot of fiery liquor; last, the drawing of the orange through his teeth. The barkeep beamed approval while he drank.

"Ver' fine *tequila*—no?"

It was vile stuff, probably the dregs from some nearby local distillery. Andy suppressed a gasp. His throat felt raw and scorched. "Your *tequila* reaches considerable distance," he paid the dubious compliment. "A little bit goes a long way. And, now, another drink of water—*pronto*!"

He hesitated over his fourth glass of water, wondering at the same time why he didn't leave. There appeared no reason for staying longer. At the same time there was a certain pull for Andy in the *cantina*, a pull he found difficult to resist. That "hunch" was working stronger than ever now. He noticed the four men at the table were talking in low tones.

While he lingered over the drink of water, the four men were looking Andy over, taking in his sandy hair and even six feet of bone and hardened muscle. Farlow was well featured, his shoulders broad in their denim shirt. Overalls of faded blue were turned up at the cuffs which fell somewhat below the tops of his high-heeled cowman's boots. A weathered gray Stetson and open vest of greenish black completed the togs.

That which had the greatest interest for the four men at the table was the single-action, Colt's forty-five six-shooter slung low at Andy Farlow's right thigh. Three of the men at the table were wondering if Andy would use it. The fourth man, being a better judge of character, was speculating as to how well he could use it—his swiftness on the draw, accuracy in shooting and so on. Three of the men had appeared considerably annoyed at Andy's entrance; the fourth man had looked a trifle relieved.

The four were talking again, in lower tones now. To the demands of three, the fourth man always shook his head.

"Cripes!" one of the three swore impatiently. "We can't talk here, Dan. You don't want strangers listenin' in on our *habla*. Let's go up to your place where we can mull over this matter in friendly fashion."

The fourth man shook his grizzled old head and laughed scornfully. "You ain't talkin' to me, Quillan. Me, I'm likin' this *cantina* better every minute. It's comfortable here. I bought you the only bottle of real liquor to be had in Ensenajo. I can't see what more you want."

One of the others cursed, low-voiced, venomous. "You known damn well what we want, Jenkins. We're going to get it, too. If we don't get it at your place, we'll do business right here and now, and if anybody gets hurt it's their own fault. Savvy? We've wasted enough time palaverin' with you and bein' stalled off—"

"Shut your trap, Porter," growled the man known as Quillan. "You cravin' to have the whole country learn our business?"

"I don't much give a hoot in hell if it does—that part of the country close by," half-snarled Porter.

11

"If anybody tries to learn too much, they're li'ble to get hurt bad. We're just wastin' time with all this talk. I'm statin' it's time we got down to business. Don't you agree, Pipe?" Without awaiting an answer, Porter turned back to the fourth man. "You see, Jenkins, we're all agreed that—"

"All agreed," the fourth man cut in jeeringly, "that I should take you saddle louses up to my house and let you try out some refined torture, eh? And not so refined, at that. Hell! Porter, I wa'n't born yesterday. Me, I'm plumb satisfied to stay right where I am."

Porter scowled. "By geez!" he rasped, "you'll come across for us with the information we want, or we'll convince you that what them Mexes done to you was just playful foolin'. Where they left off, we'll start in, and by the time we've finished with you there won't be enough left of your twisted carcass to interest a scavengin' buzzard—"

"Cut it, Porter," Quillan snapped. He was a tall, dark-complexioned man with a long, unshaven jaw and pale blue eyes which, at the moment, were gazing uneasily at Andy Farlow's back. He was in range togs like his companions; all were armed with six-shooters.

Porter snorted, shrugged his bulky shoulders, shifted his holstered gun a trifle nearer the front. He spoke directly with a certain coldness: "I always did figure you as havin' a weak streak, Quillan. If you're afeared of that hombre at the bar, why I'll—" Without finishing his statement he turned slightly in his chair and hailed Andy, "Hey, you—at the bar!"

Andy placed his glass on the wooden counter and turned slowly toward the speaker. "Meanin' me?" he asked quietly. His eyes on Porter were level and coldly questioning.

Porter was somewhat taken aback by the chill steadiness of Andy's gaze. He abruptly dropped his blustering manner, and endeavored to make his tones sound cordial, "Meet my friends, cowboy. Louie Quillan, Pipe Dinehart and Dan Jenkins. My moniker's Tom Porter."

Andy nodded coolly to the four men, caught the warning glance in the eyes of the old man known as Jenkins. The remaining three were somewhere between thirty and forty years of age. There was something about old Jenkins that gained Andy's sympathy. Something queer about Jenkins' body, too. His arms didn't seem right. Twisted, sort of, Andy mused. There were deep lines etched in his grizzled features, lines that could have been produced only by extreme suffering.

Even while Andy was considering this, old Jenkins gained his feet and came hobbling toward Andy. Andy noticed now that Jenkins' legs were rather twisted, too. In fact, his entire form seemed to possess a grotesque, tortured appearance. His fingers, as they clasped Andy's outstretched hand, were gnarled and lacked strength, giving Andy an impression that complete coordination between mind and muscle was lacking.

"I'm Andy Farlow. Glad to know you, Mr. Jenkins."

The other three men had remained at the table, glaring at Jenkins. Dinehart, a medium-sized individual with a vacillating gaze and muddy-colored hair, had started to follow old Jenkins, but had been jerked back into his chair by Louie Quillan.

The twisted man was speaking to Andy: "Glad to know me, eh?" and his voice was low. "Me, I'm more'n glad you dropped in, boy. Stick around Ensenajo a spell. Mebbe you'll find the town interestin'. I might be able to make it worth your while."

Andy nodded, released old Jenkins' fingers. His sharp gaze cut across Jenkins' shoulder, taking in the three men at the table. They appeared rather perturbed about something.

Louie Quillan spoke suddenly, anger tinging his tones: "We're waitin' for you to drink with us, Dan."

Old Jenkins turned and hobbled back to the table, one gnarled hand resting on the cedar butt that hung in a battered holster at his right leg. He sighed resignedly and lowered his crippled frame to his chair. Quillan was pouring drinks from the brown bottle. When he had finished, he glanced toward Andy standing at the bar, and said, "Have a drink, Farlow?"

Andy shook his head. "I had one once." He smiled, but his eyes held frosty lights. He didn't like Jenkins' three companions.

Porter took up the conversation. "You ridin' far, Farlow?"

"Far enough," was Andy's cryptic reply.

"Meanin' exactly what?" Porter demanded. "Where you headin' for?"

Andy smiled thinly. "From here to there," he said quietly, "and probably back again, but not in the same direction, nor on the same day."

Porter's eyes flashed angrily. For a moment he didn't speak, while he considered Andy's reply. Then he decided to change his tactics:

"Ensenajo," Porter declared flatly, "ain't no burg to stop in."

"You and your pards stopped here," Andy reminded the man.

One of the pards swore under his breath. Porter went on, "We got business here—damn' important business. What I'm makin' clear to you is this— there's better towns this side of the Border, if you're lookin' for excitement."

"I didn't come below the Border lookin' for excitement," Andy smiled easily. "If excitement comes, it'll probably be lookin' for me. It usually does."

"Uh-huh, mebbe so," Porter conceded. "Mebbe you'd better get back to the States side of the line. In case you're askin', it's only about ten miles from here—due north."

"I'm not askin'," Andy shook his head and grinned.

That grin appeared to infuriate Porter. "I'm tellin' you," he growled. "Mebbe it'd be a good idea for you to listen—and ride."

Andy's grin vanished. "That way, eh?" he said coldly. "Look here, Porter, have you got anything back of your conversation, or is this just your way of being sociable? Why should you care where or when I ride? What business is it of yours?"

"Sweet Gesis!" Porter burst out. "I'm just tellin' you. You can go or you can stay, and I don't care where you go—"

"So long as I go, eh?" Andy smiled again, but there wasn't any smile in his gray eyes.

Porter's features reddened. "All right, if you want it straight, I'll let you have it. This ain't the town for you to stop in, savvy? It ain't healthy. Now, can you take a hint or can't you?"

The eyes of the other three men were on Andy. Jenkins looked anxious. Behind the bar, the half-breed bartender was making nervous, clucking sounds.

Andy swung around to face Porter more directly, elbows supporting his lean form on the bar at his rear, left heel hooked over the footrail.

The eyes of the two men clashed across the width of the room. Quite suddenly a soft laugh parted Andy's lips.

"Your words," he told Porter in even, quiet tones, "may have held a suggestion. Considered in the light of pure reason, what you've just said might be considered a threat. And then again I'm not sure but what you were throwing a challenge." Andy's tones were mocking now, his manner nonchalant. A trace of contempt crept into his voice as he laughed suddenly. "I'm going to let you decide which it was, Porter. The next move is up to you. I'm waitin'."

II. ANDY TAKES A HAND

PORTER'S JAW DROPPED; his eyes bulged. His mouth closed suddenly as he shoved back his chair and rose from the table. Andy didn't say anything. His eyes were steady on Porter. Quillan, without removing his gaze from Andy, reached out and pulled Porter down to his chair. Porter swore under his breath. Quillan and Dinehart glared at Andy. No one spoke. The very air seemed to quiver with repressed violence.

Andy hadn't moved. He stood as before, his back to the bar, elbows resting on its edge, one boot-heel hooked over the footrail. His eyes had narrowed a trifle. That was all. Slowly, a smile of contempt widened his lips.

Quite suddenly, old Jenkins laughed throatily. "Don't let 'em bluff you out, son," he advised. "They're only skunks."

Andy laughed softly and said whimsically, "A real *skunk* might bluff me out, but not this lower breed." He was still watching Porter.

Louie Quillan said something low and vicious to Jenkins. Porter cursed, rose abruptly, kicking his chair out from behind him. Quillan swung around on his seat, snapped an oath at Porter, reached out and seized the man's arm.

"Don't be a damn fool, Tom," Quillan told Porter sharply.

Dinehart retrieved Porter's chair. Porter sat down, still eyeing Andy with hot, resentful eyes. Quillan still had hold of Porter's arm.

Andy said quietly, "Let him go, Quillan. I don't know what his grouch is, but if he's insistent, maybe I can help him get rid of it."

Quillan said testily, "Porter's grouch is Porter's concern. If he wants to work it out on you, Farlow, that's his business. But—not now. There's more important business that concerns all four of us gents. We don't want trouble with you, Farlow—" Quillan hesitated, a dark scowl clouding his face, then continued, "Not that you got us buffaloed—"

"I hadn't intended that," Andy said quietly.

Quillan's brow cleared. He nodded. "You get the idea, anyhow. Us three and Dan Jenkins, here, have been havin' a mite of argument. 'Tain't nothin' serious. It wouldn't concern you. You wouldn't be interested, even. It's private business between the four of us. When our argument's settled, me and Dinehart and Porter will be ridin' on. If you're around town when we pull out, we'd be glad of your company, if you figure to head our way. Right this minute though, we'd like to have a mite of privacy. Is that clear?"

"That's a long speech, whether it's clear or not," Andy evaded.

Quillan frowned. "I'm askin' if I made myself clear?" he insisted.

19

Andy looked steadily at Quillan. "It's clear that you're askin' me to get out," he said coldly.

"Exactly," from Dinehart, before Quillan could reply. Quillan's face flushed. "All right," he nodded, "we'll let it ride as Dinehart put it."

"Is Mr. Jenkins riding on with you when you leave?" Andy asked next.

"I am not," Jenkins put in. "I live here. I'm intendin' to stay quite a spell. Farlow, you remain just as long as it suits you to stay. These hombres ain't no more right here than you have. Stay a long time, cowboy. Yo're within yore rights."

"True enough," Quillan conceded. "Farlow's within his rights." The man was fighting hard to keep down his anger. He added, "Howsomever, said rights don't include listenin' in on a private business conversation."

"Which same isn't intended," Andy replied. "Your business is your business, and I'll be glad to get out—if Mr. Jenkins asks me to leave."

Again that throaty laugh of old Jenkins'. He said jubilantly, "I'll be more'n glad to have you stay right in here, son. It's all right with me to have you listenin' in on anythin' these hombres have to say. You stick around, cowboy."

Andy nodded. "I'm in no hurry. I was mighty thirsty when I came in here. Now that I think of it, I'm still thirsty."

The 'breed bartender interposed nervously,

"Have ver' fine *tequila*. What say, *señores*, we hav' the drink on top of the house, no?"

No one heard his offer. Quillan was saying to Andy, "You can't be very thirsty, Farlow. You already had a shot of liquor and three glasses of water."

"You keeping cases on me, Quillan?" Andy's tones were tinged with sarcasm.

"If I am," Quillan retorted, "I got a reason. You can't be thirsty—"

Andy grinned. "Ever hear of a man having a thirst for knowledge, Quillan? That's me."

Quillan said testily, warningly, "Don't you crowd me none, Farlow. This is serious business. I got a reason for askin' you to get out—"

Andy laughed softly. "Maybe you got a reason, Quillan, but have you got *reason?* I'm not strong on being crowded, myself. I've stated I'm staying a spell. What are you figurin' to do about it?"

Quillan tensed, glared for a moment, then regained hold of his emotions. He shrugged his shoulders. "Oh, hell! I ain't got time for you now." He turned disgustedly to Jenkins. "C'mon, Dan, we'll go up to your place where we can talk without being overheard. This is important—"

"It's damn important," Jenkins chuckled, "that I stay right where I am. Nope, Quillan, I just cleaned up my house before I come here, and I don't want you boys trackin' sand and dust all over my floor. We'd better stay right here."

Dinehart and Porter tried their hand at persuasion, but Jenkins was adamant before their arguments. He merely laughed at the veiled threats hurled by Quillan and the other two. The four men wrangled among themselves for a few moments. Their voices dropped lower. Andy could no longer hear the words, except for a steady, repeated, "No," on Jenkins' part.

Wondering what it was all about, Andy turned back to the bar where he could watch the four men in the cracked and fly-specked mirror back of the bar. The four weren't paying Andy any attention now. Whatever the argument was, Quillan and his two pardners weren't, apparently, getting anywhere with old Jenkins. In the mirror, Andy saw that the twisted man was giving only a negative shake of his head to everything that was suggested.

There didn't seem to be any particular reason for Andy to remain any longer in Ensenajo and this dingy *cantina*, but he was reluctant to depart. He felt sorry for old Jenkins and, somehow, sensed that Jenkins wanted him to stay. Jenkins was in some sort of a "tight," no doubt about that, but he had been too proud to ask outright for Andy's aid.

To pass time, Andy ordered another *tequila*, which he left untouched, on the bar, before him. The half-breed bartender moved moodily about his business—rinsing glasses, making futile passes at buzzing insects—his swarthy face a study in brown dismay. Finally he glanced at the drink standing untasted in front of Andy.

"Is no good?" he asked wistfully.

Andy, gaze fastened on the mirror, didn't reply. The barkeep followed his eyes, then nodded to himself. Low voiced, he said to Andy, "Is trouble coming." It was a statement of fact, not a question.

Andy removed his eyes from the mirror long enough to ask, "What's the argument?"

The barkeep shrugged fat shoulders. "I'm don' know. The Señor Jenkins, he is one good hombre. Theese othairs—" again a shrugging of shoulders and expressive shake of the head, "—bad—*malo*. Something the Señor Jenkins hav'—theese hombres *muy malo* wish to possess ver' much. *Por Dios*! I'm weesh theese three men leave my *cantina* without the gun fight. Is ver' bad." He paused, then, "If comes the trouble, you stay?"

"I'll stay," Andy nodded.

"If comes ver' bad trouble—weeth shooting of the guns?" the half-breed persisted.

"I'll stay," Andy repeated his promise.

The barkeep's brown eyes studied Andy gravely for a minute, then he nodded with some relief. "Is ver' good," he grunted, and commenced to mop the bar with a damp rag.

Andy considered the tumbler of *tequila* before him, and reached for the salt cellar, then set it down. His left hand went out to the glass of liquor. Behind him, at the table, the voices were sounding louder. Quillan was losing his temper. Porter was sweating in a hot, angry voice. Dinehart snarled and snapped, like a dog about to go mad. Jenkins faced the three, slowly shaking his head, lost in a stubborn silence of refusal. The twisted man looked a trifle nervous now.

In the bar mirror, Andy saw Porter's hand slip down to holster. He waited for Quillan to check that move. Quillan didn't stir. Andy knew that Quillan saw Porter reaching for the gun. Quillan cast a swift, furtive glance at Andy's back, then faced Jenkins again.

"No use of you actin' like this, Dan," he rasped. "Yo're stubborn as a lazy mule critter!"

"By geez!" Porter snarled, "A slug of lead would make you change your mind—"

Andy didn't hear the conclusion of the sentence. He caught the whole picture in the bar mirror, saw Quillan's quick nod to Porter. The twisted man struggled to his feet, one hand moving toward his belt. Quillan was heaving up out of his chair. Porter's gun crashed out!

A chair tumbled backwards. Dinehart and Quillan were off their feet now. Andy saw Quillan nod again, this time to Dinehart, and jerk one thumb toward the bar. The twisted man sagged back in his chair, fighting to rise again.

Andy whirled, his forty-five flashing into view. The weapon roared twice. Andy's left hand, holding the tumbler of *tequila*, shot out. Glass and

24

liquor flew through the air. Quillan cursed in frantic pain as the fiery alcohol splashed into his eyes. He stumbled back, caught one booted foot in the rungs of an overturned chair and crashed down in a heap. Dinehart had toppled across the table, blood trickling from his open mouth.

Andy whirled back to cover Porter. The twisted man's gun exploded three times. Porter was jerked off balance and nearly fell. As it was, he half ran, half staggered, across the width of the room, bringing up short against the bar. His gun had dropped from his grasp.

Powder smoke swirled lazily about the room. The twisted man was braced against the opposite wall, now, fighting to raise his six-shooter for another shot at Porter. But his strength wasn't equal to the effort. His gnarled fingers relaxed and lost their feeble grip on the weapon, and he slid gently to a sitting position on the floor.

Quillan was struggling to his feet, cursing with pain, wiping at his eyes. Porter was swaying uncertainly at the bar, his fingers gripping its rough board edge. Andy stood, wide-legged, in the middle of the room, the gun in his clenched fist thoroughly controlling the situation.

The twisted man, his back against the wall, laughed grimly from his position on the floor. His shirt front showed a dark crimson blotch.

"Nice work, Farlow," the twisted man gasped, after a moment. "You didn't waste time picking any daisies once you started into action. . . ." His voice trailed off in a throaty gurgle and he toppled sidewise. Prone, he found his voice again, "Or . . . mebbe . . . I should say . . . lilies. . . ."

Again, he lapsed into silence, eyes closed now.

Andy spied Porter's gun on the floor, gave it a kick that sent it spinning into a far corner. He crossed to Quillan. Quillan was dabbing at his reddened eyes with a bandanna and ripping out curse after curse. He saw Andy coming, but Andy was too quick for him: in a second, Quillan's six-shooter had been jerked from holster and sent to join Porter's weapon on the floor.

Andy snapped at Quillan, "Don't you move until I say so, or I'll bore you dead center!"

Quillan backed away a few paces, still wiping at his eyes. Andy moved to the table and examined Dinehart. It didn't take a second glance to tell him Dinehart was dead. Porter was still swaying at the bar. The half-breed bartender's eyes were wide; his mouth hung open. He didn't say anything.

Andy turned from the table to face Quillan. "Get out!" Andy ordered tersely.

Quillan ceased dabbing at his eyes a moment. "I'll get you for this, Farlow." Quillan's voice was low, vicious.

"Get out!" Andy repeated. "You and Porter take Dinehart with you. You can bury him outside of Ensenajo some place—"

"He's—he's dead," Porter said dumbly.

26

"Dinehart's dead." The fact seemed to stun the man. He slumped against the bar. One arm hung loosely at his side, blood dripping from the finger tips. With his good arm, Porter reached for the bottle of *tequila*, raised it unsteadily to his lips and drank deeply. A shudder shook his frame as he lowered the bottle. "Pipe . . . Dinehart's . . . dead . . ." he said again, as though unable to believe it.

A third time, "Get out!" Andy said sharply.

He gave further orders, watched closely while Quillan and the wounded Porter staggered to the street with the lifeless form of their dead companion, then followed the men outside. It was necessary for Andy to help them lift the body to the saddle of its horse, and lash it firmly across the animal's back. The business was finally accomplished, and Porter and Quillan mounted their own ponies.

Along the street, several curious faces peered from doors and windows, but no one approached. There didn't seem to be law of any sort in Ensenajo.

Quillan wheeled his horse away from the hitch-rack and momentarily drew rein, his eyes burning down into Andy's. Porter sat his saddle a few feet away, silent, holding the reins of the dead Dinehart's pony.

"You ain't heard the last of me, Farlow," Quillan threatened. "I'll find you some day."

"Is that a promise?" Andy smiled thinly.

Quillan didn't reply. He spurred his mount to Porter's side, took the reins of Dinehart's horse from Porter. The ponies trotted slowly along the winding, dusty street, until they had passed beyond the first bend.

Only then did Andy's watchfulness relax. Methodically, he plugged out the empty shells in his six-shooter and replenished the empty cylinder chambers with fresh cartridges. He shoved the weapon back into holster and turned to re-enter the *cantina*.

III. THE TWISTED MAN'S STORY

As ANDY PUSHED through the doorway of the *cantina*, the fat bartender was just lifting the wounded Jenkins to a chair. While the bartender tugged and heaved and sweated profusely, he was voicing sympathetic Spanish, or cursing fluently at his inability to get the twisted man settled comfortably. Andy crossed the floor in quick strides and lent a hand. Jenkins gave a long sigh as they got the chair settled against his back, then slumped sidewise against the table. After a moment he straightened up, with an effort, and opened his eyes.

"Looks like the finish for this tough old root," he managed to gasp out. His face was ashen, drawn with pain. He spoke to the bartender, "Felipe, I'm needin' liquor—*pronto*."

"*Si*, Señor Jenkins, I get heem."

Andy glanced about for the bottle of whisky, but it had been tipped from the table during the melee and spilled over the floor. The half-breed waddled back from his bar, carrying a bottle of *tequila*. Andy poured a tumbler, half full, and held it to the twisted man's lips.

Jenkins drank deeply. "Rotten stuff," he muttered, "but it'll serve. Farlow, we handled them skunks right. Give me a minute's rest—then I'll talk."

29

"Better not waste time in talking," Andy protested. "I'll go get a doctor. Maybe it would be best to get you to your home first—"

"Doctor? Home?" Old Jenkins chuckled throatily. A wistful look came into his faded eyes. "My home's a good—many miles—from Ensenajo."

"But you said you lived here," Andy reminded.

"Existed, is the word. Not *lived*. I got a small shack—on the side of one of them hills—just outside the town limits. I managed to get along there. But it wa'n't livin'—it wa'n't really a home. Just a place to eat in—and sleep in—them nights I was able to sleep—without the fear of torture to ha'nt my dreams—"

"I'll go get the doctor, then," Andy persisted.

"Ain't no doctor—within fifty mile o' here." The twisted man forced a twisted grin. "Felipe's the only—doctor—in Ensenajo. His *tequila* kills or—cures. Anythin' from rattler bite—to woman trouble. Just—just let me rest a mite, Andy Farlow. The shock's—passin'. I'll get my— breath—in a minute—" Jenkins' voice trailed off into silence.

"But we ought to do something," Andy frowned.

"Son," Dan Jenkins fixed Andy with a keen gaze, "don't never waste time tryin' to repair a busted ol' fence that's—outlived its usefulness. That's me—just a busted ol' fence—with a maverick soul that's—been penned up long enough. It was a good ol' fence while it lasted—

and withstood a heap of attacks, but . . ." Jenkins paused, then continued impatiently. "Get that doctor idea outten yore mind, boy. I'm finished complete. I *know*. I'm bleedin' internal. There ain't a chance to pull me through. But I got a story to tell before I slough off. Just a mite more rest—son—then we'll make *habla*."

His gnarled fingers groped for the glass of *tequila*. Andy helped him raise it. Jenkins drank deeply, shuddered. His eyes closed, his head dropped to his breast. Andy watched the twisted man in some alarm. Evidently, Jenkins sensed what was passing through the cowboy's mind. Without raising his head, he said, "Don't worry, son. I ain't gone yet. Just—just restin'—storin' up some energy—for the next few minutes."

Andy nodded. "Take your time," he said quietly.

The minutes dragged on. Felipe, the bartender, went to the door and "shooed" away the curious Mexican faces peering in through the entrance. Andy seated himself on the table, at the twisted man's side, one booted toe dangling nearly to the floor, his knees crossed. A search in his vest pocket produced a sack of Durham, papers and a match. A cigarette was rolled deftly between his lean, brown fingers. A match scratched loudly in the silence. Still, Jenkins didn't stir. Smoke curled lazily from Andy's nostrils. Felipe had returned from the door and stood helplessly by, his round swarthy features a mask of sympathy.

After a time, the twisted man slowly raised his head and smiled wanly at Andy. "Storin' up strength, son, that's what I was doin'. I ain't much time left—but I got enough. Let me have another shot—of that dynamite juice."

Andy helped him, then replaced the empty tumbler on the table.

"Yep," Jenkins smiled feebly, "good for rattler bite, and most any other trouble. But this time it fails to cure. It won't help *my* rattler bite none, and I don't reckon I got any love sorrows to drown—not that kind of love, leastways. There's a girl that—but, I'm wastin' time. I'll come to her in good time." He paused a moment, his eyes brightening a trifle. "Andy, you'n me, we gave them snakes whatfor, eh? I reckon Louie Quillan will remember that little ruckus for a long, long spell."

"I hope he does," Andy spoke grimly, "and I hope to cross his trail again."

"You will, son. It's in the cards. That thought came to me within the last few minutes. When a man draws this close to the Great Divide he *knows* things, senses stuff that a normal hombre can't understand. Yes, you'll meet Quillan again. Look sharp for that sidewinder. He's plumb *malo*. Bad clear through. He underestimated you, though. Didn't think you'd make a hand on my side. You'n me—we'd cleaned them skunks out proper—if it hadn't been for my twisted mitts. I couldn't make to get my iron into action in time—sort of weak on the trigger pull, too."

"You put Porter out of the running, anyway," Andy said. "That should be some satisfaction."

"Too damn bad I couldn't put him out of the running for good. I couldn't hold the ol' Colt's steady enough, though. . . . You'll meet Porter again, too, Andy. That's two tough jobs ahead of you, son. I could have handled 'em both, myself—once. That was a long spell ago. Right good I was with a gun, them days. Max used to swear there was none to beat me. Old Max was a right hombre—for a Dutchy—"

"Max? Old Max?" Andy queried, puzzled.

"Maximilian—Emperor of Mexico," Jenkins explained. "It was back in 'sixty-four he started roddin' that country. But he never got to be very popular. Folks didn't understand him. And Max bein' born in Austria like he was, I reckon he never did get the hang of the *mañana* people. Customs was so almighty different from what he'd known. Yep, from the very minute old Max stuck his boots into them throne stirrups, he was forced to make a rough ride. Finally, he was throwed—hard. They shot him in 'sixty-seven. Good Lord! That's nigh thirty years ago."

Andy coughed and began rolling a second cigarette. He was eyeing Jenkins rather queerly. The twisted man read his thoughts and paused. A ghost of a smile curved his pallid lips.

"Don't worry, son. I ain't ravin'—or out of my head. Nothing like that. But that's how it was. A bunch of Maximilian's relatives, in Europe, had set him on the throne in Mexico, and declared him emperor. Max was pretty easy-goin', and when they told him the Mexican people wanted him to rule, he believed it—every bit of it. He done his best—but no Austrian was ever meant to rule Mexico and get away with it. He was in wrong, right from the start—"

Andy had started to speak, but Jenkins checked the words with a tired move of one hand. "Don't you stop me, son. I know what I'm doin'. I ain't wastin' time. My head's right clear, even if my laigs are commencin' to get cold and stiffen up a mite. I ain't got leisure for words that don't count. But all this about Max is part of my story that you've got to listen to."

Andy nodded, spoke to Felipe. The half-breed brought a chair and raised Jenkins' feet to a comfortable position on it. Andy lighted his cigarette and prepared to listen further.

"It was early in 'sixty-six," Jenkins went on, "that I first got to know Maximilian. I'd been boomin' around down in Mex and ran on to some holiday doin's. The Mexes were holdin' some sort of celebration with ridin' and ropin' and shootin' at targets, and such. Well, I entered the shootin' contests and won, hands down, from a bunch of Mexican guns. Max sort of took to my weapon handlin', and hired me on as a sort of body-guard. From then on, we got right chummy."

Jenkins paused and requested more *tequila*. Andy held the glass to the man's pale lips. Jenkins' eyes brightened momentarily, and he went on, "Once I saved Max from being assassinated. That placed me higher than ever in Max's eyes—and he kept me close to him, most of the time. I got paid plenty for my job—not from the regular palace payroll, though. Max hired me on his own—paid me out of his own pocket. A heap of hombres connected with him didn't even know what my job was. A sort of secret service hand I was makin' those days."

The twisted man ceased talking to move one gnarled hand into a pocket. In a few moments the hand emerged, holding a faded photograph and a gold coin. These he placed on the table.

"After I'm gone, Andy, you take that coin and the picture. If you ain't otherwise tied up, you look up my daughter, whose picture that is. Then you go after the rest of these *pesos*—"

"Where is your daughter?" Andy interrupted. "Where will I find her? She's not here, in Ensenajo, is she?"

"I'll get to that part in a minute, son. You just listen. I'll do the talkin'. I'm sort of slippin'—so I'll have to talk fast. . . . Right from the time he took the reins of the monarchy, Maximilian had trouble in plenty. He knowed he couldn't last as emperor, but like a good fighter he hung on as long as he could. Late in 'sixty-six, some of Maximilian's influential friends in Spain got the idea they could save his throne, and eventually bring Mexico back under the Spanish flag. That news was never made public. Old Max only told a few of us. To start the ball rollin', the friends in Spain shipped Max a shipment of gold bullion, secretly, to carry on with—"

Jenkins' voice had grown weaker. He requested another drink. After a few moments his tones came stronger:

"The first thing Max did was to have the bullion stamped into money. He spread that job between three mints—San Luis Potosi, Guanaxuato, and Chihuahua. If he'd had all of the bullion converted into money at one mint, it might have aroused suspicion. I don't know when the money at San Luis Potosi and Guanaxuato was sent out—or where it went to. Spread all over Mexico, I reckon. Maximilian never got to see any of it. The coins minted at Chihuahua, I had charge of. I was the head of the escort that was to bring the money back to Maximilian's treasury—plenty money, Andy—to be exact, one hundred thousand *pesos*."

"Phew!" Andy whistled softly. "That would be around fifty thousand dollars in United States money."

"Wrong again, son." A ghost of a chuckle escaped Dan Jenkins' lips. "Yo're thinkin' of silver. I'm talkin' about *gold pesos*—and a gold *peso* is worth one dollar of any man's money."

He leaned back in the chair, breathing with difficulty, then continued, "There's nearly a hundred thousand dollars to split with my daughter, when you get it. It's half yours, boy—"

"Hey!" Andy protested, somewhat awed by the figures, and at the same time, half doubting the story, "You haven't any call to give me that money. If I can find it for your daughter, I'll be glad to try, but—"

"It won't be hard to find, son. I can tell you right where it is. And you'll be entitled to your half. Hush up now, boy. Yo're honest. You done yore darndest to help me out of a scrape. I like you. . . . Felipe, you get another bottle of yore forty-rod. This un's nigh to empty. I may need it before I get through."

The half-breed hurried to obey. The twisted man took another drink and went on, "Spanish *pesos*, that's what they are, Andy, just waitin' for you to come and uncover 'em. But I'll get on with my yarn. . . . We'd heard rumors of a revolution brewin' in Mexico, and I was set for trouble of some sort before I left the mint in Chihuahua. I pulled out with the gold *pesos* and my escort in January 'sixty-six, but I never got back to Maximilian. Just before we left the mint, a messenger arrived from old Max, telling me that his game was up and that he was trying to escape to the town of Querétaro. Max said, in the letter he sent me, to get the gold *pesos* over the line, into United States, and cache 'em until I heard from him. He added, in the letter, that the money was to be mine, if anythin' went wrong. That was the last word I ever had from old Max. The revolution set in in real earnest. Maximilian was captured, court-martialed. He died in front of a firing squad in June, eighteen-sixty-seven—executed. . . ."

The twisted man closed his eyes for a moment. His breath was coming faster and faster. After a time, he continued, "There's no use of my going into too many details, son. I had a hell of a time getting those *pesos* across the line, into the States. I had a dozen men with me and several pack-mules. The news of what I was doing leaked out. The revolutionists commenced looking for us, trying to head us off. We had to hide day and night, traveling a little at a time, when we could. Once we were cornered and had to stand a two-days' siege. We wiggled out of that hole, after I had lost seven men. There were other fights. One by one, my men were picked off and killed. Our mules were shot down. Finally, there was only the gold and me left—and three pack-mules. I pushed on with the *pesos*, and finally crossed the Border with three lead slugs in my carcass."

Andy held the tumbler of liquor to Jenkins' lips. He barely moistened his tongue this time, before continuing, "I hid out for three months, gettin' cured of my wounds. When I heard the news of Maximilian's execution, I pushed on toward the west. I was purty weary of fightin' by that time. I wanted to settle down. I took some of the money and started a cow outfit. I needed supplies. Other outfits sprang up, here and there, in my vicinity, so I opened a general store. That store developed into a town, eventual, and I named that town—"

Andy moved quickly enough to catch old Jenkins as he started to topple from the chair. The old man smiled wearily.

"My works is runnin' down, awful fast, son. There ain't much more to tell, though. . . . No—no more *tequila*—not right now. I got enough strength to finish, I reckon, without further insultin' a stomach that was raised on prime bourbon. I'll make to carry through. Just sort of— brace me—though."

He closed his eyes. Andy waited for him to resume. The words came slowly, after a time:

"I should have stayed on my cow ranch, but I was plumb *loco*. I'd hid the *pesos* away, figurin' to expand my outfit in real earnest, when I got goin'. Meanwhile, there was a girl I'd met. I married her. She died when my daughter was born. That purty well broke me up. I wanted to get away from everybody I knew. I fought off the itchin' foot until my daughter—Deborah, we'd named her— was able to toddle around, then I drifted away for a spell, leavin' Deborah and the ranch in good hands. From time to time I returned to my outfit, then lit out again. The last time I was there, was ten years ago."

For a short time, Jenkins' voice came clearer: "Now here is where I made a damn fool of myself. Word reached me from Mexico that the *pesos* minted at San Luis Potosi were also cached away. I decided to find 'em. Hell! I didn't need the money, but gold will make a feller do queer things, sometimes. I headed down into old Mexico only to learn the whole thing was a ruse to get me back there. Some of Maximilian's old followers knew I'd made a getaway with the *pesos* minted at Chihuahua, and they wanted a share. They captured me. I refused to tell where I'd hidden the gold coins. That's somethin' I never told anybody. I'll tell you though—"

"Doesn't your daughter even know about the *pesos*?" Andy queried.

Jenkins went on as though he hadn't heard Andy's words, "After my capture I was held captive in an old Mexican dungeon for two years. From time to time I'd be taken out and tortured. They were afraid to kill me outright, for fear I'd die before they learned the hiding place of the gold. Them Mex hombres shore know how to make a man suffer. There were Americans helped 'em, too—I mean men of my own race. Louie Quillan's father was one of 'em. Louie is just as bad as his old man was. One by one, they broke

40

damn nigh every bone in my body. But I wouldn't talk. Finally I made my escape. That was the time I killed Louie Quillan's father. But Louie had had the story of my *pesos* from his father, long before I gunned out the old coyote."

The twisted man's face was the color of ashes now. His breath came and went with extreme difficulty. His shirt front was wet with a slowly spreading stain.

"Look here, Mr. Jenkins," Andy said anxiously, "you'd better take a good rest. We'll stretch out some blankets and—"

"I'll do my restin' later, boy. I've got a good long rest coming. But I've got to talk—now. I'll cut this yarn as short as possible. After old Quillan was dead and I'd escaped, Louie Quillan took up the chase. I kept away from my home ranch. Hell! I couldn't go back home lookin' like this. I didn't want Deborah to see her father all twisted up like a damaged corkscrew. From time to time, I've heard indirectly about her. She thinks I'm dead."

"I don't reckon she'd mind your looks," Andy said earnestly. "You should have gone back—"

"It was *me* that minded—*me* that used to ride like I was part of the horse. I was too proud to go back. I was afeared folks might laugh at me. Besides I was afeard Louie Quillan might learn of my connection with Deborah and do something to hurt her, so as to make me talk. You see, Louie had never learned where my ranch was located—"

"Never troubled to learn before you killed his father, I suppose," Andy nodded. "Does he know you own a ranch—and about your daughter?"

Jenkins gave a slight, negative shake of his head. "So long as I remained away from home, there wasn't any danger of Louie Quillan trackin' me there. For the past five years, Louie and his pards have been on my trail. Every so often I'd give 'em the slip. But I couldn't move fast enough to get far away. They always caught up with me, sooner or later. The human wreck that was Dan Jenkins ain't so spry at makin' getaways. Today, Louie and his snakes found me here. I'd slipped 'em, two months back, but today there wasn't a chance of a getaway. They was plumb impatient to learn where I'd hid the gold money. I could see it in their eyes they were set to torture me, if necessary. Then you showed up. They were sort of afeared to pull anything here in town. I'd refused to take 'em to the shack where I lived. They were figuring to kidnap me when you came in."

"Thank the Lord I arrived," Andy said fervently.

"I'll do *that* for you when I get finished talkin'." Jenkins managed a dry chuckle. "Yore showin' up here, sort of put a crimp in Quillan's plans. They were afeared to start anythin', until they knew how you'd act. Well, I fooled 'em again—with yore help. Don't ever let Louie Quillan get you in a tight, son. Only for Porter losin' his temper and pullin' on me, today, I might still be alive, with them sidewinders houndin' me for information. It'll be good to rest. . . ."

The old man's eyes closed wearily. A bloody froth was exhaled out on his chest. Jenkins was holding himself together through sheer will-power. Andy knew he couldn't last much longer. He tried to make him more comfortable in the chair.

Jenkins opened his eyes, a triumphant light shining in them. "Told you I'd last long enough to finish the story," he half whispered, "but I'm shore gettin' winded. I'd sort of like a last drag on a cigarette, if you'll twist one for me, Andy. Let Felipe brace me up, while you get out yore makin's. Then, I'll tell you how to find Deborah—" His voice broke for an instant, but he quickly continued, "Just one more rest, then I'll call it a day. You roll me that twisty, Andy."

Felipe came around to the chair, placing his right arm about Jenkins' shoulders. Andy moved away a pace, reaching for tobacco and brown papers. He sifted the tiny golden grains into a paper, deftly turned the cigarette and ran the tip of his tongue along the edge of the paper. Turning back to the dying man, he said, "Here you are, Mr. Jenkins." He scratched a match. "I'll hold a light for you."

One hand advanced to place the cigarette between Jenkins' colorless lips. Then, Andy slowly checked the movement. He drew back the hand proffering the cigarette and placed the cylinder of tobacco between his own lips, as his gaze fell on Jenkins' still features. Still looking at Jenkins, he raised the lighted match to the cigarette, then inhaled deeply. Twin spirals of gray smoke ascended from Andy's nostrils.

The twisted man's eyes were wide open, glassy, staring. . . .

Felipe stared at the cigarette in Andy's mouth, then down at the crippled, lifeless form. "Is dead, no?" Felipe said stolidly.

"Is dead," Andy nodded, echoing the half-breed's words. Slowly, he walked to the door, opened it, glanced out along the quiet dusty street and the surrounding brown hills. After a few moments he turned back into the room.

"Is dead," Andy said again. This time there was a note of finality in his voice.

IV. GOLD EAGLE AND RATTLESNAKE

THE WESTERING SUN WAS dropping toward the brown, dusty hills by the time Andy Farlow had rolled the last boulder on Dan Jenkins' grave, which the cowboy had dug a short distance to the rear of the hillside shack the twisted man had called home—or at least, the place in which he had existed. There was a certain satisfaction in the look Andy cast on the low, rocky mound.

"There you are, old timer," Andy spoke softly, "I don't reckon the coyotes will do any digging under that heap of granite. Rest a long time, Dan Jenkins. You deserve the peace that's come to you."

His eyes strayed down the slopes to the roof-tops of Ensenajo with its single winding street. A few figures moved here and there across the dusty thoroughfare. The lowering rays of the sun cast red lights on the flat roofed adobe build-ings; the shadows were deeply purple.

"Mighty quiet and placid down there now," Andy mused. "A heap can happen in a few hours. I didn't know, when I rode into Ensenajo, I was going to meet a *man*. Life's a queer set-up, sometimes. A feller can go along, day after day, seeing certain men and never growing to know them. Then, again, he'll meet one man and within the space of a few hours grow to feel he's known him all his life, grow to like him as a brother . . . or a father." Unconsciously, his eyes came back to the heaped mound of rocks. "I'm mighty thankful I arrived in time to meet you, Dan Jenkins."

With a sigh, Andy picked up the shovel he'd found in the twisted man's ramshackle, temporary home. "Dan," he murmured, "you've fought the good fight. You can lay down your guns. I'll take up where you left off and you can rest your weary bones, knowing I'll do my best. I swear it! If I fail, it won't be because I haven't tried. God knows there should be some sort of prayer said over you, but I haven't got the right words. Maybe I can make that up to you in the days to come. All I ask is that I may ride the straight trails as you've traveled them—as you've pointed out the way for me to ride—in straight man-fashion—fighting the square fight and looking every man in the eye. God rest your soul, Dan Jenkins."

Andy Farlow's eyes were moist as he turned away from the grave and set his steps toward Jenkins' one-room shack. He entered the open door softly and set the shovel down in one corner. Then he glanced about the room with its single paneless window. The shack was scantily furnished—a small sheet-iron stove, a cot bed with neatly folded blankets at one end, two straight backed chairs and a rickety table. A shelf on one wall held two cans of peaches, a partly depleted sack of flour and a smaller sack of salt. On a low bench stood a wash basin and a bar of soap.

Andy shook his head. "With a hundred thousand bucks at hand—almost—this was the sort of dump he was forced to spend his last days in. Poor hombre. I reckon he sure paid for his gold." Andy swore softly under his breath. "If he only hadn't died before he could tell me the way to find his daughter. Shucks! I don't even know the name of his iron, or where his outfit is situated. For all he said to the contrary, his spread might be 'way up North in Idaho or Wyoming or Montana. . . . Still, I don't know. . . . He was Southwest, cow-country, stuff. At least I know the daughter's name— Deborah Jenkins."

Some worn clothing hung on a peg driven into one wall. In the hope of finding some clue that might lead him to Deborah Jenkins—letters or something of the sort—Andy searched a coat, slicker and a pair of faded overalls, but the investigation proved fruitless. He next reached to his hip pocket and brought out the photograph the twisted man had given him. It was scratched and somewhat blurred, the outlines of its subject having weakened over a period of time and exposure.

But the photograph was plain enough for Andy

to distinguish the likeness of Dan Jenkins' daughter. The cowboy found himself looking at a tall, slimly built girl with honest eyes and dark hair plaited into twin braids that hung down over either shoulder. It was a full length portrait.

"Hmmm," Andy speculated. "Good eyes. Her jaw looks like she might have some of old Dan's determination. Not much to look at, otherwise, though. All arms and legs—skinny as a starved yearlin'. She's got a mess of hair. Those two braids comin' down on each side of her face are sort of pretty, though. Maybe it's those big ribbon bows that sets 'em off. . . . I'd reckon her to be about thirteen or fourteen, here. Let's see . . . Dan said it'd been ten years since he'd been home. Probably this picture was taken thereabouts. That makes Miss Deborah Jenkins somewhere in the vicinity of twenty-three or -four, now. Huh! Dang near my age. Probably got a husband and kids by this time. Still, if she had, Dan would most likely have known about it."

Andy gazed at the photograph a few moments longer, then replaced it in his pocket. Next, he took out and examined the gold coin which Jenkins had given him. That too showed the effects of wear.

"I reckon it got worn down some," Andy nodded, "scratching and knocking against other things in Dan's pocket. He's probably carried it for years and years."

One face of the gold coin showed a likeness of Maximilian—the head of a man with a long, pointed beard, divided in the center. "If old Max was fatter," Andy mused, "he might pass for Santa Claus—in Mexico, but not in the United States." On either side of the head of Maximilian were the words: *Maximiliano* and *Emperador*, the lettering running around the edge of the coin. Further lettering, below the head, was too badly worn for Andy to read. He tried for some minutes to decipher the words, but at last gave it up and turned the coin over.

Here was to be seen a coat-of-arms, surmounted by a crown stamped in the golden surface. In the center of the device was a spread-winged eagle, holding in its beak and claw a writhing rattlesnake. On either side of the eagle was a fabulous animal possessing the head of a horse and the body of a lion, from the shoulders of which sprouted wings.

Andy smiled. "I wonder what sort of a mount that would make, if I had one here to throw a rig on," he mused. "Could he buck or couldn't he?"

He continued his scrutiny of the coin. On this side, also, there was certain lettering around the edge of the gold piece: over the device in the center were the words, *Imperio Mexicano*; to the lower left was stamped, *20 pesos*; and to the lower right, the date of minting, *1866*. There was more lettering directly below the device in the center of the coin, but it was too blurred and worn for Andy to read.

The cowboy turned the coin over a few times before replacing it in his pocket. He rolled a cigarette, lighted it and strolled slowly to the doorway of the small shack. Below him was a long slope and a group of scattered roof tops, but Andy wasn't seeing Ensenajo now.

"Twenty *pesos* to the coin," Andy muttered. "Nearly one hundred thousand dollars. Gosh!" making some mental calculations, "There must be dang nigh five thousand yellow boys, like this one in my pocket. Phew!" more mental figuring. "They'd weigh up mighty close to four hundred pounds—better than three-fifty, anyhow. . . . It just don't seem possible. If I hadn't felt that Dan Jenkins was throwing a straight loop, I'd sure suspect he'd run a whizzer on me."

Andy dropped his cigarette on the earth, outside the shack doorway, then stepped on the butt to extinguish the fire. He frowned. "In a way, I wish I'd never run into this. That gold never brought any luck to Dan Jenkins. It's going to be one hell of a job breaking the news of his death to his daughter. I don't like it none. Still, I promised Dan. I'll ride it to a finish. But I don't even know where to start looking for her."

He gave a last glance around the shack, then drew the door shut. "I reckon I'd better drift back and say good-bye to Felipe," he mused, moving out to his waiting pony. "That 'breed isn't such a bad hombre. He was real broke up over Dan's death. Damn funny he refused to help me with the burial, though. Wouldn't even come along to lead Dan's horse, carrying the body. What was it, he said? Oh, yes, something about having important business to attend to." Andy smiled. "Important business in a dump like Ensenajo! That's downright funny. I reckon Felipe was just plain superstitious about getting too close to a corpse."

Andy mounted and jogged his pony down the long slope into town, drawing rein before the *cantina*. To his surprise he found Felipe seated on the edge of the plank sidewalk, both feet planted squarely in the dusty road. To Felipe's right hand was tethered a pair of scrawny, squawking chickens, held captive by rawhide thongs bound about their legs.

Felipe glanced up, as Andy drew the pony to a halt. He didn't say anything for a moment. From the doorway of the *cantina*, at Felipe's rear, floated sounds of revelry. Glasses clinked against bottles, lusty voices bawled loudly for drink; there was much ribald laughter and joking in Spanish. A voice was raised in a bawdy, Rabelaisian song, to the accompaniment of a guitar strummed with considerable violence and little art.

Andy frowned, shifted in his saddle. "What goes on, Felipe?"

Felipe ignored the question, eyed Andy with gravity. "Hav' you finish'?" he queried.

"It's all done, Felipe. I'll be riding on as soon as I've said good-bye—"

"Where ees the *caballo* of the Señor Dan Jenkins?"

"I left Dan's horse under the shelter, at the back of the house. I figured you'd go up and take care of it."

"*Socorro*! Señor Andee, you could have sav' time by bringing that *caballo* weeth you."

"What are you talking about, Felipe?"

"You weel see. I'm go now to get that *caballo* of the Señor Jenkins. You make the wait for me—right here on theese spot. When I'm return, weeth theese horse, we will get on our way."

"We?" Andy looked blankly at the half-breed.

Felipe nodded. "I'm intend going weeth you, Señor Andee."

"T' hell you are!" Andy exploded violently.

"That ees not the place we go to," the breed explained earnestly. "Eet is to find the Señorita Jenkins. An' the gol' *pesos*."

"Huh!" Andy's eyes widened. "You got gold fever, Felipe?"

A sorrowing expression passed across Felipe's swarthy, round features. "I like go—is all. Dan Jenkins was my *amigo*—as well as yours. I'm like to help find the gol' for hees daughter. For myself—*por Dios*!—I geeve not the hangnail of

52

my leetle finger for gol'. What does gol' bring?" Felipe shrugged expressive, fat shoulders. "A man can ride only the one horse at the time. Hees belly will hold only so many of the *frijoles*. Eet require' only one sombrero to cover the head from the sun. A horse, food and a hat. For theese, much of gol' is not require'."

Andy chuckled at the simple philosophy. No, Felipe wasn't after Spanish *pesos*. Andy eyed him gravely, struggling to keep the smile from his lips. "Gold would bring you many sweethearts, Felipe," he suggested.

Felipe exploded into a fiery Spanish oath. "Bah! From the woman comes always the trouble. Eet is best that a man tie hees affection to a good horse." The breed added, more quietly, "I will go get the Señor Jenkins' horse. Then, together, we make the long travel, no?"

"No," Andy said flatly. "I'll ride alone."

Felipe commenced a long, earnest protest. From his position on the sidewalk, he gazed up at Andy with pleading brown eyes. His swarthy features perspired profusely. Andy heard him through in silence, gazing down on the fat 'breed's disturbed face. After all, Andy considered, Felipe's eyes were straight, his teeth were white. True, his face was round and fat and greasy. His paunch stretched shirt buttons to the snapping point.

Felipe's argument waxed stronger, his voice grew louder. As he talked, he waved both arms vigorously, without rising from his seat on the sidewalk. He appeared to have forgotten the two chickens clutched in one hand, though how he could, in the face of their frantic squawkings, is beyond belief. As the two hens were snapped through the air at the end of his arm, their frightened utterances almost drowned out Felipe's words. In addition, the sounds of revelry from the *cantina* had increased. Suddenly, Andy found himself laughing outright.

"Whoa!" he exclaimed. "Take your time, Felipe. I can't hear myself think."

The half-breed's arms dropped to his sides. His face brightened in a white-toothed smile. "Eet is that you will allow me to go weeth you then?" he asked more quietly.

"Now, you listen here, Felipe," Andy said kindly. "You couldn't stand up under the ride I'll be making. You're hog-fat—all out of condition. Your saddle muscles have gone soft. It'll be tough going. I've got a mite of money, saved from wages, but that won't last long. Mostly, I'll be riding steady—taking jobs now and then, for a short time—and then riding on again, until I find—"

"*Válgame Dios!*" Felipe broke in, again thrashing his chickens through the air. His eyes flashed angrily. "Do you theenk I'm ask to live on your money? Am I look to you like a blood-socker? *Madre de Dios*! Me, I can work the cows.

Look you, Señor Andee, at one time—and not so many years ago—I am consider' the bes' *vaquero*—cowman—in theese country. Eet is true I am—how you say?—plump, but—"

"Fat is the word," Andy grinned.

"All right! Fat! Too fat, maybee. But I am still the young man. Geeve me the chance. You shall see."

Felipe fell silent, pleading brown eyes bent on Andy's face. Andy looked the man over more carefully, noting that the half-breed's hair was slicked down and that he had recently donned clean overalls. A pair of old shoes fitted his feet loosely. Gradually, as Andy considered this offer of partnership, the sounds from the *cantina* bore in on his consciousness. He glanced quickly toward the doorway, then back to Felipe.

"What in the name of the seven bald steers is going on in there?" Andy demanded. "Sounds like a fiesta had got under way."

Felipe smiled broadly. "The owner of the *cantina* celebrates the gran' opening of hees place. All drinks are on the top of the house. To all of Ensenajo he gives the drink—free gratis for nozzin'—and no money to be pay'."

"Free drinks?" Andy looked startled. "And you're not in there, drinking your share—" He broke off, then, "Sa-a-ay, I thought you owned that joint."

Felipe's smile broadened. "Did I not tell you,

before you bury the Señor Jenkins, that I hav' the important business? That was eet. I'm sell my so-fine *cantina*, so can accompany you when you ride away."

"Sold the place?" Andy almost shouted. "Well, you double-dyed, sun-twisted idiot! Throwing up a good business so you could—say, did you get a good price?"

"Enough, under what I'm call the circumstance." A tinge of sadness crept into Felipe's smile. "See—" holding up the mangy pair of hens, "—theese are the price I am paid."

Andy's jaw dropped. "Cuckoo as hell," he thought, then said to Felipe, "Do you mean to sit there and tell me you sold your saloon for two flea-bitten, scrawny chickens, just so you could go with me?"

"Eet was the bes' price I could find in all of Ensenajo," Felipe explained apologetically. "True, the birds are not so fat—but then, neither was the business. Is enough. I am satisfy. I can go weeth you—no?"

Andy groaned. "Of all the persistent, stubborn, single-minded hombres I ever met up with, you top 'em all. . . . What's your name—I mean your full name?"

Beaming proudly, Felipe pronounced, "Don Vicente Felipe del Ordoño y Celestino Rey—"

"Hey, hey!" Andy shouted. "Wait a minute—"

But there was no stopping the half-breed now.

Felipe had leaped to his feet. Spanish names bubbled and spewed from his lips like pebbles rolling down an open trough. ". . . and I am of the pures' Castilian strain," he rushed on, arms and hens revolving in the air, "and relate' to the once King of Spain through—one minute—I tell you just wheech king I'm speak of. Eet was—eet was King Cortes—that ees eet—King Cortes—"

"Seems to me," Andy chuckled, "Cortes was a conqueror—not a king."

Felipe looked sadly at Andy. "Do you insis'," he asked, "that I'm upset the history of the Spanish throne, jus' because you are make the mistake? But what difference does eet make whether he ees king or conqueror? I'm am relate' to him through—"

"You're related to Ananias, or I miss my guess," Andy grinned. He tried to look stern but failed. "Let's you and me get down to cases. I'm askin' you for your name."

Felipe suddenly beamed broadly. "Oh, you do not ask for the purposes of—how you say heem?—publicity. Eet is my real name you require. Well, that is a matter that is not known in Ensenajo. I'm leave my real name in another town. There was a little matter involving an argument when I nicked the edge of a man's knife I'm borrow. I was force' to leave hurriedly. I came to Ensenajo where I was not known—"

"Nicking the edge of a man's knife—a knife you

borrowed?" Andy frowned. "That doesn't sound serious enough to—"

Felipe made regretful explanation. "You see, the knife struck the man's rib, first. It was a fair fight—after I had taken away this knife with which he attack' me. But he had many friends who also commenced grinding their knife'—so I'm theenk maybee I better go to more healthy climate. You understand—no?"

Andy chuckled. "I understand. And now, your real name?"

"*Seguro*. The real name. Eet is Felipe Pico. I weel not mention to you the names of any places, Señor Andee, but if you evair find yourself in a town named Rayecco, do not say to any man that you hav' seen Felipe Pico. . . . Now, when do we start?"

By this time Andy was laughing outright. He couldn't hold out any longer. Somewhat reluctantly, he gave his permission. "All right, Felipe, get your hat. And I promise never to mention that Rayecco business to anybody. Anyway, Felipe Pico is a pretty common name in these parts. I don't think you've got anything to worry about. . . . Get your hat and we'll be leaving."

"The sombrero I have not, Andee," Felipe said gravely.

"What, no hat! . . . All right, hop up behind me. We'll ride to Dan Jenkins' shack and get his horse.

Seems to me I remember an old hat, hanging there, too. Then we'll push on." Andy paused, then, "I just happened to think of something. I haven't any idea what direction we should head to find Deborah Jenkins. You got any ideas on the subject?"

"One minute." Felipe disengaged one of the hens and handed it to Andy to hold. The other he threw on the ground. Wildly, the chicken scrambled off along the dusty road, in an effort to escape. With a yell, Felipe took after it. Chicken and man met in a cloud of dust, frantic squawkings and Spanish verbiage, from which Felipe emerged triumphantly bearing the bird under one arm.

He came puffing back to the side of Andy's horse, beaming proudly. "The hen, she heads toward the northwes'. Who am I to doubt the wisdom of a hen who already brings me the good fortune of accompanying you?"

Andy stared, chuckled, then shrugged his shoulders. "All right, northwest we'll make it. That's the quickest direction back to the States, anyway. Besides, one way is as good as another. . . . Take your damn hen and hop up behind me."

The horse, bearing its double burden, moved back up the slope toward Jenkins' shack. Here, but a few moments' halt was necessary. Felipe saddled the dead man's pony while Andy was finding a hat to fit the half-breed. With Andy's permission, Felipe buckled on Dan Jenkins' six-shooter. Again the two pushed on, following a little-worn trail across the dusty brown hills.

An hour in the saddle was torture to Felipe, so long unaccustomed to riding, and overweight besides. Andy glanced at the half-breed from time to time, but always a weary smile broke through the mask that was Felipe's face.

"Want to stop, Felipe?" Andy asked once, feeling sorry for his companion.

"Me, I am stop now," Felipe answered with grim humor, "but the horse is keep moving. I'm think I go along."

It was well after dark when the two crossed the international boundary line that separated the United States from Mexico, and pulled to a halt, near a small water hole, to make camp. Andy watched Felipe dismount stiffly. The man nearly fell at his first step, and for a few moments was forced to brace himself against the side of the horse. But not a word of complaint reached his lips. He glanced up, saw Andy watching him, and forced a white-toothed grin.

"The son-of-a-gun's takin' it standin' up," Andy thought. "There's not a spot of yellow in that fat body. I'll say that much for the gamey cuss. Maybe he'll prove a good hombre to tie to." Which was a lot more than Andy had expected to say at the beginning of the ride.

He unsaddled both horses and staked them out, while Felipe worked to get a fire blazing. The necks of the two chickens were wrung and the birds picked by Felipe, then roasted over the glowing embers. There was scarcely enough meat on the pair of fowls to satisfy the two men, sitting cross-legged, side by side.

Andy chuckled. "Yep, you're sure addlepated, Felipe—trading these two scrawny hens for your *cantina*, bad as it was."

Felipe grinned. "Again, you make the mistake. Eet was not my *cantina*, bad as eet was—as you say. Would I, Felipe Pico, operate so miserable a *cantina*, if—"

"Hey, what you saying? Not your *cantina*? Weren't you the owner?"

Felipe made patient explanation: "The real owner of the *cantina*, he ron away with my woman, when firs' I come to Ensenajo. When he is leave, I take the charge of his place. Some day, he and the woman will come back, but I weel not be there—"

"Lord," Andy chuckled, tossing away a chicken bone, "what a trade! A woman for a *cantina*. . . . Was she a pretty good woman, Felipe?"

Felipe chuckled fatly. "I am think, Andee, it was a pretty good *cantina*."

Andy howled with laughter. "That's one to sleep on, waddie. Speaking of sleep, I reckon we'd better unroll our blankets and turn in. You'll need plenty rest. You're going to be mighty stiff and sore in the morning."

"An' for many mornin' to come," Felipe said ruefully.

"Think you'll be able to stick it?" Andy asked.

"There is nozzing else to do," Felipe said stolidly. "I'm leave everytheeng behind to follow you. Andee, I'm don't think you evair get rid of Felipe Pico."

"I'm commencing to think," Andy said sincerely, "that will suit me right down to the ground."

The two men shook hands on that.

V. WINGHORSE

A MONTH IN THE SADDLE accomplished wonders for Felipe Pico. The fat peeled from his bones as though by magic and was replaced by firm, healthy flesh. His muscles hardened, his features took on stronger lines, his eyes grew clear and bright. With the shedding of avoirdupois, he seemed to drop ten years from his age. Andy was finding the *mestizo*—which is Spanish for half-breed—a better man, in every respect, every day.

At the end of the month, the two took a job breaking horses for an outfit in the Texas Panhandle, and Felipe thoroughly proved, to Andy's satisfaction, his ability to "peel rough broncs." The job lasted three weeks, at the end of which time they drew their pay and pushed on, ever heading west and ever asking information regarding the whereabouts of a girl named Deborah Jenkins.

Two months later, they took another job, which lasted but a short time, then they rode on again. They headed north and returned to the south; they rode east and west. Jobs never detained them very long. A week here, a day or so there. Once they lost ten days, prospecting for silver—and found none. Andy had hoped to gain some money for advertising purposes. Another time, they spent a week in a railroad section gang, adding to their rapidly thinning bankroll. They found friends and they found enemies in their travels, and the latter soon learned that Andy Farlow and Felipe Pico could whip their weight in wildcats, if need be.

A year passed in this manner, and Andy was commencing to lose hope of ever locating Dan Jenkins' daughter. By this time, Felipe had purchased new overalls, riding boots and spurs, a shirt of vivid green and a tall, steeple-crowned sombrero of which he was extremely proud. There was a certain swagger in the *mestizo*'s confident bearing. His good humor was always uppermost. More than once his infectious smile and humorous speech had lightened the load of responsibility the twisted man had placed on Andy Farlow's heart. There were moments when Andy was tempted to give up the search, but doggedly he adhered to the task that had been given him.

The two were approaching the Border Country again, one day, and had drawn rein in the shade of a boulder at the side of a twisting mountain trail to roll cigarettes and rest their ponies. They had been climbing steadily all morning. Noon was nearly upon them, before the pair had reached the crest of a great mountain range and commenced the downward descent. Far below lay rocky slopes still to be negotiated, and beyond was a wide sweep of undulating grazing lands.

Andy ran the edge of a cigarette paper along the

tip of his tongue, as his gaze surveyed the vast terrain spread out before his eyes. He pointed with one arm. "Town, down there. See it, Felipe? Fair-sized, I'd say. Know what it is?"

Felipe shrugged lean shoulders. "Does it matter? One town is like another, *amigo*. We know eet is not a town named Jenkins."

"Dammit!" Andy sounded impatient, irritated. "Where in the name of the seven bald steers is this town named Jenkins? We've found two small burgs of that name, but neither had a Deborah Jenkins livin' there, or a Jenkins ranch. Dan Jenkins told us he'd founded and named a town— of course, we've still got Utah to cover. Howsomever, the map of Utah doesn't list a town named Jenkins, neither."

"Maps are not always correc'," Felipe pointed out. "Nozzing made by human hands is perfec'. Pairhaps, theese town of Jenkins is not show' on the maps."

Andy sighed and nodded. "Well, we're seeing a heap of country, anyhow," he observed philosophically. Again, he glanced at the plain, far below at the foot of the mountain slopes. "Cattle country. That town—whatever it is—backs up against some right fair-sized hills, too. I reckon those hills are an offshoot of this range we're crossing—Entonces Mountains, according to that feller we met yesterday. I don't remember him mentioning any name for those big hills back of the town, or saying what the town was we'd find over this way."

Without taking his eyes from the scene below, Felipe said, "Three *ranchos*—all within fifteen mile of the town."

"Yeah, I noticed 'em. There's enough grazing land down there for a dozen outfits—providing they can all get water. . . . But I don't reckon we'll be interested in any of those spreads, Felipe. Ten to one, none of 'em is owned by a Deborah Jenkins."

"You geeve only ten to one odds, *amigo*?" Felipe smiled.

"Cripes no! A hundred to one, anyway. This is a wild-goose chase again, or I miss my bet."

Felipe frowned. "I am no so sure, Andee. I have the honch in my back."

"Hunch in your back?"

"The honch like same as you get sometime'— the feeling that here we weel fin' something different."

"Oh, you got a hunch, eh?" Andy smiled dubiously. "Well, I hope so. . . . Let's slope on."

They extinguished cigarettes and again mounted their ponies. From this point on, the descent was steep and twisted and turned every fifty yards or so. It was almost impossible to make any sort of speed. The town they had seen dropped from sight behind huge masses of red-speckled granite. The trail widened. Prickly pear and *cholla* jutted from the rock walls on either side. The floor of the trail was strewn with broken chunks of rock.

By mid-afternoon they were in the foothills. The going was more level now. Mesquite and other growths common to this section of the Southwest were passed from time to time. Occasionally the trail flattened out; again, on a gradual descent, it wound among huge outcroppings of jagged rock.

Another half hour of travel brought them to a second trail that crossed the one they were traveling, at right angles, and headed off toward the southeast. This second trail appeared to be well traveled and was deeply wagon-rutted.

"Looks like there was considerable freighting, along here," Andy commented, half twisting in his saddle to face Felipe who was riding a few paces to the rear. "I wonder how far that town is from a railroad—"

He broke off, hearing the sounds made by an approaching wagon. Considerable profanity also reached his ear from the direction of the unseen teamster who was tooling the team through the low-walled canyon.

"We'd better wait here," Andy proposed, pulling his pony to a stop. "Maybe we can get a mite of information from this freighter we hear coming."

Felipe drew up beside his companion. "It is," he commented humorously, "that we can hear nozzin' else. Is enough to make deaf—no?"

Andy nodded. Undoubtedly, the approaching

wagon was noisy. It came nearer, accompanied by the screeching of brakes, shouted curses from the driver, squealing of axle spindles, and the sharp *crack-crack* of a long whip. Andy could hear the jangle of harness and the sounds made by the panting team as it dug slipping hoofs into uncertain footing.

In a few moments, the first mules appeared around the bend in the trail. Four more followed the first animals—six mules in all, puffing and straining against the weight of the wagon at their rear. The wagon rumbled and groaned and carried within sight of Andy's vision a dour-faced, bewhiskered individual in tattered clothing and a flop-brimmed disreputable hat. A pair of keen black eyes peered out from under the hatbrim, from the small portion of sunbaked features showing above the whiskers.

The mules pulled abreast of Andy and Felipe, moving more easily now, and passed on. As the huge, cumbersome vehicle drew opposite the two riders, the freighter on the wagon roared at his mules. The big wheels slowly ground to a stop.

"Howdy, gents," came in bellowing accents from the freighter, as he put down his long whip. "By cripes and criminy! I like to bust my neck, wagon and six mule critters on that grade back yonderly. She shore curves bad at one point, an' when we struck that turn my wheels commenced slippin' to beat all Hades an' its imps. For a few minutes I was plumb irritated—that's a fact. But we made 'er—just like we been a-makin' 'er for the past seven year."

"We heard you having some trouble," Andy smiled.

"*Heard* is correct as hell! Haw-haw-haw! I reckon folks can hear me comin' for miles. It's this here off front wheel. Th' spindle is wore nigh to bustin' and makes that hub screech like an old maid capturin' a burglar under her bed—that's a fact. I'll get around to gettin' it fixed one of these days, but it'll last quite a spell yit. Only been thataway for a coupla year."

"You need of the axle grease maybe," Felipe put in.

"Axle grease?" A deep chuckle ploughed its way through the freighter's bearded lips. "I finds my axle grease where I freights, in this country."

He leaped down from the wagon and approached a huge clump of prickly pear growing at the side of the trail. Disregarding the sharp spines, he thrust his horny hands into the clump and wrenched loose a couple of pads. These he brought back to the wagon and packed into the hub, around the axle spindle. Then he remounted to his seat on the wagon. His eyes twinkled merrily at Felipe. "Thar's more'n one use for cactus, eh, gents?" he observed.

"*Madre de Dios*!" Felipe exclaimed. "You have the tough hands like the rhinoceros—no?"

The freighter considered the question and scratched his head. "I dunno," he finally said dubiously, "as I ever knowed them rhino critters had hands—that's a fact. Mebbe they have though. I've heard about 'em, but never seen none in this country."

"I reckon if there was any rhinos ever to be found in the Southwest," Andy observed gravely, "they're extinct now."

"That's possible," the freighter nodded, "but if they smell any worse than a goat, I'd be surprised."

Andy smiled. Felipe chuckled. The freighter looked from one to the other, then went on, "You two headin' for the Rafter-V—Vaughn's spread?"

"Hadn't intended to," Andy replied. "We were aiming for town."

The freighter nodded. "You'd better turn here, then, an' follow this road I just come over. That'll lead you right into Winghorse."

Andy said, "Thanks. Winghorse, eh? We were wondering what town it was. We passed a hombre yesterday who told us this was the Entonces Range, but he didn't remember, or didn't say, the name of the town this side of the mountains. He was more or less a stranger to this country, I reckon, and had never been over this way."

"That's the town—Winghorse—for a fact. She ain't a bad burg, 'specially now that I get some jobs freightin' stuff from the other side of the mountains where the rails end at Bodieville."

"We could see the town, and three cow outfits," Andy commented, "from a point where we stopped to breathe our ponies, this forenoon. There's a smaller range spread out back of the town, which sort of juts out from the Entonces—"

"That's the Casa de Leonés Range," the freighter promptly supplied the information.

"Home of the Lions, eh?" Andy translated. "Mountain lions, I reckon. Plenty of 'em around these parts?"

The freighter pondered the question while he produced a plug and bit off a huge chew of tobacco. "Wal, now," he said at length, his jaws slowly masticating the weed, "I don't rec'lect as how I ever seed many of them critters in these crags—that's a fact. There mighta been plenty once. I dunno. But not recent. I've only lived in Winghorse the past eight year. The town has boomed a heap since I come here. County seat, now—"

"You crediting the town's growth to your residence?" Andy smiled.

The freighter didn't reply at once. He eyed Andy with some suspicion, as though he were being joshed. After a moment he spat an unerring brown stream that splashed wetly against the hindquarters of the off mule. Quite suddenly he chuckled.

"Didn't know what you was meanin', at first—for a fact," the freighter rumbled through his whiskers. "Now that you mention it, mebbe I did have somethin' to do with the town's expandin'. It was me freighted in every stick of buildin' material, the past seven year. . . . You gents lookin' for jobs?"

"We might be," Andy replied. "Anybody hirin'?"

"Wal," after some consideration of the question, "I sort of doubt it. Ethan Vaughn has got a full crew on his Rafter-V. I'm plumb shore the Crown outfit ain't doin' no hirin'. Reece Rudabaugh might take you on. He's got expandin' notions regardin' his spread. He might pay you to stay come round-up time, when there'll be a-plenty to do."

"Who's Rudabaugh?" Andy wanted to know.

"Runs the 2-R. He'd run Winghorse, too, if folks didn't sort of object. Still an' all, he's plumb ambitious to get big holdin's—that's a fact. He already operates the Winghorse Bar, an' he's plannin' to shove up a big dance hall and gamblin' parlor with mirrors around and carpet on th' floors. I'm headin' for Bodieville for th' timbers, now, an' before he gets through I'll prob'ly have to farm out some freightin', like I've done before. . . . Yep, Rudabaugh is shore after cash. He'd like to get holt of the Crown outfit, but so far the owner refuses to sell."

Something was clicking in Andy's mind, but he couldn't make his thoughts dovetail. What was it?

Casa de Leonés. Winghorse. Crown Ranch. He glanced at Felipe. The *mestizo* was talking cattle and horses to the freighter. Andy swore inwardly. His mind was revolving in a feverish whirl. House of the Lions, an iron known as the Crown, a town named Winghorse. What was it all about . . . ?

"—no, the freighter was telling Felipe, "there ain't never been ary gold found hereabouts. There was some silver mined a few years back, but it didn't 'mount to much—for a fact. The minin' company sunk a heap of money in useless equipment. Nope, this is cow country. Won't never be nothin' else. Ary gold a man finds here is already minted and paid in wages or over a bar—" The freighter rambled on, giving Feline his impressions of the surrounding country.

Abruptly, Andy's right hand slipped into his pants' pocket and touched the gold twenty-peso coin he'd had from Dan Jenkins. A thrill of excitement ran through him. He glanced up to find Felipe's puzzled eyes scrutinizing him.

"What ees it, Andee? I can almos' hear the wheels in your head go click-click."

"I reckon mebbe we've found somethin', *amigo*," Andy replied calmly, though inwardly he was seething with excitement. He turned toward the freighter and though he spoke easily, he felt as though the fate of a world depended on the reply to his next question: "Is the Jenkins girl still running the Crown outfit?"

73

Felipe's jaw dropped. He started to speak, then, apparently speechless, closed his mouth again.

The freighter looked at Andy with new interest, then nodded, "Yeah, Deb's still runnin' the Crown. Do you know her?"

Andy could scarcely suppress an exultant yell, but his voice was casual when he replied, "Not personally. I've heard about her from—from a friend."

"You drop in and visit her for a spell," the freighter advised. "Any friend of Deb Jenkins will be welcome. You'll find there ain't no sweeter gal from hell to breakfast, than Deb—for a fact. She's got a right outfit, too, and knows how to handle affairs. She ain't no wishy-washy female critter that faints if she don't have ice cream in bed for breakfast. No, sirree! Deb's genuine an' can stand on her own two laigs, 'thout nobody to brace her up. Now, you be shore to pay her a call. Tell her hullo for me. This here freightin' keeps me outta town, mostly, and I don't get no chance to make society calls no more. If I don't see folks on Winghorse's streets, when I'm in town, I don't get to see 'em—for a fact."

"Does Deborah Jenkins live alone," Andy pursued, "or do her folks live with her?"

"She's got a crew on her spread. Her maw's dead. Been dead ever sence Deb was a babe in arms. Her paw—Dan Jenkins—left the ranch nigh onto ten 'leven year ago. He never did come back. Died while he was away, I understand. Deb never seed him again. I never knowed him, of course, but if Deb takes after him, he was shore one white, upstandin' hombre. After he left, Deb sold some of her holdin's to Reece Rudabaugh— that was just about three year back. Before that, she let Ethan Vaughn have a piece of land. Until them two come in, the Crown was the only ranch within spittin' distance of Winghorse. There's other outfits, farther south, down nigh the Border. They come to Winghorse for all their supplies."

"I reckon," Andy agreed absently. He was eager to be on his way now, but the freighter was anxious to make conversation:

"If you boys should stay in Winghorse a spell, I'll likely be seein' you some more. 'Course, I won't be returnin' for three-four weeks, and I'll pro'bly be linin' right out again, no sooner'n I get in. I'd like to see you land a job with the Crown. They might be needin' help."

"Needin' help?" Andy queried. "I thought you said the Crown was full up."

The freighter chewed in silence a few minutes before spitting a long brown stream. Then he said frankly, "That was before I knowed you come from a friend of Deborah's. It's this way— Rudabaugh would like to get control of the Crown. He's tried to buy, but Deb won't sell. A hombre like Rudabaugh don't give up easy. One way or t'other, he'll get what he wants, or die a-tryin'—that's a fact. He's had a coupla tough-lookin' hombres workin' for him, the past three weeks. If they ain't hired killers, I'm the Angel Gabriel—and I ain't got the sign of a wing sproutin' and I never could toot no trumpet!"

Andy frowned. "Range war brewin'?"

"Mebbe yes, mebbe no. If there was just the Crown to buck, there wouldn't be no war. Deb's outfit is too small to buck Rudabaugh. On the other hand, if Vaughn's Rafter-V took sides with the Crown, it might develop into somethin' mean—for a fact. Still an' all, there ain't no actual range war brewin', as yet—no open break of horstility, if you know what I mean."

"I know what you mean," Andy nodded impatiently. He picked up his reins. "Well, we'd better be slopin'."

"Goin' to see for yourself if they's a range war brewin', eh?" the freighter chuckled through his whiskers.

Andy smiled, shook his head. "Mebbe I'll find a job keepin' the brew flat," he remarked. "Well, we'll be seeing you again, mebbe. It'll be dark now, before we strike Winghorse."

"The sun's droppin' fast—that's a fact," the freighter admitted. "I reckon I'll camp right here for the night, an' get an early start, come mornin'. S'long."

He leaped down from the wagon and commenced unhitching his mules. Felipe, his face a study in perplexity, spurred up beside Andy, and the two trotted their ponies around the bend and along the trail over which the old freighter had brought his wagon.

VI. "DROP THAT IRON!"

Andy and his companion were scarcely out of hearing of the old freighter's activities, when Felipe demanded excitedly, "Andee! *Amigo*! Tell me—how did you know? Soch a surprise! When you ask did the Jenkins *señorita* still make the operation of the Crown Rancho, I'm nearly expire from the shock!"

Andy chuckled. "Nothing to it, old wasp," he returned modestly. "I just put two and two together—"

"And made twenty *pesos*—no?" Felipe's tones were vibrant with emotion. "Yes, yes, I know that, but where did you get the 'two and two' to put together? That ees what I'm not understanding."

"You said it, Felipe. That twenty *pesos* piece. Look here." Andy jerked the golden coin from his pocket, spurred stirrup to stirrup with Felipe. He held out the coin for inspection. "See this design—"

"Already I'm see him one hondred time already," Felipe almost shouted. "Where ees hees brothers? That is what I'm want to know. An' how could you tell—?"

Andy laughed. "Calm down, and I'll explain. Look at the design on this side of the coin—where it says *Imperio Mexicano*. . . . See this coat-of-arms? Look at these animals, rearin' up, on either side—a horse with wings and the body of a lion. There's your town—Winghorse. Why shouldn't Dan Jenkins have named the town Winghorse? Trouble was, we went looking, taking it for granted he'd named the town after himself. Look at the crown on top of the coat-of-arms—Crown Ranch—"

"*Poder de Dios*!" Felipe's eyes bulged in their sockets. "And these hills hear the town of Winghorse—the *Casa de Leonés*—the Home of the Lions—the hills where lay hidden the brothers of theese golden twenty-peso coin. *Socorro*! You have struck it, Andee—"

"I hope so. But we struck it together, *amigo*."

"No, no! Nevair in theese world would I think of figuring all that from the suit of clothing."

"Coat-of-arms, you mean."

"What *I* mean is nozzing. Eet is you who have the mind that is quick like the lightning rod. Now, we hav' nozzing to do but find the gold and geeve it to the Señorita Jenkins."

"And there's the rub," Andy laughed softly. "You must remember, Felipe, that those coins won't be laying in plain sight, up in those hills. For all we know, someone else may have located them by this time. Folks have stumbled on buried treasure, more than once."

Felipe's face fell. "That is so. Anyway—" brightening once more, "—we hav' at leas', found the Jenkins *rancho*. That is something."

"It's a great deal," Andy nodded soberly. "It sort of looks, Felipe, like we might have run into some fighting, too, if this range war breaks."

The *mestizo*'s features became animated. "At leas', if I can not think, I can fight. Surely, Andee, we could not come so far, and still not find those golden coins. Fate could not be so unkin'."

"I don't know," Andy said slowly, frowning. "That's one thing we'll have to be prepared to face, anyway. One thing at a time, Felipe, and we'll face it as it comes. We've located the town and the ranch and the girl, anyway. C'mon, let's speed up and see what comes next."

They spurred their ponies into quicker action and loped along the trail which by now had flattened out considerably. In time they had descended to the open plain. The sun had dropped below the western horizon, but by this time the two riders could see the lights of Winghorse reflected redly above the town and against the night sky.

It was dark when they trotted their ponies along the main street of Winghorse, which proved to be a typical Southwestern settlement made up of squat adobe houses and false-fronted frame structures. Near the center of the town stood a two-storey brick building, known as the Court House, which housed the sheriff's office, jail and other offices. An almost unbroken line of tie-rails ran along each side of the main street.

"She's quite the good-size' town," commented Felipe, as he and Andy walked their ponies, side by side, down the unpaved street, "to be keep going by only three *ranchos*."

Andy nodded. "There's more outfits to the south," he remembered the old freighter's words. "They use Winghorse as a source of supply. Then, this town is the county seat, too."

Rectangles of yellow light splashed from doors and windows along their path. Two saloons were passed—the Winghorse Bar and the Brown Jug Saloon. The swinging sign of a general store showed ahead, then a one-storey frame building of warped, unpainted boards which laid claim to being the Winghorse Hotel. The Lone Star Livery was farther on. There was a barber shop, a harness-and-saddle store, a pool room, and other miscellaneous places of commercial enterprise.

Andy and Felipe drew rein in front of the New York Chop House, which proved to be a small restaurant with a counter and three tables. Here, the two proceeded to loosen their belts and make up for a meal-less day in the saddle.

On the street once more, three-quarters of an hour later, they stood at the hitch-rack, rolling cigarettes. Pedestrians sauntered by; now and then a rider trotted his pony along the street. Andy frowned. He wanted to ask questions relative to the Crown Ranch, but with a range war brewing, he didn't care to say too much until he knew to whom he was talking.

Felipe's cigarette butt formed a glowing curve through the night as he tossed it out to the road. The final inhale floated lazily from his lungs. "Where to, now?" he asked.

"Reckon we'd better feed and water our broncs," Andy said slowly. "We can pro'bly leave 'em at that Lone Star Livery we spotted, coming in. I don't know, though. Maybe we should leave 'em saddled. Might be we'll ride out to the Crown outfit, after I catch some directions. The best place to find information is a saloon. Let's try that Brown Jug place. The Winghorse Bar is bigger, but I remember that freighter said it was owned by this Rudabaugh hombre. There's no use giving him our trade, if he's bucking the Crown iron."

They fed and watered their ponies at the livery, then returned to the street. Leaving the horses tethered at a tie-rail, the two started out on foot for the Brown Jug Saloon. Now that the supper hour had passed, there were more pedestrians to be seen on the street. Andy and Felipe strode along the plank sidewalk, passing the Winghorse Bar from which came sounds denoting a flourishing business. A block farther on, they crossed over and pointed their steps toward the Brown Jug Saloon.

The Brown Jug was much smaller than the Winghorse Bar. It was constructed of adobe and boards, with a wooden awning jutting out above its swinging doors. A small window was situated in the front wall, to the right of the entrance. In comparison to the Winghorse Bar, the Brown Jug seemed quiet and orderly.

"Looks like Rudabaugh's place got most of the business," Andy commented, as he and Felipe stepped toward the platform that fronted the building. "This place seems plumb peaceful—" He broke off suddenly, then, "Nope, I reckon I'm wrong."

Loud, angry voices, from the interior of the Brown Jug, had suddenly formed a decided contradiction in his mind. He and Felipe paused outside the swinging doors, listening.

"I think, Kimball," the tones that floated through the opening were hot, savage, "that you're a damn liar! You knew you were faster'n Zach. You crowded him into that fight, knowing you weren't running any risks. Nobody but a yellow dog would do that—"

"You can't call me a liar! I ain't takin' that yellow dawg talk from no son—"

A sharp, vicious voice cut in: "Take him, Kimball!"

Andy jerked Felipe to one side. "*Amigo!* That last sounded like Louie Quillan's voice—"

"I am theenking exactly the same—"

Felipe was interrupted by further words from the interior of the saloon:

"Jerk yore iron, Devers!" The voice was challenging, murderous.

"Iron hell! You don't outsmart me, like you did Zach. You want to fight, eh? How does this suit you, you lousy, killin'—" The words weren't finished.

Spat! Crack!

Andy chuckled. "Somebody's jaw collided with a bunch of knuckles, sounds like—"

There came a swift rush of footsteps, yells. The swinging doors banged wide apart. A man came stumbling out, his back to the street. Following him closely was a veritable young tiger in cowpuncher togs.

The young tiger stepped swiftly in, arms working like pistons. He slammed out a right swing to his opponent's face. Blood spurted! The youngster closed in, hit the larger man again as he started to go down, and followed up with a savage one-two that sent the fellow sprawling.

Other men came plunging from the interior of the saloon. In the light from the small window, Andy recognized Louie Quillan's long-jawed, unshaven features, as Quillan followed closely behind the young puncher.

The man on the ground was scrambling up, now, clawing at his holster. Andy noticed blood trickling from his open mouth as he came barging back to the platform that fronted the saloon. Andy swore softly, wondering why the youngster didn't pull his own gun. But it seemed the young tiger had no time for guns. Again he leaped in, striking with savage ferocity. The bigger man lost his gun and his balance at the same time and went tumbling once more on his back, in the dusty road.

"Damn you, Kimball!" the tiger cub panted. "I'll make you wish you never saw a gun. If you want more, get up and take it—"

That was as far as he got. Quillan, coming in swiftly at the youngster's rear, forty-five in hand, struck viciously with the gun-barrel at the young puncher's head. The puncher half-sensed the blow coming and dodged, but the heavy barrel struck him a glancing blow that was staggering. He swerved back and half around, nearly losing his footing.

"Now, will you pull iron?" Quillan snarled. "By geez! I'll blast you wide open—"

"Quillan, you put that gun away *pronto*!" Andy's words cracked sharply through the blur of dust and noise. His six-shooter leaped to hand.

Quillan cursed, whirled around. The light from the saloon window fell full on Andy's face. Quillan's jaw sagged. He said, "Christ! Farlow!" He lowered the gun in his hand.

A crowd had gathered. The young puncher pushed through to face Andy. "Much obliged, cowboy," he jerked out. "Now, let me have this

Quillan skunk. I'll give him what I handed Kimball—"

"Quillan's my meat," Andy spoke sharply. "You take care of that Kimball hombre, Button. . . . Quillan, put that gun away—or use it! Quick! Make up your mind."

Quillan hesitated. Sullenly, he slid the six-shooter back into his scabbard and raised his arms in the air. "You ain't got no call buttin' in on a private scrap this way, Farlow," he rasped. "This is the second time you've butted into my affairs. You'll do it once too often."

"Mebbe this is that time," Andy said softly. "I'm waitin' to see. Whether it is or not—well, Quillan, I'll do the same thing every time I see a man outnumbered by sidewinders—"

A new voice cut in, meanly triumphant, "Yeah, you've done it once too often, Farlow. Drop that iron, or I'll blow you to hell!"

It was the voice of Tom Porter—Tom Porter who had killed old Dan Jenkins! Jenkins, before dying, had prophesied another meeting with Quillan and Porter. Now it was coming true.

Andy felt something round and cold and hard boring savagely into the small of his back. He felt Porter's hot, liquor-laden breath on his nape, heard Porter's vicious curses and the repeated order to drop his gun.

Slowly Andy lowered the six-shooter clutched in his right hand.

VII. QUILLAN BACKS DOWN

A CROWD OF curious onlookers milled around the group on the saloon porch, ready to scatter if shooting broke out, but morbidly interested in seeing what strange fate lay in store for the strange cowboy who had come to Winghorse. Felipe had gone entirely overlooked in the throng.

"Looks like a showdown, at last!" Tom Porter's voice, viciously triumphant. "We'll even up for that little ruckus in Ensenajo, Farlow. Drop that six-shooter. Dammit! Yo're all through!"

Quillan's gun was out again. His teeth were bared in a snarling smile of hate. He came slowly toward Andy, killer lights gleaming in his pale blue eyes. The young puncher who had knocked Kimball into the road was still occupied, trying to kick Kimball's gun out of reach and at the same time, come to Andy's aid.

Quillan's finger was quivering on gun-trigger. Porter's forty-five barrel still bored into Andy's spine. Both were cursing Andy in a steady, vicious monotone. . . . The crowd commenced to back away. This couldn't go on much longer. Hell was due to break loose.

"I'm think," Felipe's voice cut clearly through the night air, "that eet is time for Porter and Quillan to put away the gons, before I puff them both to the hell that freezes over."

There were sudden exclamations of surprise at this new voice.

"Nice work, *amigo*," Andy laughed softly.

Quillan went white, cursed, and lowered his gun. Porter half turned, then stiffened as Felipe's gun muzzle was jabbed into his back ribs. He, too, lost no time holstering his forty-five. Andy again brought his gun into play. The young puncher who had downed Kimball also appeared to have remembered his gun.

"Looks like a new deal for the Crown," he chortled. "Kimball, what say you and me continue our fight? You too, Quillan. And my invite includes Porter. We'll start all over again—and this time, we'll use six-guns, if you like!" He laughed joyously, coming to stand at Andy's side.

Kimball, Porter and Quillan were now standing with raised arms. Quillan rasped, "You've got the upper hand, this time, Farlow, but yore luck can't last forever. Yore finish is in sight, if you stay in Winghorse. You'd better travel—"

"Want to end it right now?" Andy invited coldly.

Quillan shook his head. "My time will come. I'll get you yet."

Porter had turned and was looking at Felipe. He spat disgustedly toward the *mestizo* and snarled at Andy, "Trailin' around with a greaser, now, eh, Farlow? I don't admire yore taste none—"

"Greasair, ees eet!" Felipe's dark eyes snapped.

He holstered his gun, stepped swiftly up to Porter. His open palm as swiftly left white marks on Porter's cheek.

"Now, son of a pole-cat," Felipe snapped, "pull your gon on the greasair, an' I show you how queeck the grease helps the fast draw-shoot!"

Porter backed away, the marks of Felipe's strong fingers livid against the crimson of his features. "Not now, Mex, but I'll get you—later. See if I don't."

Felipe spat contemptuously, held his arm far out from his side, and hurled a certain unprintable challenge. Still Porter refused to go for his gun. Felipe looked disappointed, but at a word from Andy ceased goading the cringing Porter.

Quillan was looking with puzzled gaze at Felipe. He failed to recognize in this fiery *mestizo* the slovenly fat bartender of the previous year.

"Yes, we'll get you, too, Mex," he said slowly, struggling to keep his temper. "I've got a hunch I've seen you before—some place."

"Pairhaps," Felipe nodded calmly. "I have been there. Maybee it was the same place you hav' seen me."

Kimball, standing next to Quillan, growled something in thick tones, then, after spitting out a couple of loose teeth, managed to make his words understandable: "We goin' to stand here arguin', all night?" he said through swollen lips.

"You can leave any time you like," Andy said

coldly. "I'm not stopping you." He added, "The same goes for Quillan and Porter too."

Quillan and his two companions paused but a moment before starting away. Quillan called back over his shoulder, "We'll meet again, Farlow, and—"

"I'll be disappointed as hell if we don't," Andy snapped, "and you can expect trouble any time you cut my trail."

Quillan stopped and half started back. Porter swore and caught at his arm. Finally the two men, with Kimball walking ahead, strode angrily away from the scene of the fight. The crowd before the Brown Jug commenced to disperse.

Andy glanced around, smiling grimly, "Well, looks like the show is over for tonight."

The young puncher who had precipitated the trouble moved closer to Andy. "I'm Denny Devers," he introduced himself, "ridin' for the Crown outfit, at present. You sure helped me out of a tight. What say we have a drink on that neat little ruckus? I'm buyin', and I'm plumb dry, and I can't think of anythin' better to do."

"We were heading for a drink when we saw you coming out of the Brown Jug," Andy smiled, adding, "you and Kimball that is. You looked plumb occupied, so we didn't take a hand until it looked like you might get the worst of it."

"And just in time, cow-poke," Denny Devers grinned.

Andy gave his name and Felipe's. The three shook hands and entered the Brown Jug. The small barroom was empty, save for an undersized, slick-haired bartender, most of its former customers having followed Quillan and his friends to the Winghorse Bar.

"This here half-pint portion behind the bar," Denny Devers introduced, "is Toby Byers, barkeep and proppy-teer of this here Brown Jug den of sin and iniquity. Only us hombres that take pity on Toby drinks his swill. He's got to make a living somehow and charity begins at home—"

"And stays there," cut in the dapper little bartender, "so don't be hinting that I buy the drinks. Though I must admit the Brown Jug was home for half this town, also includin' the Crown, 2-R and Rafter-V outfits—to say nothin' of henpecked husbands—until Rudabaugh opened his Winghorse Bar." Byers stuck one hand across his counter, "Glad to meet you, gents."

"And then," Denny Devers again took up the conversation, "Rudabaugh bein' of a hoggish nature, he makes things so unpleasant here, every time he can, that trade naturally gravitated to his place. Peaceful folks don't like to drink in a barroom where fights occur frequent."

"Which statements," Toby Byers intervened, "don't quench no thirst. What'll it be, gents? I'm so pleased the 2-R took a beating a short spell back, that I'll buy the drinks."

"Now that's news!" Devers exclaimed. "The Brown Jug hasn't bought a drink for so long that I can't remember—"

"Can't afford to give drinks away," Toby Byers said seriously, "not when I don't get trade. It's getting so every time I get a customer, some of the 2-R waddies come in and start an argument with him—"

"Which same is undoubtedly done by Rudabaugh's orders," Devers stated, his lean features looking serious. "Folks are gettin' so scared of Rudabaugh, they're afraid to come here. It's just about time him and his 2-R outfit got their comeuppance."

"Sounds like this Rudabaugh was related to skunks," Andy smiled.

"What you got against the skunk family that you make such slanderous statements?" Devers complained. "Nope, that Rudabaugh outfit is worse'n skunks. Toby, set out those drinks. I want to wash the taste of that name out of my mouth."

"I'm waiting for you to call your shots," Toby said.

The men gave their orders. A bottle and tumblers were set out. Drinks were consumed. Replacing his glass on the bar, Andy said, "I'm still waiting, Button, to hear what your argument with Kimball was based on."

Denny Devers grinned, his dark eyes sparkled.

He glanced fondly at his bruised and battered knuckles on one hand. "I sure did give that Kimball hombre what-for," he said reminiscently, "and by the same token, Andy Farlow, I just about figure I've outlived that Button moniker."

"Right," Andy chuckled. "You've proved yourself man-sized, Denny. I take it all back. But what was the argument?"

Denny explained, "Kimball was trying to crowd me into reaching for my gun. He knows he's a heap faster'n I am. I know it too. I don't crave a sudden demise nohow, so I declines to draw against him. Some words was passed—fightin' words. Well, there's a limit to what I'll take. While he was waitin' for me to draw my gun and get plugged, I hit him. That was the only way I had an even break. If I'd pulled my gun, I'd have had more than I could handle. As it was—say, you'n Porter and Quillan had met before, someplace, it sounded like."

Andy nodded. "There's a grudge between us from a year back. Give me a line on this Rudabaugh. I'll tell what I know later on."

"There ain't much to tell," Denny said slowly. "What I mean, it won't take long to tell it, though it's plenty important. Rudabaugh is greedy for money and land. For some time now, he's been trying to crowd Deb—that's my boss, Miss Deborah Jenkins—into selling out. He don't offer a fair price, and, anyway, Deb don't see it thataway. Rudabaugh has a rough crew. They been sort of crowdin' us, tryin' to force a fight—"

"Figuring to frighten the Señorita Jenkins out of the countree—no?" Felipe put in.

"That's the plan, Pico," Denny nodded, "but it ain't goin' to work. Miss Deb, she don't scare easy. But Rudabaugh is sure tryin' to make things uncomfortable—sa-a-ay, Farlow, I just thought of something."

"Spill it," from Andy.

"You and Pico looking for jobs?"

Andy said, "Maybe. What's offered hereabouts?"

"We-ell—" Denny hesitated, then went on, "mebbe I spoke too soon. I misdoubt that Miss Deb would hire *two* hands, at present. But she might take on one. Say, did you ever have any experience roddin' an outfit?"

"Some," Andy admitted. "I was foreman of a small spread down Santone way. Once I was boss of an outfit on a trail herd travelin' from south Texas to—"

"You'll do, I'll bet," Denny cut in. "Deb's going to need a rod—"

"Howcome?" Andy asked, noting that Devers had suddenly lost his boyish grin.

"That's what started my fight—or helped to start it," Devers explained. "Herb Kimball—he's foreman of Rudabaugh's 2-R spread—crowded old Zach Watson, rod of the Crown, into an argument. Zach's fingers is sort of crippled from

94

rheumatics, and his hand don't draw fast. Natural, Kimball beats him to the shot. The Crown is without a rod."

"Watson killed?" Andy asked.

Devers shook his head. "Hit purty serious, though the doctor thinks mebbe he can pull Zach through."

"When did this happen?" Andy queried.

" 'Bout four this afternoon. They took Zach to the doctor's. The doc says if he does live, Zach won't be able to leave his room for quite a spell."

"Is ver' toff," Felipe put in sympathetically.

"Damn right it's tough," Devers growled. "That's what started my scrap with Kimball tonight. I was in here, talkin' peaceful to Toby, when Herb Kimball comes in, followed by Quillan and Porter. Kimball wants to know if I'm ready to take up Zach's fight. I told him not right away. I also told him he didn't have enough nerve to pull iron against a man of his own speed—"

"Which same," Andy nodded, "I'm bettin' is true. Kimball looked yellow to me."

"Anyway," Devers continued, "one thing led to another, Kimball gettin' more abusive all the time, and Quillan urgin' a fight. I reckon they had it planned out, to put me out of the running. That would cut down the Crown crew some more. I had my choice of drawing my gun, usin' my fists, or backin' water. To keep from showin' yellow, or bein' shot to death, I used my fists. It was my only chance."

"You done a good job," Andy commented dryly. "Kimball's face won't look natural for some time."

"Just the same," Denny said ruefully, "if it hadn't been for you and Pico backing my play, I'd have been rubbed out. With Porter and Quillan sidin' in with Kimball, they'd have finished me—"

"Where do Porter and Quillan fit into Rudabaugh's scheme?" Andy interrupted.

Devers shrugged. "You got me. They're both professional guns, or I miss my guess. I reckon Rudabaugh just hired 'em on in case."

"In case what?" from Andy.

"In case professional guns is needed. Besides, I understand they knew Rudabaugh a long time back. . . ." Devers returned to the former subject, "The Crown needs a foreman, Farlow. Why don't you apply for the job?"

Andy said, "I don't know as it would do any good. Your boss will probably want to promote somebody from her own crew."

"Ain't much crew left," Devers said. "Now, with Zach out of the running, there's just me and Kitten left—"

"Kitten?"

Devers grinned widely. "That's what we call him. His name is Elmer Kittenger, but he don't like to be called Elmer. There wasn't much left to call him, 'ceptin' Kitten."

"Is like a kitten—no?" Felipe asked.

Devers chuckled. "Tiger kitten, mebbe. Now, if elephants had .kittens, I'd say—well, you see, when they built Kitten, they weren't stingy with materials. You'll know what I mean when you see him. Anyway, there's just me and Kitten and the cookie—Beanpot Reardon. Beanpot's a dang good cook, if you're interested. Now, me'n Kitten, we admit we make good hands, when old Zach Watson is on the job to tell us what to do, but neither of us is fitted to rod an outfit. With Zach laid up, we feel sort of lost. Farlow, I got a hunch you might fit into our needs."

Andy considered. "I reckon I'd better talk to Miss Jenkins. As a matter of fact, we came here to see her."

Denny Devers looked surprised. "That so? Well, you won't have to wait much longer. She's in Winghorse—at the doctor's house. I rode in with her as soon as word was brought about Zach being shot up. Zach had druv the wagon in to get supplies. I'll have to tool the team back to the Crown. It's plumb spirited at times—"

"Look here, Devers," a pompous voice interrupted, from behind the men, "you've been starting a fight again."

Denny looked lazily over his shoulder at the portly figure of Winghorse's sheriff, who had just entered the barroom.

"Why, hello, Puffy," Devers drawled insolently.

"Did you just hear about that ruckus? Shucks! That was 'way last Christmas—or was it Fourth o' July? I disremember which, though I'm certain shore it was a holiday of some sort. Anyway, I felt like it was a holiday—"

"That's enough," the sheriff said impatiently. He was a pot-bellied man with bug eyes and a dirty gray mustache. A black Stetson covered his bald head. He was in flannel shirt, corduroys and riding-boots. A star of office was pinned to his open vest; a holstered six-shooter dangled sloppily low on his right leg. "Devers, that's enough," he repeated.

"I reckon Kimball thought it was too much," Devers grinned. "But you shouldn't jump me, Puffy. I tried to avoid a fight—"

"Don't lie to me, Devers," the sheriff puffed angrily. "Rudabaugh has told me all about it."

"What does Reece Rudabaugh know about it?" Devers snapped. "He wa'n't there. He only give the orders that started the fight."

"You ain't got proof of that," the sheriff said angrily.

"And you," Devers said evenly, "ain't got proof that I ain't. So that makes us quits."

"I won't have any fightin' in Winghorse—" the sheriff began, his fat face reddening.

"T'hell you won't," Devers denied vehemently. "If you don't control things more, you won't have anythin' but fightin'—and it'll get worse as it goes along. So it's up to you. Puffy, you know how to stop fights after they're started, don't you?"

"What do you mean?" the sheriff queried cautiously.

"Just what I said," Devers snapped. "It was a simple question. Even you should be able to understand it. I asked if you knew how to stop fights—"

"Well, I don't see—" the minion of the law commenced uncertainly.

"Do you or don't you?" Devers barked.

The sheriff commenced to get flustered. He wasn't sure exactly what Devers was getting at, though he felt the young puncher was poking fun at him. "Why—er—er—" the sheriff stammered at last, "I guess—"

"That's just the trouble," Devers flashed, "you always guess, but you never guess right. You're never certain and you're never on hand when a fight is takin' place. Take my advice, Puffy, and get your facts pat before you go to blaming me."

"Rudabaugh said," the sheriff continued doggedly, his face crimson, "that Kimball and them two new men of his, Quillan and Porter, was drinkin' peaceful here and you started a row. Then you and a coupla strangers pulled guns—"

"Just a minute, Puffy," Devers interrupted, "I want to introduce two friends of mine—Andy Farlow and Felipe Pico. Boys, meet Sheriff Puffy Baggs. He's Puffy by name and puffy by nature, and as fine a peace officer as ever accepted hush-money from a crooked politician—"

"Devers! That's enough," Sheriff Baggs said indignantly.

"It's too much," Devers contradicted. "There's far too much of you, Puffy. If fat was fightin' weight, you'd be a battleship—only you ain't. Now, get this straight. Kimball forced me into a fight, tried to make me pull my gun. I hit him with my bare fists. Quillan struck at me with his gun and him and Porter was just about to lend a hand in my extinctin', when Farlow and Pico cut in, preventin' my sudden and untimely demise. That's all. Now you can go back and play with your marbles—but don't play for keeps with any bad boys."

"Well—well—well—" sputtered Baggs. "I—"

"Yeah, all three of us," Devers grinned. "We're all well. You've been introduced to the strangers, heard about the war, and now you know the condition of our respective healths. There ain't anythin' else to keep you. We ain't asked you to have a drink and we don't intend to. S'long, Puffy."

"Now, look here, Denny," Baggs said weakly. "I wa'n't tryin' to make trouble for you or yore friends. I'm just checkin' up on Rudabaugh's statements. No hard feelin's, I hope. You boys just try to keep out of trouble, and everythin' will be elegant. I aim to keep the peace at all times." He started to back toward the door, then spoke to Andy and Felipe: "I'll see you again, gents."

"You will, if they don't see you first," Devers laughed.

Andy and Felipe exchanged grins. The sheriff disappeared through the swinging doors.

"Important cuss, isn't he?" Andy said ironically.

"Important ol' windbag," Devers said resentfully. "I'm dam'd if I know why folks put up with him. Political appointment, of course. Oh, yes, there was an election, but everything was in the bag beforehand. Nobody pays any attention to Puffy Baggs, though Puffy pays considerable attention to anythin' Rudabaugh says. He's afeared of Rudabaugh—"

"You figure Baggs to be crooked?" Andy asked.

"You mean in cahoots with Rudabaugh?" from Devers. "No, Andy, I don't think so. I never figured Puffy Baggs as downright dishonest, but he ain't got any mind of his own—nor any backbone. If Winghorse had a sheriff with a spine, things might be different."

"Another drink, gents?" Toby Byers put in.

"I've had enough," Andy shook his head. Felipe and Denny Devers also refused further refreshment. Andy bought cigars for himself and two companions. When they had lighted up, Andy said, "Denny, what say we go down to that doctor's place and see if we can find Miss Jenkins? I'd like to talk to her."

101

"It's an idea," Devers agreed. "You won't get a job hangin' around Toby's place. All right, let's go. It won't be necessary to pick up your ponies. Doc Griffin's ain't five minutes walk from here. S'long, Toby. I'll see you in the cemetery."

Toby said good-night and the three men departed.

VIII. A FIGHTING FOREMAN

DENNY DEVERS LED THE WAY from the Brown Jug Saloon, with Andy and Felipe at his shoulder, Denny talking in a steady stream every moment, as the three strode along the street. The young puncher hadn't as yet recovered from his elation at besting the men from Rudabaugh's 2-R outfit.

"You see," he was explaining earnestly to the other two, "us Crown hands have been taking plenty slurs from the 2-R for quite a spell now. It wasn't that we didn't want to fight back—we didn't dare to mix it with 'em. We've been outnumbered, right along. And if anything happened to us—well, there's no saying what might become of Deb. She depends on us a heap, and knows we'll back her play to the last ditch."

"I imagine so," Andy returned gravely. "Felipe and I still have a score to settle with Tom Porter and Louie Quillan. I'll tell you about that sometime. Maybe we can help even matters a little."

"Maybee now comes the new deal," Felipe's white teeth flashed through the night gloom. "We take chips in theese game, eh, Andy?"

"If Miss Deborah will have us," Andy nodded.

"It sounds *muy elegante*," Denny said enthusiastically. "We been actin' like worms long enough. I crave to kick the 2-R around some."

"Worms? Kick?" Felipe looked puzzled. "To kick you must have the legs. I'm theenk you mean centipede—not worm—Denny. We prove to the 2-R, we are poison like the centipede—no?"

"It sounds good, anyway," Andy smiled, "but we don't want to forget the 2-R may have some ideas of its own on that subject. They're already on the prod, apparently. And there's no certainty that Miss Deb will want any help from me. She's probably got her own ideas about who she puts on her payroll."

"I'll bet a stew of fried rattlers," Denny said enthusiastically, "she takes you on, Andy. Wait until I tell her how you—"

"Whoa, boy, whoa! Don't lay it on too thick—"

"I won't have to," Denny cut in. "I'll just tell Deb the truth. I've seen you in action. I know yo're just what the Crown needs for a foreman. Don't you worry, Andy, Deb's got a mind of her own. Nothing I'll say will persuade her either way, but I just know she's going to feel the same way I do about you."

"You sound flattering, anyway," Andy said dryly.

"I mean every word of it."

The three men turned at the first corner, into Hereford Street. Doctor Griffin's house and office, surrounded by a white picket fence and with a big cottonwood tree in the front yard, was but a short distance farther on.

Andy and Felipe waited near the gateway in the

fence, while Denny went to the door and was admitted by the doctor's wife. Andy and his companion puffed quietly on their cigars while they waited. Neither had a great deal to say; each was wondering how Reece Rudabaugh and his outfit would react to the evening's activities.

The doctor's door opened after a time and Denny appeared on the porch, accompanied by a tall, slim girl in divided corduroy skirt, flannel shirt and spurred riding boots. In the light cast by the open doorway, Andy could see she wore a tan Stetson covering her coiled dark hair. After a moment the door closed and Denny and the girl came down the steps.

On the sidewalk, Denny performed the introductions. Deborah gave her hand to the two men. There was something cool and firm about her handclasp that warmed Andy's heart. Even in the faint starlight, Andy could see that Deborah Jenkins, while she still bore a faint resemblance to her photograph, had developed into a mighty pretty woman.

"Denny tells me," the girl spoke to Andy, "that he has found me a fighting foreman to run things until Zach Watson recovers."

Andy laughed. "I'm not just sure where he gets that 'fighting' idea."

"Denny didn't say," the girl smiled, "but he takes a lot of interest in fighting—too much, I sometimes think."

"I didn't get a chance to tell Deb," Denny said defensively, "just how we happened to meet. We were talking to the doc about Zach, most of the time."

"How is your foreman, Miss Jenkins?" Andy put in.

Deborah Jenkins' forehead wrinkled into a frown. "I don't know what to say," she stated slowly. "Doctor Griffin has him in the spare bedroom and Mrs. Griffin is acting as Zach's nurse. Doctor Griffin thinks he can pull Zach through, but I'm not so sure. Zach isn't a spring chicken any more. His heart is none too strong."

"Hoping for the best is all we can do, I reckon," Andy nodded.

"At any rate," Deborah went on, "I'm needing a foreman until Zach recovers—or—" She paused, then added, "We'll face that part when we come to it. Mr. Farlow, Denny tells me you're looking for a job."

"Felipe and I are both looking for jobs," Andy said, "but Denny didn't know as you felt like hiring two men—"

"It isn't how I feel, but what I can afford, Mr. Farlow. However, it might be wise for me to take on both of you."

"Don't let wages bother you," Andy said quietly. "Felipe and I can get along on what you'd pay a new foreman, very easily. Besides, I didn't come here to talk 'job' as much as I did—"

"You understand," Deborah broke in, "—Denny has told you, of course—how affairs stand with us, that you may encounter trouble if you go to work for the Crown."

"Denny explained," Andy nodded. "I'm not thinking of that. Felipe and I have come a long distance to find you. I—"

"What I been tryin' to tell you, Deb," Denny interrupted impatiently, "is that me'n Herb Kimball had a little run-in—"

"Oh, Denny—" it was almost a wail from Deborah Jenkins, "—I asked you particularly to keep out of trouble. If you don't, I won't have any crew left."

"Yes'm," Denny said meekly, "but it wasn't my fault. Kimball backed me into a corner and used some words I couldn't take. I had to fight or be shot—"

"You killed him?" Deborah's voice was firm.

"Shucks, no," Denny replied. "I just used my fists on him, that's all. I remembered what you said about gunfights. Beside, Kimball is faster'n me on the draw. So I give him a knuckle massage and—"

"Denny! Didn't his friends help him?" The girl's sole concern was for Denny now. "Or weren't they with him—?"

"Sure. They tried to, but—"

"And you aren't hurt, at all?" The girl's tones were sharply questioning.

"Not none," Denny laughed. "That's what I've been trying to tell you. Louie Quillan and Tom Porter took a hand, but Felipe and Andy cooked their goose—geeses—for 'em, plenty pronto. That's how I come to meet Andy. You see, it was like this. I was in the Brown Jug, mindin' my own business, when Herb Kimball come in. . . ."

From that point, Denny continued and told Deborah the story of what had taken place.

When he had concluded, Deborah heaved a great sigh. "Denny, you never said a word at the doctor's—just that you had found me a foreman that was a fighting fool—or something like that. I—"

"Dang it!" Denny said aggrievedly, "I kept tryin' to tell you, but you kept tellin' me to 'hush.' You were too interested in Zach's condition and what Doc Griffin was sayin' to pay me any attention."

Deborah raised one protesting hand. "All right, Denny. I'm sorry. No, you weren't to blame." She turned to Andy again, her face earnest under the starlight. "It seems the Crown is already under obligations to you, Mr. Farlow—you and Señor Pico. You have my thanks for helping Denny—"

"Forget it," Andy laughed. He could see Deborah thought a great deal, in a sisterly fashion, of Denny Devers.

"Eet was nozzing," Felipe said, shrugging his lean shoulders.

"It was a great deal," Deborah said simply. "I'm commencing to think I'll be lucky if I can get you two to work for the Crown."

"Look here, Miss Jenkins," Andy put in, "Felipe and I have traveled a year to find you. Let's not talk job until I've had a talk with you, first."

The girl looked startled. "You—you come from my father." It was more a statement of fact, than a question.

Andy was slightly taken aback by her directness. "Why, yes, we do. You—you sort of figured him as being dead, all these years, didn't you?"

Deborah nodded. "In a way—yes. At other times I couldn't believe he was dead. Still, this past year, I've felt more sure of it. Somehow, I've grown to accept it. But now, if you know, tell me. Don't be afraid. It won't come as a shock, now. You see, the last twelve months, I've felt so sure I wouldn't see him again. But, tell me."

Andy told her, as gently as he knew how, leaving out the facts of Dan Jenkins' death. It required little more than a few moments. The girl remained dry-eyed.

"There's a lot to tell," Andy added, "a long story to give you. It might be best if we found some place where you could sit down. There's a hotel in town. Perhaps—"

"We'll head for the Crown immediately," Deborah said. A wistful smile formed on her lips.

"No, I don't have to be pampered. I got over that a long time back—even if I am a woman. A girl has to forget she's a girl when she has an outfit like the Crown to operate. . . . Denny, where did Zach leave the wagon, before he was shot?"

"It's down the street a spell," Denny replied. "I'll take you to your horse and then get the wagon, while Felipe and Andy are getting their broncs."

Denny accompanied the girl to her horse, then went after the wagon the wounded foreman had driven to town. Andy and Felipe headed in the opposite direction to get their ponies. When they came riding back along the main street, the girl was mounted, waiting for them beside the wagon. Denny was seated on the driver's seat, his own mount tied on behind.

Andy couldn't help admiring the ease with which the girl turned her pony and spurred to his side. She and the two men rode out of town, followed by Denny and the buckboard. Neither Andy or Felipe offered to break the silence that enveloped the girl, as they left Winghorse behind.

They were a mile out of town, before Deborah said to Andy, "I didn't realize it until now, but it's considerable relief to have with me a man sent by my father. He generally had pretty sound judgment." She smiled wanly, but there was a lot of sincere friendliness in her tones.

"Even the best of men make mistakes of

judgment, now and then," Andy said slowly. "I aim to do my dangdest, though, to live up to Dan Jenkins' trust—and Felipe's backing me in that."

"He was, good man—your fathair, *señorita*," Felipe said simply, "an' I'm ver' proud to do anyzing for hees daughter. For you, the only thing now—is not to make worry. Andy and Felipe—we take the care of everything. Is all."

They fell silent again. Behind them, the wagon rumbled over the rutted trail that led to the Crown Ranch. After a time, Felipe dropped back to ride at Denny's side, thinking the girl might feel more free to talk with Andy.

But only the steady drumming of horses' hoofs and the bumping of the buckboard at the rear, broke the silence. Deborah didn't speak again. She seemed to have drawn into herself to nurse, dry-eyed, the grief the news of her father's death had brought.

It wasn't until they reached the ranch buildings, some time later, that the girl spoke again: "Come up to the house, Mr. Farlow. I'm prepared now to hear anything you can tell me."

IX. "I'LL WIPE OUT FARLOW!"

MEANWHILE, IN A BACK ROOM of the Winghorse Bar, the owner of the 2-R Ranch, Reece Rudabaugh, sat arguing with Louie Quillan and Tom Porter. Herb Kimball also sat at the table around which the men were gathered, but Kimball was too busy nursing a set of badly battered features to take any part in the conversation.

Reece Rudabaugh was a big man with ponderous, freckle-covered hands and hulking shoulders. His head, with its scanty, mud-colored hair, seemed too small for his huge, muscular frame. His eyes were small and almost lost in his skull, though a cunning gleam, from time to time, brought them to light. His large nose showed evidence of having been broken and poorly set; Rudabaugh's mouth, under the nose, was wide, thin-lipped. He was clothed in rather soiled-appearing range togs.

Rudabaugh's voice was cold when he spoke: "Howcome, Louie," he demanded of Quillan, "that you haven't told me about these gold *pesos*, before? Nice square deal you're trying to put across on me, ain't it? Christ, I should have known better than to trust you. You and Porter come here—broke. I give you jobs. And now, look how you try to pay me for my kindness. I suppose you figured to get this gold money and then leave me in the lurch. T'hell with that! Men don't treat Big Reece that way and get away with it. I won't stand for double-crossing."

"Dammit!" Quillan snapped. "Ain't I told you, we never dreamed this was the place. How was I to know this Jenkins girl was old Dan Jenkins' kid, growed up? Jenkins is a mighty common name. There's hundreds of Jenkinses. Cripes, we ain't getting any place, arguin' thisaway—"

"You ain't, you mean," Rudabaugh interrupted meaningly.

"Have it your own way," Quillan growled. "We give it to you straight. Me'n Tom needed money. We happened to be riding in this country and run across my old friend, Reece Rudabaugh. Reece needs a couple of guns, in case some trouble breaks that he's expecting. And he hires us on. Reece, you ain't no kick comin'. You got value received for your money. Hell! Believe it or not, we didn't even know there was a Jenkins in this country, until after you'd took us on."

Rudabaugh considered the matter coldly. He knocked the ash from the long black cigar clamped between his jaws through the simple medium of cocking it suddenly to one corner of his wide mouth. The ashes sprayed down and across his shirt front and vest, adding to the man's generally untidy appearance. Finally, he spoke:

"I think," Rudabaugh said skeptically, "that you're a liar, Louie."

Quillan half rose from his chair. "Think all you want, Reece," he snapped, "but don't put yore thoughts in words. It ain't healthy—not when yo're talkin' to me."

The two men glared at each other a moment. Rudabaugh's laugh, when it came, was distinctly unpleasant. "All right, Louie," he said, "don't get sore. I'll give you the benefit of the doubt. . . . But what makes you so certain, now, that you've uncovered the right Jenkins?"

Quillan dropped back to his chair. "Why not, Reece? Farlow was with Jenkins when Tom killed the old man. Undoubtedly, old Jenkins told Farlow where the *pesos* are hid. Fallow has come to Winghorse to give the girl the information. All we got to do is watch the girl."

"If Jenkins gave Farlow this information a year back," Rudabaugh wanted to know, "how come Farlow ain't showed up before this?"

Quillan shrugged his shoulders. "I ain't got the answer to that one. I don't see as it makes any difference, anyhow. Mebbe Farlow has been tracking me'n Tom and just caught up with us. We've rambled around the country plenty in the last year, and it might be Farlow was looking to get even after that fight we had. I already told you about—"

Rudabaugh's scornful laughter cut in, "Yeah, you told me how Farlow and a cripple outgunned three of you. I wouldn't take any pride in repeating that story, was I you, Louie. This Farlow hombre must be right smart, at that, if he—"

"Give me an even break and I'll—" Quillan commenced hotly.

"Don't talk so much, Louie," Rudabaugh grunted. "I'm interested in facts. Are you certain sure about these gold *pesos*?"

"I had the story from my old man," Quillan replied promptly, "before Dan Jenkins killed him. The money is hid someplace. The old man never could learn where, though he done his best to pry it out of Jenkins. We could never hold Jenkins in a tight long enough to make him come through with the information. If I'd only learned more from my old man before Dan Jenkins rubbed him out, I'd—"

"No use you wastin' time, cryin' over spilt milk," Rudabaugh cut in sourly. "If you'd used your head, you'd thought of all these things, long ago, before your paw got gunned out. For that matter, you two hombres ain't even sure old Dan Jenkins died."

Tom Porter's raucous laugh denied that statement. "That's one thing I'm certain definite on. Jenkins couldn't live long after the forty-five slug I thrun into him."

"You told me that Jenkins and Farlow run you out of Ensenajo—" Rudabaugh began, his tones more skeptical than ever. "

"They did," Quillan admitted reluctantly. "But

they had all the luck. It would be different another time. Dinehart was killed, plumb off the bat. Tom was wounded. Me, I was half blind from the liquor that Farlow hombre had thrun in my eyes. It was a dirty trick. Just the same, I was watching when Tom slung his lead into Dan Jenkins. It hit vital."

Porter nodded, taking up the story. "Jenkins was dying on his feet. It was just luck he got his iron into action and winged me. He was nigh finished then. My slugs ripped in right where he lived. A healthy man couldn't have stood such a jolt, and Jenkins' constitution wa'n't over strong. Hell! Jenkins is dead, all right."

"I'd stake my life on it," Quillan chimed in. "Look here, Reece, you need us as much as we need you—"

Rudabaugh laughed nastily. "Big Reece," he said scornfully, "don't need help from no man in particular. I get what I want in my own way. How do you figure I need you, Louie?"

"For the job you hired us to do—usin' our irons if a range war breaks out on this range," Quillan snapped.

Rudabaugh yawned sleepily. "There's plenty gunfighters in this country would be only too glad to earn Reece Rudabaugh's cash, Louie. I don't have to depend on you and Tom. Besides, I ain't so sure there'll be any range war."

"Just the same," Quillan countered, "things are

pointing thataway. You're crowding the Crown outfit. You ain't any too popular with the Rafter-V. Gunning the Crown foreman, Zach Watson, ain't goin' to set so well. There'll be trouble, or I miss my guess."

Rudabaugh's face clouded. "There wouldn't be trouble, if you dumb buzzards knew how to follow orders. I give instructions to wipe out that damn Devers kid, told Kimball just how to go about it. Kimball knowed what to do. Instead of doing it, he lets young Devers work him into a fist fight. Haw!" Rudabaugh's laugh sounded ugly. "Kimball in a fist fight. That's a joke. Kimball tryin' to be a boxer when he don't know a jab from a kidney punch. Kimball that thinks a swing is something for kids to play on, and an uppercut a sort of a beefsteak."

"Hell, Reece," Kimball protested through swollen lips. "I ain't that bad. I know how to use my fists—"

"Any looking-glass in the country will prove you're a liar," Rudabaugh said brutally. "Now, shut your trap!"

Kimball subsided into a sullen silence. Rudabaugh went on, "That's a small matter, though. If I take it into my head to wipe out the Crown, I'll do it, without any trouble. I outnumber 'em, without help from you and Porter, Quillan."

"Yeah, you do," Quillan conceded, "so long as the Rafter-V don't take sides with the Crown. If

117

that happens, you'll be damn glad to have our guns."

"Where'd you get the idea that Vaughn's Rafter-V might throw in with the Crown?" Rudabaugh growled.

"Common sense would tell Vaughn what to do," Quillan snapped impatiently. "Naturally, if he sees you gobblin' up the Crown, or trying to, he's going to figure you'll be after his scalp next. You know, Reece, you ain't as popular in the Winghorse Country as you might be. Folks don't take to you a-tall."

"I'll make the buzzards like me!"

Quillan shook his head. "It can't be done, Reece. You can't force that sort of a move. Folks have seen you try to grab money and power, right and left. They're wise to you. They're gettin' uneasy too. . . . You can't lick the world, and when you think matters over, you'll see that you need me'n Tom."

Rudabaugh grunted something unintelligible, glared at Quillan, and finally said more quietly, "Just for the sake of argument, Louie, we'll say I do need your help. Now, you tell me why you need me?"

"That's easy," Quillan smiled coldly. "Me'n Tom are after those Spanish *pesos*. We're going to have 'em. With Farlow coming here, we're li'ble to run into trouble with the Crown outfit. Me'n Tom want your backing if that trouble breaks."

"What do I get out of it?" Rudabaugh rumbled.

"One-quarter of what we find," Quillan said promptly. "That'll run around twenty-five thousand dollars."

"You're crazy! Half or nothing," Rudabaugh clipped out.

"You're the crazy one, Reece." Quillan's voice was like ice. "Winghorse is right. You're greedy as hell. Any time you figure to cut yourself in for half—"

"Half or nothing," Rudabaugh spat.

"You push me too far," Quillan threatened, "and it'll be nothing for you, Reece."

"I don't like the way you say that, Louie."

"I'm saying it," Quillan snapped, now thoroughly angry. "Me'n Tom can go ahead on our own. We can get along without your help if we have to. We'll find somebody else who ain't got ideas about hoggin' it all. But you need us, and you know it. . . ."

That started another long argument, that ended when Rudabaugh finally agreed to be satisfied with a third of the treasure when it was located. "All right, we got that settled," Rudabaugh grunted. "Now, where's the gold coins?"

"That's something we got to find out," Quillan said in quieter tones. "We've got to trail Farlow and the girl."

"Hell's-bells!" Rudabaugh exploded impatiently. "I thought you already had some information.

What's to prevent me from taking *all* of this gold for myself. I can have Farlow and the girl trailed as well as you—"

Quillan and Porter leaped to their feet. Kimball looked uneasily at the pair. For a brief instant, Rudabaugh read murder in Quillan's eyes. He laughed nervously.

"Aw, I was only kiddin' you," Rudabaugh said. "Tom—Louie—sit down. Can't you take a joke?"

Quillan calmed and slowly sank back to his chair. When he spoke his voice was low and vicious. "I hope that was only a joke," he said slowly. "If it wasn't, and you try to get that gold on your own, Reece, *I'm* the one who'll prevent you. So help me, Reece, if you try to double-cross us, I'll kill you. Shore as hell, I'll kill you!"

The smile faded abruptly from Rudabaugh's features. He shrank back from the venomous glare in Quillan's eyes. Tom Porter dropped back to his chair, jeering at Rudabaugh's manner.

Quillan said shortly, "Shut up, Tom. Rudabaugh knows we won't stand crooked dealing." He repeated to Rudabaugh, "I'll kill you, Reece. You mind what I say. Don't try any double-crossing, or I'll get you right where you live."

Herb Kimball looked from his boss to Quillan, but kept his mouth shut.

Rudabaugh forced a thin smile and commenced placatingly, "Now, take it easy, Louie. You don't want to take my jokes to heart, thataway. I didn't mean—"

"I know exactly what you meant, Reece," Quillan cut in, "but I aim to watch you. Your word don't mean any more than it did a few years back when you played that dirty trick on—"

"Never mind that," Rudabaugh said hastily, casting a warning glance toward Kimball.

Quillan looked at Kimball and fell silent.

Rudabaugh nodded. "Quillan," he went on, in more confident tones, "you were in that business as deep as I was, so it wouldn't pay to talk too much."

"Sure I was," Quillan agreed readily, "but I didn't cross-up a pal and send him to his death. That hombre didn't mean anything to me, one way or another. But he thought you were a pal of his—"

"Let's drop it," Rudabaugh said shortly. "No use bringin' up past history. That's all done and finished. . . . Let's get back to those *pesos*. I'm not figuring to cross you and Tom. You can talk out. What's your ideas in the matter?"

"Here's the way it looks to me," Quillan continued, "after we left Ensenajo, Dan Jenkins lived just long enough to tell Farlow where to find the gold and where to find his daughter. Farlow is here. Like's not he's already told the girl."

"Maybe not," Rudabaugh considered. "Farlow may figure to keep that gold for himself and not let the girl know—"

"Not Farlow," Quillan sneered, shaking his head. "You don't know him. He's the type that would go to church, if there was one in Winghorse. Nope, he'll tell the girl. That puncher you had watching the Brown Jug already told you he saw Farlow and the girl and the Mex riding out of town, with young Devers behind—"

"Where does that Mex fit in, anyway?" Rudabaugh wanted to know. "Was he in Ensenajo that day?"

Quillan shook his head. "I been wonderin' about him, though. I reckon he's just somebody Farlow picked up in his travels for company. Still, that Mex looked familiar. I've seen him some place."

"I'll take a look at him, someday when he comes to town," Rudabaugh said. "Mebbe he's from this part of the country. I may have seen him in Bodieville, or someplace around here. What's his name?"

Quillan shrugged his shoulders. "Damn' if I know. I reckon he don't matter one way or the other, anyhow."

"Probably not," Rudabaugh agreed.

"Yeah, we can forget him," Quillan nodded. "The fact I want to bring out is, there wouldn't be any reason for Farlow looking up the girl, if he planned to keep that gold for himself. Am I right?"

"I guess maybe you are," Rudabaugh nodded, after a few moments' thought: "That being the case, the girl is the important one to watch. We won't have to keep such close cases on Farlow. When they go to get the *pesos*, the girl will want to be along—"

"Exactly what I figured," Porter cut in, "so I don't know of any reason why we shouldn't rub out Farlow as *pronto* as possible. If we can put him out of the way—"

"We'd better go slow on Farlow for a spell," Quillan objected, "until we get our dew-claws on those *pesos*—"

Rudabaugh sneered. "Go slow on Farlow, eh? 'Fraid of him, Louie? 'Course, you've got a right to be—"

"That's enough, Reece!" Quillan flamed. "You know why I want to hold off Farlow's finish. Suppose he's the only one who knows where the gold is, suppose he ain't told the girl?"

"Yeah?" Rudabaugh's sneer was tantalizing. "You already said, Louie, that Farlow is the sort to tell the girl, right away. You can't go back on that. Now, you're getting cold feet. If Farlow has thrun in with the Crown, he'll be bucking me next. I hired you two fellers to put Crown hands out of the running. Now, you're showing a streak of yellow. Porter's game to go after Farlow, but you ain't, Louie. What can I lay it to, if not the fact that you got a bad attack of cold feet. If a hombre had ever thrun liquor in my eyes, I'd be keen as hell to square the score. He didn't even waste his lead on you, did he, Louie? Judas! That *is* an insult. Put you out of the running without even using his gun—"

"Damn your hide! Stop!" Quillan half yelled. His face was the color of ashes. Anger had drained all of the blood from his features. He pounded crazily on the table. "Stop, I tell you! I'll show you if I'm yellow. I'll wipe out Farlow, as sure as—as—as—" Quillan choked on the words, his voice trembling with rage. "I tell you I hate him. Who's got more cause than me to hate him? I'll cut out his heart—"

"Actions are more convincing than words," Rudabaugh said coldly.

The statement acted like a dash of cold water on Quillan. He sank back in his chair, cursing under his breath. "All right, I'll show you," he promised, his tones quieter. "Farlow can't be finished too soon to suit me. I'll get him!"

"That's the talk, Louie," Rudabaugh said heartily. "Now, you got the right spirit. It's all agreed. Farlow's to be rubbed out—but you ain't goin' to do it, Louie."

"Huh! What do you mean?" Quillan and Porter stared at Rudabaugh. Kimball was listening without saying anything.

Rudabaugh smiled thinly. "I was just testing you out, Louie. For a spell I thought mebbe you might be afraid of Farlow—but I can see you're not—"

"Hell, no!" from Quillan.

"That's fine," Rudabaugh went on, his eyes

gleaming slyly. "You see, Louie, I'm due to get one third of those *pesos* when they're found—"

"Sure, sure, I agreed to that," Quillan said impatiently.

"So I got to safeguard my interests, Louis. Now I don't doubt your honesty, but there's just a chance you've forgotten to tell me all you know—"

"You're crazy, Reece—"

"No—just careful, Louie. Until those *pesos* are found and divided, I aim to see you don't run any risks. You might beat Farlow in a fight; again you might not. I'd hate to see you rubbed out before we'd completed our business—you or Tom, either one."

Quillan and Porter looked bewildered. Quillan said slowly, "I don't get what you're hitting at, Reece. We've already agreed that Farlow has to be put out of the way, haven't we?"

Rudabaugh smiled thinly and nodded his head. "Yes, we have, but now that I know you hate Farlow too much to go over to his side, I feel better—"

"Ain't Farlow to be killed?" Porter asked dumbly.

"As quick as possible," Rudabaugh said.

"Well, if I don't do it," Quillan snapped, "who is going to?"

Rudabaugh laughed softly. "Ever hear of Diamonds Beck?"

Quillan started. "Hell, yes! There ain't a man in

the southwest can match Diamonds Beck for speed. But he's in—"

"Sure, Diamonds Beck," Porter interrupted eagerly. "Fast as a rattler. He should be called Diamond-back."

"But Diamonds Beck is in the penitentiary," Quillan frowned. "I heard he was serving a life sentence for murder."

Rudabaugh laughed. "He's been paroled—for good behavior. Isn't that a joke? Some of these parole boards are funny. You're right, Tom, he should be called Diamond-back. He's got all the instincts of that reptile. . . . Anyway, when I read in the paper where he was going to be paroled, I wrote and offered him a job, figuring he'd come in handy if a range war broke. He's out of the pen, by this time. I sort of expect him to ride into Winghorse any day now, and the first job I give him will be—"

"Andy Farlow!" Quillan exclaimed.

"Andy Farlow," Rudabaugh nodded. "How does it sound, boys?"

"Reece, you've got a head on you," Quillan said.

"And besides," Rudabaugh grinned slyly, "it saves you running risks, Louie. . . . Now, wait a minute. Don't get sore. Let's understand each other. You're a good shot and you got brains besides—you and Tom. Diamonds Beck ain't got brains—except for shootin'. He carries his brains in his holster. We'll use him for the one thing he's good for. You boys will come handy for other things—"

"What say we have a drink?" Herb Kimball mumbled.

"Right," from Rudabaugh, "we'll drink to Farlow's sudden and abrupt ending. Go to the bar, Herb, and have a bottle sent in."

Kimball rose and made his way from the back room to the bar. In a few minutes he returned with a tray holding a bottle and four glasses.

Rudabaugh pulled the cork and poured four drinks which he passed around. He raised his own glass in the air, saying, "Here's to those golden Spanish *pesos*. May we find them soon."

"And here's to a quick death for Farlow," Quillan proposed. "Success to Diamonds Beck!"

The four men gulped down the toast.

X. TROUBLE BREEDERS

ANDY HAD given Deborah Jenkins the complete story, almost as soon as they arrived at the ranch house. The girl had heard him through in silence. Toward the end of the story, her eyes had grown misty, but there had been no weeping, no sobs, much to Andy's relief. The girl had courage, no doubt on that point.

"And—and this Porter," she said after a time, "you say he's the one who shot my father—the same Tom Porter you encountered in Winghorse?"

"The same," Andy nodded. "Right now, there's little can be done about him. You'll have to remember, Miss Jenkins, that your father shot him, too. Besides, it all took place on Mexican soil. If you expect the authorities to take up the business, you'll encounter a great deal of red-tape. I doubt if you'd be able to bring Porter to trial."

"I suppose you're right," Deborah said quietly.

"Don't think—" Andy's voice was grim, "—don't think that Porter is going to escape justice. One way or another, that man is due for a reckoning, along with Quillan. But for the present, I think it best if we move quietly, until the gold has been secured. That's to be my first duty—"

"Oh, the gold." Deborah made an impatient movement. "Is that all men think of—gold?"

"It was what your father thought of," Andy

replied quietly. "He wanted you to have it. I gave him my promise to get it for you. I've got to keep my word."

"I'm sorry, Mr. Farlow," the girl said impulsively. "I don't mean to be so disagreeable. You're right, of course. My father knew what was best. I should see it that way, too. If that gold can be located, it will lighten my burden—but, oh, I'd sooner have had father than all the gold in the world. I wish—I wish he had come home. He was so foolish about being crippled. It wouldn't have made any difference—I wouldn't have cared how he looked."

Deborah and Andy were seated in the main room of the ranch house, in large comfortable chairs. A lighted lamp stood on the table between them. Mesquite roots blazed in an open fireplace built of rock. A deer-head ornamented each wall; on the floor were animal skins and Navajo rugs.

The two sat watching the flickering flames in the fireplace. Andy moved uneasily in his chair, at last, saying, "Well, you've got the story, Miss Jenkins. We'll talk more tomorrow. I'd better be getting down to the bunkhouse, with Felipe and Denny. I want to meet the rest of your crew, too—"

Deborah Jenkins raised one protesting hand. "Don't go yet. I realize I'm not very good company. I haven't been talking. But there's so much to think of. Don't go. I'm—" she smiled wistfully at Andy, "—I'm not quite ready to face the night alone, yet, after all you've told me. Besides, it's not late."

Andy sank back in his chair and rolled a cigarette. After a time, the girl reopened the subject of the gold: "Naturally, I haven't the least idea where to commence looking for those *pesos*. I knew father had wealth hidden some place: he told me the last time he was here that he had enough money to make me rich some day. But he didn't say where it was—just that it was placed in safe-keeping, and that I'd have it when the proper time came. I suppose he figured I was too young to be trusted with the secret."

Andy shook his head. "I don't think that was it, Miss Jenkins. Your father was afraid that such knowledge might be dangerous for you to possess. The men who tried to make him speak wouldn't hesitate at working on a woman—and in the same way." He hesitated, "I reckon we'll just have to wait for something to break to lead us to those *pesos*."

"If we find it, it's to be half yours."

"Nothing doing. I—"

"Look here, Andy Farlow, I knew my father. I know he wouldn't ask you to do anything like this, without offering you an equal share—"

"Now, Miss Jenkins—"

"I won't be interrupted. Didn't Dad say something of the sort—?"

"We-ell, yes," Andy admitted reluctantly, "but that's no sign—"

"Fifty-fifty, Mr. Farlow," Deborah stated firmly. "You've earned it."

"Not yet I haven't, and besides I'm not going to take one cent of—"

"Oh, yes, you are. Anyway—" the girl smiled suddenly, "—there isn't any use of us arguing about something we haven't yet laid our hands on, is there?"

Andy grinned. Deborah liked that grin and the clear eyes that went with it. Andy said, "Anyhow, there's one thing we can argue about."

"What is that?"

"This 'mister' you've tacked onto my name. Mostly, my friends call me Andy. Are we going to be friends?"

"Mostly," the girl mimicked, "my friends call me Deb. Are we going to be friends?"

They both grinned this time.

"Looks like we are," Andy chuckled. After a time he went on, "About this gold, I don't suppose your foreman, Zach Watson, would know anything about it, would he?"

"I doubt it. Father hired him, a good many years ago, to run this outfit, but Dad and Zach never knew each other well enough to become fast friends. Of course, father was never home long enough to get well acquainted. I do know he had a high opinion of Zach's ability as a foreman. . . .

That reminds me, are you ready to take Zach's job, until he returns to work, or—"

"We'll hope Zach doesn't die," Andy cut in. "Meanwhile, I'll do what I can to keep things running. I suppose I should know all about the situation here. I've heard some talk of trouble between you and the 2-R spread."

Deborah frowned. "It sort of shapes up that way. Still, we may avoid trouble. Perhaps I'd better go back to the beginning. You see, mother died when I was born. Dad had to hire a woman to look after me until I was able to take care of myself. But he was never at home a great deal. He'd come and go—"

"I'm acquainted with that part of your story," Andy broke in. "Maybe we'll save time by telling me what happened since the last time your father was here."

Deborah nodded. "I'll get to it. I was just a little girl when I last saw him—it must be eleven years ago. I never heard from him again. Three years after he went away, a cowboy, riding through, brought me word that Dad had died. This cowboy had had the word from somebody else who in turn had had it from a third person. I tried to run down the truth of the matter, through a detective agency, but about all those detectives did was spend money. I realize now, Dad sent the word himself, so I wouldn't expect to see him again. Of course, he left his will with me, so I inherited the ranch at once. The county judge knew Dad, and knew me, so affairs were closed up in short order."

"When did you sell to Vaughn, of the Rafter-V Ranch?"

"About a year after I'd inherited the Crown. I wanted a neighbor and I wanted to build up this Casa de Leonés country, as Dad always called it—though I never knew why until I'd heard your story of the gold. Vaughn has been a good neighbor. I only charged him what was reasonable for the land, and he appreciated that, I think. He knew I'd had larger offers. I think you'll like Ethan Vaughn."

"What do you know about Rudabaugh?"

Deb's face clouded. "I'm disappointed in that man," she said severely. "He came to me a trifle over three years ago, and said he wanted to buy enough land to start an outfit. Like a fool, I trusted him and figured he'd keep up the payments on what he bought. He made a down payment and was to pay more each year."

"He hasn't kept up his payments?"

"Hasn't paid me one cent since he made the down payment. Last fall he took a nice beef herd south. In a month he was back with a long yarn about the herd stampeding over a bluff and getting killed. I believed him, at the time, and told him not to worry about payments. I could kick myself when I think how sorry I felt for the man."

Deborah grinned. "Anyway, he took me at my

word: he hasn't worried about the payments. I know, now, he has money, because he bought property in town and at present is erecting a big honky-tonk. That'll be a nice thing for Winghorse, won't it? Not that folks shouldn't have some amusement, but I shudder to think of the sort of place Rudabaugh will run."

"I heard about that dance-hall building he was putting up," Andy nodded. "He must have money, all right."

"I'm sure he has. He couldn't afford to pay that large 2-R crew, if he didn't have money."

"It seems to me," Andy said, "he could be forced to pay."

"Yes, he could," Deborah said. "I could go to court, have the 2-R holdings returned to my ownership, or make him pay up. There's scarcely a doubt but that I'd win my case. But," the girl smiled wryly, "it costs money to carry your troubles into court. The Crown isn't overly burdened with coin of the realm, Andy. If Rudabaugh chose to put up a fight, he might cost me a lot of money, worry and trouble. Later, after beef round-up, I should have a few dollars to call my own, but until then, I'm sitting quiet. I'll just let Mr. Rudabaugh get away with his scheming for a time. Later, I'll settle the score."

"Is the Crown carrying a mortgage now?"

"Thank the Lord, no! That's why I'm short of ready cash. I don't operate a very large spread, but it's in a healthy, flourishing condition, particularly in view of an epidemic of black-leg that cost a good many ranchers in this state a lot of money when it struck their herds, about three years back. We're all just commencing to get back on our feet. But the Crown hasn't been forced to borrow one cent—and I don't intend that it shall, if I can help it!"

"You're wise, Deb."

"I try to be. Right now, if I had to have money, I wouldn't have the least trouble borrowing on my holdings, but I don't want to borrow money to spend on lawyers—though that is exactly what I figure Rudabaugh would like me to do."

"Counting on breaking you in a court fight, eh, if he can force you into one? What is he driving at?"

"He wants the Crown," Deborah said grimly, "but he's not going to have it while I'm able to fight him off. He's offered to buy the outfit from me."

"What! And him already owing you money—"

"Owing me money for the present property he controls," Deborah nodded. "Oh, that man has more nerve than a ton of brass monkeys. You see, both the Crown and Vaughn's Rafter-V get their water from two streams that head up in the Casa de Leonés. Rudabaugh has to depend for his water on waterholes. I warned him of that when he bought his land from me, told him his waterholes couldn't always be depended on. But I guess he thought he knew more than I did. He learned differently. Now, he'd like to get the Crown, so he'd have plenty of water for his herds. In fact, he had the nerve to tell me he could pay me up within two or three years, if he had my water. He claimed I was preventing his ranch from developing the way it should, when I refused to sell him water rights."

"That cuss sure has got nerve. What did you tell him?"

"I told him to get back to the 2-R and stay there while he could." The girl's face was flushed. "In fact, I told Mister Reece Rudabaugh that if he didn't mind his step, he wouldn't have any ranch to develop." Deborah suddenly laughed at the memory. "Good grief! I was certainly mad clear through that day. But he's stayed away from the Crown, since then."

"Denny Devers tells me he makes trouble for your crew whenever possible."

The girl nodded. "Yes, he does. That whole 2-R outfit is composed of trouble-breeders. His crew is always trying to start fights with my crew. Today, they shot Zach Watson. That makes it look as though serious trouble was breeding, Andy. I don't like the looks of things. Rudabaugh is probably figuring to frighten me out of the country—make me glad to sell out at any price. But I don't scare easily. If he wants a fight, I'm likely to give him one." Deb's jaw set determinedly.

Andy considered. "Suppose a range war between your outfit and the 2-R did break out, Deb, would the Rafter-V take sides?"

Deborah replied promptly. "Not with the 2-R. I feel sure Vaughn would trail with me, if I asked for help. But I hesitate to do that. Vaughn is a good man, and I wouldn't want to get him into anything of the kind. But I do know he doesn't like Rudabaugh."

"Vaughn," Andy said quietly, "may find himself forced to fight, if a range war breaks. If Rudabaugh could win out over you, his next move would be toward seizing the Rafter-V. Common sense will show Vaughn that. How many men has he on his payroll?"

"Let's see . . . there's his foreman, a cook and three punchers. . . . I've been getting along with a cook, Zach Watson as foreman and two hands. Now that you've taken Zach's place, we'll have an extra hand, if Felipe stays here with you."

"Felipe will stay. He's a mighty good man, Deb."

Deborah nodded. "He looks capable. Come beef roundup time I'd have had to hire one or two extra men, anyway."

"How is your herd sizing up—losing any cows to rustlers?"

Deb shook her head. "I don't think so—that is,

no more than we all lose, every year. There haven't been any serious losses. Denny and Kitten have been riding regularly, and they haven't reported any big shortages, like there'd be if a big gang started to rustle me."

"We can be thankful for that," Andy said. "Usually with a skunk like Rudabaugh to contend with, there's rustling besides."

"I don't think for a minute he's above rustling a beef animal, now and then," Deborah nodded. "But so far, things don't look bad in that direction. Lucky for me, they don't. If I had cowthieves to contend with—" She broke off, then resumed, "Anyway, you know how things stand now. You can understand how much I'd like to locate those gold *pesos*. In short, the Crown needs money, if it's to be kept out of debt."

Andy frowned. "And we haven't the least idea where to start looking for them. Hang the luck!" He chucked his cigarette butt into the fireplace and faced the girl, "You don't happen to remember your dad mentioning a cave, at any time, do you?"

"Cave? What cave? Where?" Deb shook her head.

Andy shrugged his shoulders. "I don't know exactly. It was just an idea I got. Hidden treasure is sometimes found in caves. I got to thinking there might be a cave up in the Casa de Leonés Range, someplace. You know, Home of the

Lions—meaning hiding place of the gold pieces."

Deborah frowned. "You might have the right hunch, Andy. Only father always called all of this country, roundabouts, the Casa de Leonés country. That money might be most any place. I've never heard him mention any cave in particular, either."

Andy smiled ruefully. "Looks like we're up against it. Just the same, there's bound to be caves in those hills. I figure to give 'em all a good combing. Anyway, those hills are a good place to start looking. . . . Is there anybody in Winghorse your Dad knew well enough to trust with the secret?"

The girl shook her head. "There's scarcely anyone living in Winghorse now, that Dad knew. For that matter, practically all of the original buildings have been wrecked and new ones erected. The first buildings of the town were but little better than shacks, anyway. That is, excepting the Brown Jug Saloon. Dad built that building himself, to house the general store, when Winghorse was founded."

"Yes, Dan Jenkins mentioned starting this town with a general store."

He built every bit of that building with his own hands."

"He sure built for keeps," Andy said. "Those adobe walls where Toby Byers has his Brown Jug, must be nigh to three feet thick. The timbers and boards look solid too."

The girl smiled reminiscently. "Dad always had a soft spot in his heart for that place, because it was the first in Winghorse. He never would sell it, as he did several other places in town. Toby Byers pays his rent to me regularly, though I guess business isn't so good since Rudabaugh opened the Winghorse Bar. Oh, well, if Toby goes out of business, I won't mind, so much, though I'd hate to see him lose money. But I never did like the idea of a saloon in that building. Still, the men want such a place, and Toby runs a quiet, orderly business."

"I wouldn't worry about that, if I were you," Andy advised. "The thing we've got to think about is finding those *pesos*."

"For you as well as for me," Deborah put in quickly.

Andy sighed. "Have we got to open that old argument again?" He grinned suddenly. "Let's postpone the argument until we actually find the gold, then you and I can have a reg'lar slambang, knockout and drag-down battle of an argument."

"All right," Deborah smiled. "I won't say another word about it—tonight. Just the same, Andy Farlow, I'm mighty glad you're here to help me locate the money. It must have been just good luck that took you to Ensenajo, that day. Or had you headed there on business?"

Andy shook his head. "Pure luck, as you say. I'd been working pretty hard for three years and saving most of my wages. Finally, I quit the job and decided to see some new country. I was heading west and had dipped down into Mexico when I come to Ensenajo. I'm mighty glad things worked out to bring me there—" Andy broke off suddenly and consulted a large, silver watch that he carried. "Holy sufferin' bald-headed steers! It's past midnight. I've got to be drifting down to the bunkhouse."

The man and girl talked a few minutes longer, before Andy said good-night and headed down to find his bunk. When he arrived, Felipe and the rest of the Crown crew were already in blankets, snoring lustily. Andy found an empty bunk and his blankets, where Felipe had spread them, blew out the lamp and rolled in. But for once he failed to find sleep promptly. His mind was roving futilely through the *Casa de Leonés* hills, groping for the spot where a man would be most likely to hide one hundred thousand dollars in gold. . . .

XI. SHOWDOWN CALLED FOR

THE MORE ANDY pondered the question, the greater became his determination to avoid trouble, if possible, with Rudabaugh's 2-R outfit, until such time as he had located the hidden *pesos*. As he explained to Deborah, the morning following his arrival at the Crown Ranch:

"It's this way, Deb, if a range war should break out, there's no telling where it might end, or how long it will last. That being the case, we've got to do our best to avoid trouble."

Deb said, "You mean, let Rudabaugh run all over us?" The girl looked queerly at Andy.

"Not exactly that, Deb. But we don't need to go around with a chip on our shoulders, looking for trouble. We can keep out of his way—"

"I don't like that either," Deborah said, hard-voiced. "The Crown will fight for its rights."

"If it has to, yes," Andy conceded patiently, "but—"

"Look here, Andy, what are you hinting at?" the girl said abruptly.

The two were standing near the back door of the ranch house, right after breakfast. The bright morning sun picked out highlights on Deborah's dark, shining hair. Andy glanced off, across the ranch yard, toward the signs of activity about the bunkhouse, where the men were commencing to get ready for the day's work. He didn't answer the girl at first. Deborah repeated her question.

"What am I getting at?" Andy smiled wryly. "It's this way, Deb, if war breaks out, somebody's going to get hurt. I don't want to be that one, not until after I've had an opportunity to find that hidden money. I promised your father I'd help get it for you. While I'm alive, I've got a chance of keeping my promise. If I was to get laid up—well, I wouldn't be much help to you. Do you see what I mean?"

"I see. At the same time, Andy, I'd rather not find that treasure than have the Crown knuckle under to Reece Rudabaugh. No foreman of mine will ever do that—" she broke off, saying hotly, "You've got to understand, Andy Farlow, that I won't take another thing from that crooked—"

"Now, wait a minute, wait a minute," Andy grinned. "Don't you go to flyin' off your high-horse. I know just how you feel. I want to fight just as much as you do. But I'm trying to show common-sense. All I ask is that we try to sidestep trouble. If it's forced on us—then we fight back the hardest we know how. I'm not aiming to take anything from Rudabaugh—"

"But—"

"Wait a minute, let me finish. If there's a range war coming, nothing we can do will stop it. But we'll be in a far better position to do battle, if we can stall that range war off, until we've found the money your Dad left."

"I don't see why?"

"You probably don't," Andy said calmly. "You've never been messed into anything of the sort, have you?"

"N-no, I haven't."

"A great general once said that God is on the side of the heaviest artillery. Well, I don't know about that, but I do know that, in a range war, the side who has the money to hire the most gun-fighters, generally wins. Now do you know what I mean?"

The girl looked at Andy, wide-eyed. "I think I do," she said slowly. "I hadn't thought of it that way. Would Rudabaugh hire professional gunmen, if we had trouble with him—"

"Certain. We'd have to do the same thing—or be wiped out. So you see, Deb, if we can find those twenty-peso coins, we'll be in a better condition to buck Rudabaugh, if he decides to cut loose. Meanwhile, we'll try and keep out of his way— unless he forces our hand—"

"Oh, I hate it! I hate it all!" the girl burst out angrily. "Why can't we live in peace? Why do men have to be always fighting over land or gold? Why can't they live quiet lives? Why do men like Rudabaugh have to come here and—and—?"

"I haven't got the answer to that one," Andy broke in quietly.

"What have you the answer to?" Deborah flashed.

Andy spoke quietly, "I'm not sure, as yet, I have the answer to anything. The last few hours have been tough on you. I'm realizing that. I'm hoping you'll see my way, after you've calmed down some. If I'm going to be your foreman, you've got to let me run things. You don't want war; neither you don't want to knuckle under to Reece Rudabaugh. I don't blame you. But sometimes a person finds his hand forced. Well, we're not going to knuckle under, but we are going to do our best to avoid an open break as long as possible. If a break is unavoidable, I aim to be prepared."

"I'm sorry, Andy." The girl was suddenly contrite. She smiled ruefully. "I sort of lost my head for a moment. I'm truly sorry."

"Nothing to be sorry for. I know how you feel."

"You said something about being prepared. What are you going to do?"

"I'm going to ride over and see Vaughn this afternoon, find just where he stands, and if he'll side with us, in case of an emergency. To avoid trouble, I'm going to have your men stay away from Winghorse—"

"But some of us will have to go in town—"

"I'll take care of going in for mail and so on—"

"Taking all of the risks yourself, eh?" Deborah snapped.

Andy grinned. After a moment the girl relaxed and smiled.

Andy went on, "There'll be less risk, I figure, if

I go in alone. I even plan to have Felipe stay here. Some of the 2-R crew might use Felipe, a Mexican, as an excuse for starting a fight. Felipe is hot-headed. If I keep him here, he won't be the fuse to set off the dynamite. The 2-R men probably travel in groups. If I'm alone, they'll hesitate to pick a quarrel with me, while I'm in Winghorse. Public opinion, there, might resent that, as I'd be one lone cowhand against two or three. So you see, I'm not running any risks."

"I hope not," Deborah sighed.

Andy continued, "If supplies are needed, your cook can drive in for them—unarmed. I'll accompany him, if I feel it is necessary."

The girl finally admitted, somewhat reluctantly, that Andy's plans were best. The two talked a few minutes longer, before Deborah returned to the house.

Andy strode down to the bunkhouse, where Denny Devers and Elmer Kittenger, known as Kitten, were just picking up their saddles and starting out for the corral. Kitten was a big giant of a man with mild, blue eyes and an easy-going manner. He was slow of speech and deliberate of action.

Felipe and Beanpot Reardon, the Crown cook, stood nearby. Reardon was elderly, with a skinny frame and long white mustaches. An old flour sack, in lieu of an apron, was tied about his bony hips.

"Reckon I'm a hell of a foreman," Andy grinned as he came up. "Here, the morning's half gone, and I haven't outlined any work for you."

"Denny and me was just aimin' to continue with orders Zach gave us yesterday," Kitten said slowly. "There ain't much to do, right now, but we been a-ridin' over near the Casa de Leonés, just to sort of keep an eye on the cow critters, to see that none don't get to missin' sudden like. Them orders all right with you, Andy?"

Andy nodded. "I reckon Zach Watson knew what needed to be done. You two go on as before. If anything different turns up, I'll figure then what's to be done."

Denny Devers said somewhat disappointedly. "I was sort of figuring you might want us to go to town with you, Andy."

"What for?" Andy asked.

Denny's manner was evasive. "Oh, I dunno. I just thought maybe you might want us to ride in with you and look Winghorse over."

Andy chuckled, "And see if we couldn't find some of the 2-R to throw lead at, eh? Nothing doing, Denny. My orders is to avoid trouble with 2-R, as much as possible."

"Purty sens'ble, I calls it," Beanpot Reardon said in crabby accents. "Don't never go seekin' trouble, or yo're li'ble to find a bucketful." He knocked the dottle from a smelly brier pipe. "Well, I can't stand here a-gabbin'. I got breakfast dishes to scrub an'

147

bread to set. Andy, any time any of these cowhands gets reckless at inactivity, you send 'em to me. I allus got plenty work in my kitchen."

"I'll do that, Beanpot," Andy laughed.

The old cook nodded, spat, and stomped off in the direction of his mess shanty. Denny and Kitten continued on their way to the corral and within a few minutes had saddled and were loping their ponies out of the ranch yard.

Felipe and Andy stood in front of the bunkhouse. "You go to Winghorse—no?" Felipe asked hopefully.

"No," Andy replied. "And neither do you, Felipe. I want you to stay away from town." He explained his reasons, adding, "You saddle up, *amigo*, and ride around the Crown holdings a mite. Get the lay of the land. When you get over near the *Casa de Leonés*, keep your eyes peeled for caves. We've got to comb those hills plenty. If we're lucky, we'll locate what we're after. Meanwhile, don't mention anything to Denny or Kitten or Beanpot about the gold. You see—"

"You don't trust those hombres?" Felipe asked disappointedly.

"I'd trust 'em until hell freezes over," Andy said promptly. "At the same time, there's no use letting too many in on the secret. A careless word dropped at the wrong time, might upset things considerable."

"You are ver' wise," the *mestizo* nodded. "I'm

theenk you hav' somezing like that in the mind, so when Denny asks me regarding your othair meeting with Porter and Quillan, I'm pretend I don' know."

"Good. Porter and Quillan will probably tell Rudabaugh. Rudabaugh might come over on the Crown holdings, looking for that treasure. That's another reason I want to keep you in the saddle, riding around. You can warn off any strangers you might see trespassing Deb's land."

"What you do now?"

"I'm going to look over Zach Watson's accounts and sort of get an idea of things, here on the Crown. This afternoon, I figure to ride over and get acquainted with Vaughn. We've got to move mighty cautious, Felipe. We don't want any range war interrupting our search for that gold."

"I'm theenk you are correc', Andee."

Felipe left to saddle up. Andy saw him leave a short time later, from the bunk-house window over Zach Watson's roughboard desk.

It wasn't quite noon when Andy rose from the desk, after putting the papers and books to one side. He buckled on his gun, then sauntered over to Beanpot's cook house. Here, refusing to wait for dinner, he bolted down a couple of slices of bread and cold beef, then headed for the corral to get his pony. A few minutes later he was pounding his saddle across the range in the direction of Ethan Vaughn's Rafter-V Ranch.

It was shortly after two o'clock when, topping a rise of land, he spied the Rafter-V buildings, huddled in a clump of cottonwood trees. Andy touched spurs to his pony and the animal stretched its stride. It was all good grazing country, hereabouts, and as Andy rode, he passed a small herd of steers, bearing a Rafter-V brand on the left ribs.

As he drew near the house, Andy saw a solitary figure seated on the porch that fronted the building. The man rose as Andy brought his pony to a stop near the porch railing, and called out,

"Light a spell and rest your saddle, stranger."

"I'll do just that. Thanks," Andy nodded, as he swung down from the pony's back, dropped reins over its head, and stepped to the low porch. "You Ethan Vaughn?"

"That's my name." Vaughn had dragged a rocking chair up beside his own and motioned Andy to be seated.

"I'm Andy Farlow."

"T'hell you say." Vaughn seemed glad to meet Andy. The two shook hands.

Vaughn was a tall, spare, grizzled man with steady eyes. His legs in their clean overalls were bowed somewhat, attesting many years spent in the saddle. He was smoking a corncob pipe.

Andy seated himself. "I figured I might as well ride over and get acquainted," he opened the conversation. "Miss Jenkins took me on as Crown foreman."

"That so. Well, from what I hear that ought to work out satisfactory all around."

Andy smiled. "What did you hear?"

"I rode into Winghorse, this mornin', for my mail. Stopped to see how Zach Watson was. He's just about the same. Anyway, I dropped into the Brown Jug. Toby Byers tells me that one Andy Farlow staged a little ruckus there last night and sort of set a couple of Rudabaugh hands on their haunches."

"It didn't amount to much," Andy grinned. "Besides, I had a pardner with me. Then, Denny Devers was there too."

"Pshaw! That Devers would get a preacher into trouble. That button is always ready to fight. But tell me about it. All's I heard, I got second-hand."

Andy briefly related the happenings of the night before. Now and then, Vaughn nodded his head in satisfaction, or put in a word of his own.

When Andy had concluded, Vaughn said, "I'm mighty glad to hear you come out topside."

"You don't like Rudabaugh."

"He's a skunk," Vaughn said explosively. "If you hadn't come here today, I'd been at your place, come night fall."

"Any particular reason?" Andy asked.

Vaughn looked grim. "Farlow," he stated,

"there's a showdown being called for. Either we wipe out Rudabaugh, or he'll wipe us out."

Andy asked quietly, "How you figuring?" He hadn't expected Vaughn to be so belligerent.

"I've been figuring," Vaughn said more quietly, as he shoved fresh tobacco into his corncob. "Ever since I got back from town, I been sittin' here, just figurin'. Farlow, Rudabaugh would like to control the Crown holdings."

"That so?" Andy said quietly. "What makes you think so?"

"It's pretty well rumored around town. He's got to be stopped."

Andy considered. "Have you figured how it's to be done?"

"I'm not sure yet. Here's the proposition in a nutshell. The 2-R outnumbers the Crown; it also outnumbers the Rafter-V. However, the Crown and the Rafter-V together, could, I think, just about handle Mister Rudabaugh."

"You hinting we should throw in together?" Andy asked.

"No, by Godfrey! I'm not *hinting*. I'm suggesting it's the safest thing we can do."

Andy nodded. "As a matter of fact, Mr. Vaughn, I rode over here with something of the kind in mind. I wanted to feel you out, see if you'd side us in any trouble that might arise."

"You're damn right I will," Vaughn snapped. "I got three cowhands. I can still handle a gun. If

152

necessary my cook will do his share. I'm glad this thing is sifting down to facts. We can just about put Rudabaugh in his place—"

"Just a minute," Andy interrupted, smiling. "I didn't expect to find you so all-fired ready for battle. Howcome?"

"Ain't I told you I've been figuring? It's the only sensible thing to do. If Rudabaugh can dispose of the Crown, he'd start on me next. Together we can whale the hide off'n him and his gang. When I was in the Brown Jug this morning, three of his crew come in—"

"Porter and Quillan?"

Vaughn shook his head. "No, I didn't see them two. These were fellows by the name of Hannan and Welch. The other's name was Beck, I think. He's a newcomer, must have just been taken in by Rudabaugh. I saw Rudabaugh talkin' to him on the street, 'bout half hour before I went in the Brown Jug. Anyway, Hannan and Welch started talkin' mean about how their boss was goin' to run this country. They cast some slurs in my direction, but I didn't take 'em up on it. I was outnumbered."

"You were sensible."

"Shore I was. But I'd sooner pulled iron on the dirty sons. I left the Brown Jug as soon as I'd finished my drink, but I tell you this, Farlow, there's going to be trouble—"

"There is," Andy cut in, "unless we can avoid it."

"Why should we?" Vaughn bristled. "Have I got to take a lot of slurs and not fight back—"

"Just a minute, Mr. Vaughn. Are you prepared to start a range war?"

"What else can we do?"

"I'm not sure yet, but—"

"But hell!" Vaughn said wrathfully. "The best defense is an offense, every time."

"Granted, but I'm not sure it's necessary, the way you're going at it. Are you prepared to spend money to hire gunfighters and—"

"I can handle a gun myself—"

"Now, wait a minute. I don't doubt that. But if this thing gets flaring too high, there'll be more guns than your own required—and I'm counting your crew's guns, too. And the Crown's. It'll get out of hand. We'll be forced to bring hired guns into the country. We'll spend money like it was water. We might even win. But where'd we be? Blood would flow like water, too. Lives would be lost. We've got to consider all of that."

"Well! Well!" Vaughn looked disappointed. "I didn't expect you to take that attitude."

"I'm only trying to use common-sense, Mr. Vaughn," Andy pleaded.

"Look here, Farlow," Vaughn accused directly, "you're trying to fight shy of trouble, aren't you?"

"Yes, I am," Andy replied, just as directly.

"Why?" Vaughn barked.

"I have certain reasons of my own," Andy evaded, "besides the ones I've already given you."

"What are they?"

"I'm not ready to say—just yet."

"Paugh!" Vaughn spat disgustedly. "All right, your business is your own, but I can tell you this much, if you don't want trouble, stay away from Winghorse. It's waiting for you there."

"I suppose so," Andy said idly. "You talking about anything in particular?"

"Yo're damn right I am," Vaughn snapped. "I judged from certain things I heard in the Brown Jug, this mornin', that the whole Rudabaugh crew is out to get your skin. Hannan and Welch were laughing pretty sneery, about what this Beck feller was going to do."

"Beck, eh? The new man Rudabaugh hired?"

"He's a mean lookin' cuss, Farlow, so you'd better stay out of Winghorse, if you want to avoid trouble."

"Maybe so," Andy nodded carelessly. "And then again, maybe those 2-R hands were just making talk."

"Beck wasn't," Vaughn insisted. "He spoke right out plain, once. Raised his voice more than he intended, perhaps, but I heard him."

"Just what did Beck say?" Andy asked interestedly.

"I heard Beck say," Vaughn stated, "that the only thing he loved more than diamonds was to see a man squirm with a forty-five slug in his middle, and that—"

"Wait!" Andy said suddenly. "Was this Beck—?"

"And that a hombre named Farlow," Vaughn rushed on, "would give a demonstration of said squirming the first time he rode into Winghorse!"

XII. BLANK WALL AHEAD

ANDY STIFFENED. "This Beck hombre," he asked, "was he called Diamonds Beck, by any chance? Do you know?"

"That's the name!" Vaughn exclaimed. "Welch and Hannan called him Diamonds. He's got a mean eye. Got diamond cuff links and a tie pin. He doesn't dress like a cowhand. He looks more like one of these city sports from Kansas City or Denver. The only natural thing the man wore was a holstered forty-five—and the butt was notched until it looked like a wash-board—"

"Diamonds Beck," Andy spoke half to himself.

"You know him, Farlow?"

"I—I know of him," Andy said hesitantly. "He's bad clear through. Treacherous. Fast with a gun. A killer at heart. He—he killed a friend of mine once. Outguessed him."

Andy put one hand to his face, lowered it again. He looked rather stunned. Vaughn rose swiftly and strode into his house. In a moment he returned, bearing a bottle and two glasses.

Andy looked at the man as he poured a stiff drink.

"You're looking sort of pale and shaky, son," Vaughn said. "I figured a drink might help. I'll take one myself to keep you company. Looks like news of this Beck hombre threw a scare into you."

"I—I wouldn't say that," Andy forced a weak smile. "It—it was just a shock to hear it, that's all. You see, I was under the impression that Diamonds Beck was in the state penitentiary, serving a life sentence, for another of his murders."

"He may have been," Vaughn said dubiously, "but he's certainly on the outside now. Is he bad, Farlow?"

"Pretty bad," Andy nodded.

"And fast with a gun, you say?"

Andy gulped. "I never saw a faster."

"You've seen him in action, then?"

"Once. That was enough. Saw him shoot a man in a street duel, in El Paso. He had friends with him. His horse was ready. He made a getaway before anyone could stop him. Shortly after he was caught for another killing, in another state, and went to the pen. He should have been hanged, but there was a slip-up some place."

Andy was still holding the drink Vaughn had tendered him. Now he took a drink. Vaughn raised his glass, lowered it and settled back in his chair. Slowly, Andy relaxed, his features a mask of profound thought.

"I've been thinking," and Vaughn looked queerly at Andy, "that you've got a fight ahead of you, Farlow. There's no way out of this. You're up against a blank wall. You may—"

"Yes, a blank wall ahead," Andy muttered, "in more ways than one."

"You may not like the idea," Vaughn went on, "but you've got to climb it to get any place. Either that, or turn and run back the way you've come."

Andy, lost in thought, didn't appear to have heard the words.

Vaughn frowned and went on. "You're cornered, Farlow. You've got to fight or show a yellow streak. How would it be if we waited until supper, when my boys come in off'n the range? Then, with them to back us, we'll ride into Winghorse. Instead of waiting for Rudabaugh to strike the first blow, we'll strike it, carry the fight to him. In that way, this Diamonds Beck hombre may be kept busy enough to leave you alone. One of us can get him."

Andy smiled ruefully. "You're right certain I'm afraid of Beck, aren't you?"

Vaughn said bluntly, "Well, how does it look to you? Not that I blame you, if he's as bad as you say—and already killed a friend of yours. You're no gun-fighter, from all I can see—not an expert gun-slinger, leastwise."

"I reckon not," Andy agreed.

"Well, then," Vaughn nodded impatiently. "You'll have to agree to my scheme. Good Lord, Farlow! Rudabaugh will ride rough-shod over the whole country if he isn't stopped. As foreman of the Crown, you've got to take some action."

"When I do," Andy said, suddenly quiet, "I'll take it in my own way. No, Mr. Vaughn, I'm still against open warfare—at least until it is forced on us."

Vaughn spat disgustedly. "Yore way spells ruin."

"I hope not."

"What you hope and what you get," Vaughn said angrily, "are li'ble to be two different things. You won't throw in with us, then?"

"Certainly I will," Andy said promptly, "if Rudabaugh forces us into it. Not otherwise—at least, not for a time yet."

"Why not?"

"I said before," Andy replied a trifle wearily, "that I had my own reasons. I'm not yet ready to state them."

"By God!" Vaughn snapped. "You're making it tough for me as well as the Crown. You know I don't dare tackle Rudabaugh alone."

"It wouldn't be wise," Andy smiled thinly. "Be patient. All I ask is that you give me a chance to work this out in my own way. You'll find I'll fight, quick enough, if nothing else offers."

"A rat will fight when it's cornered," Vaughn snapped angrily.

Andy's face went scarlet. He rose from his chair. Vaughn rose too, biting his lip.

"I'm taking that back, Farlow," Vaughn said. "I didn't mean it that way. I lost my temper."

"Forget it," Andy smiled, though there wasn't any smile in his eyes. "Maybe neither one of us is normal. We've got to think things over a mite."

"I reckon so," Vaughn said lamely, then added, "I'm still against your plan of holdin' off, Farlow, but you've got my hands tied. I can't buck Rudabaugh alone, and if you won't help, well—" He broke off, then, "Perhaps I could get Miss Deb to see things my way."

"Perhaps you could," Andy said courteously. "After all, the Crown is her ranch. She pays the wages. If she cares to join you in a war on Rudabaugh, that is her business. But I'd suggest, Mr. Vaughn, that you think twice before putting your finger in the pie and messing it up."

Abruptly, Vaughn said, "Will you be stayin' to supper with us, Farlow?" His eyes were hot, angry.

Andy took the hint and arose. "Thanks, no I'll be pushing off, right *pronto*."

He stepped from the porch, gathered his pony's reins in his hands and mounted.

"You won't reconsider my offer?" Vaughn asked.

"What offer?" Andy gazed down, level-eyed, from his saddle, to the man on the porch.

"I'll gather my men. We'll ride into town with you, and see that Diamonds Beck don't take unfair advantage of you." There was a taunting note in the words that Andy didn't overlook.

Andy smiled and shook his head. "Nope, thanks again. That might precipitate a range war. If I go in alone, nobody else will be responsible."

"You going in alone?" Vaughn said.

Andy smiled slowly. "What do you think?"

And then Vaughn exploded, "I know damn well you won't!"

Andy didn't say anything—just turned his horse and started back toward the way from which he had come.

Vaughn remained seated on the porch, muttering curses under his breath and watching Andy until the horse had topped the first rise of ground.

"Damn it to hell!" Vaughn swore. "I'd hoped for better from Farlow. After what I'd heard about him, I never dreamed he'd show yellow in a tight."

A step sounded inside the house. Spareribs Pryor, the Rafter-V cook, appeared at the door. He was a weather-beaten individual with a long jaw and a dour countenance.

"Shucks!" Spareribs said, disappointedly, "I thought I heerd voices out here."

"Mebbe you did," Vaughn grunted.

"I heerd a horse nicker, leastwise."

"Mebbe you did," Vaughn repeated.

"Who was it?" Spareribs demanded with the familiarity born of long association.

"What difference does it make?" Vaughn growled.

Spareribs looked his exasperation. "I thought mebbe we was goin' to have company for supper."

"Since when does a cow cook take to welcomin'

extra mouths to feed?" Vaughn asked skeptically.

"Don't get sarcastical," Spareribs snapped. "I asked a civil question, and look at the way I get answered. If you got to know, I was hopin' it was that Farlow hombre you heard about in Winghorse."

"It was."

"And you didn't offer him his supper?"

"Sure, I asked him."

"And he wouldn't stay?"

"He refused with thanks."

Spareribs pondered the reply. Finally he said shrewdly, "What did you two argue 'bout?"

"Did I say we argued?" Vaughn said sourly.

"You don't have to say it. It's writ all over your face."

"Oh, my Gawd!" Vaughn groaned. "Do I have to tell you everythin' I know?"

"Why not?" Spareribs snapped. "It wouldn't take more'n a couple of minutes."

Vaughn growled. "Go on back to yore pots and pans and leave me be."

"I won't stir a step until you've told me what happened."

"You can stand there all night then."

"I'll tell you," Spareribs stated. "Farlow wouldn't fall in with your scheme of makin' war on Rudabaugh."

Vaughn stiffened. "How do you happen to know so much?"

"I know you. You come back from Winghorse, this mornin', with a lot of talk about getting the Crown to join up and wiping out Rudabaugh, didn't you?"

"Mebbe I did."

"Mebbe my eye. There was no mebbe about it. You was plumb enthusiastical. Now, yo're crabbier'n a houn'-dawg with a cactus thorn in his sit-spot. So-o! That's what happened. You wanted to make war and Farlow suggests caution. So you flied off'n your handle. No, don't tell me. I know you did. I know you. I think Farlow is right and if you don't like that you can give me my time and I'll get out. But you won't. I know you. And you pro'bly insulted him. Ethan Vaughn, at times you ain't no more sense than a doodle-bug with woman trouble. I'm demmed if I know why I worked for you all these years. You'd drive a man crazy—"

"If you're the man you wouldn't have far to go," Vaughn said testily.

"The longer I work for you," Spareribs said, and there was a wicked light in his eye, "the longer I think I'm already there."

"I've known that for a long time," Vaughn said, a chuckle breaking through his tones. "Look, Spareribs, there's more to it than you think. Farlow's yellow as gold and not so fine."

"You're sure you haven't misjudged him?"

"Not I. Look, let me tell you . . ."

From that point on, Vaughn related all that had passed between him and Andy Farlow. When he had finished, the ranch cook shook his head.

"You missed it again, you old fool," Spareribs said testily. "That boy ain't yellow."

"I tell you he got pale as a ghost, when I mentioned the name of Diamonds Beck."

"I ain't called you a liar. Mebbe he did get pale. Mebbe he was scared. I would be under similar circumstances. But that ain't no sign he's runnin' away from Beck. Cripes, Ethan, if he'd been yellow, he'd have taken you up on your offer to accompany him to town—you and the boys. Nope, he wouldn't do that. He's wise enough to stall off the war such a move would bring. So he refuses yore help and goes in to meet Diamonds Beck alone. It's his problem and he'll settle it his way—and alone."

"My God, Spareribs, do you think that's it?"

"I feel it in my bones."

Vaughn shook his head. "If you're right, I sure owe that boy an apology. I'll make it, too—first time I see him."

"You will, if you ever see him again—alive," Spareribs growled. "And that same I doubt, if Beck is as bad as Farlow says he is—"

"Lord, I hope not." Vaughn's face was a study in concern. "I'd never forgive myself if it's like you say, Spareribs. Why I practically called that boy yellow to his face."

"I'm damned if I can understand your delicacy in sech matters," Spareribs said ironically, "any more than I can understand why he didn't knock yore backteeth down your throat. S'help me—"

"Dammit, Spareribs!" Vaughn half groaned. "I've told you I'd apologize, if Farlow rides to meet Beck."

"That will fix everything up lovely," Spareribs snapped, "if and especially we hear word tonight that Diamonds Beck thrun lead through Farlow. Ethan, you'd better do some damn fast thinking!"

XIII. THE KILLER BRAND

SUNDOWN WAS STILL an hour distant when Andy trotted his foam-flecked pony into Winghorse. He kept to the middle of the road, eyes alert for the first sign of Diamonds Beck, but the man was nowhere to be seen on the street. Once, Andy heard a man on the sidewalk call, "There's Farlow," but he paid little attention, beyond turning slightly in the saddle to see who had spoken. The man was a stranger to him; probably someone who had been in the crowd, the previous evening, at the Brown Jug.

At the tie-rail of the Brown Jug, Andy drew rein and dismounted. He tossed his reins over the rail and strode through the swinging doors to the interior of the saloon. Excepting for Toby Byers, seated on a high stool behind the bar, the place was empty.

Toby slipped down from the stool. "Hi-yuh, Farlow."

"Hello, Toby. How's business?"

"Rotten, thanks. What'll you have?"

"Nothing to drink, right now, Toby. I'm looking for information. I half expected to find a hombre named Diamonds Beck here."

Toby swore. "He's been here. I was just about to warn you. He's made some war-talk about what he intends to do to you. Ethan Vaughn of the Rafter-V was in here, this morning, and—"

"I heard about that. Thought maybe I'd find Beck here."

Toby said bitterly, "He and a couple of 2-R punchers named Welch and Hannan have been in here half a dozen times. They just stay long enough to drive out any customers I might have. If you stay here long enough, they'll be in again, likely."

"Rudabaugh in town?"

"He was in, this morning," Toby replied. "He pulled out for his ranch, around noon time."

"Quillan and Porter with him?"

"I ain't seen those two since last night—nor Herb Kimball neither. I reckon you and your pards threw the fear o' Gawd into 'em, and they're fightin' shy of Winghorse."

"I hope so, but I doubt it," Andy said shortly. "Quillan and his pards won't scare as easy as that."

"Look here," Toby said suddenly, "if you and Beck meet, will there be any gun-play?"

Andy said grimly, "I'm lookin' forward to it."

Byers looked rather concerned. He didn't say anything. Andy took the forty-five from his holster and revolved the cylinder to make certain the mechanism was in efficient working order.

Toby finally said delicately. "Business hasn't been so good."

"I suppose not," Andy replied mechanically. He was standing sidewise at the bar, his eyes on the swinging doors.

"I'd hate to have to buy another bar mirror," Toby went on.

Andy finally "got" what Byers was driving at. He smiled thinly. "You figuring my shots might go wild?" he asked.

"Nobody's succeeded in putting a slug into Diamonds Beck yet, from all I understand. He's fast—and bad."

Andy nodded. "If he's the Beck I'm thinking of, he's all of that. Just to make sure—what sort of looking fellow is he?"

"Slim, sort of dandified. Wears a lot of diamonds. Pale complected."

"Black mustache, curled at the ends? Black wavy hair, sort of oily?"

"Not now he ain't. I understand Beck was paroled recent out of prison. He's got a prison hair-cut. No mustache," Toby said.

"I reckon. I'd forgotten that," Andy nodded.

"You know him?" Toby asked.

"I've seen him," Andy evaded, "quite a long spell ago."

"He's sure dressed dudish—keeps pullin' a handkerchief out of his inside coat pocket to fleck the dust from his sleeve, or somthin' like that."

Andy said, tight-lipped, "Yes, I've seen that too." He added, a minute later, "Well, I reckon I'll drift outside. There's no use getting your place shot up."

"Look here, Andy," Byers said uncomfortably,

"I don't want you to get the idea I'm putting you out."

"Sure not, Toby. I know how it is."

"Look, Andy, how'll it be if I close up the Brown Jug? I'll get a gun, and go with you, see that you get a square deal?"

Andy shook his head. "Thanks, just the same. Beck is my problem. I don't figure you're much good at shootin', Toby. You stay here and run your business. I'll drift. S'long."

Toby said faintly, "S'long. And good luck."

"I'll need it."

Andy left the Brown Jug, walking slowly. In front of the saloon, he paused on the sidewalk. There were several pedestrians to be seen, but no sign of Diamonds Beck.

Five minutes passed while Andy waited for some sign of the man who had vowed to shoot him on sight. After a minute more he reached to a pocket and drew out a length of rawhide thong with which he tied his holster firmly to right leg, thus lessening the chance of his gun sticking in its holster in the event a fast draw became necessary.

"It looks," Andy mused impatiently, "as though I'd have to go looking for Beck. It might save time."

He waited but a few moments longer, then started off along the sidewalk, traveling at an easy stride, arms swinging at his sides. He had scarcely left the Brown Jug's vicinity when Toby Byers slipped outside, locked the door behind him and followed Andy down the street. Toby's curiosity could be denied no longer. He wanted to see the prospective gun-fight between Farlow and the notorious Diamonds Beck. From time to time, Toby paused to speak to friends along the way. Swiftly, news ran through Winghorse that Andy Farlow was seeking Diamonds Beck. Men gathered on corners, talking in undertones, alert for the first sound of gun-fire.

The sun was touching the western horizon by the time Andy came to the Winghorse Bar, the most likely spot, now, at which to find Beck. Andy didn't hesitate as he drew abreast of the saloon, but turned in and pushed through the swinging doors. Here, just inside the entrance, he paused to look the place over.

There was quite a line of customers at the bar, drinking, and talking loudly. Oil lamps in their brackets cast a yellow light over the scene. The Winghorse Bar was considerably larger than the Brown Jug. The bar ran along one wall; tables and chairs were lined on the opposite side. A few men sat playing cards; smoke from their cigars and cigarettes floated half way to the ceiling. At the long counter there was a continual clinking of glass tumblers and bottles.

After a moment, looking through the haze of tobacco smoke, Andy picked out Diamonds Beck at the bar, talking to two hardbitten men in punchers' togs whom he took to be the 2-R hands, Welch and Hannan. Beck was slim, of medium height. His skin looked pasty and the black eyes in his triangular-shaped skull were small and glittering, set too closely together.

Mostly, it was his attire that set Beck off from the others in the barroom: he wore slimly pointed shoes, tight, leg-fitting trousers. His coat had short lapels and was thrown open at the moment to display a low-cut fancy velvet vest, with a heavy watch chain stretched across the front. Set at a jaunty angle on Beck's shaven head was a roll-brimmed derby hat, the fashion of the time.

Beck seemed covered with diamonds. There were two diamond rings on each hand. Diamond cuff links shone with a dull glitter when he moved his arms. A diamond stud shone in his white shirt front and a diamond pin was thrust through the knot of his black string tie. The stones were of poor quality, as yellow and full of flaws as their owner's warped character. It was a known fact, in the Southwest of that day, that Beck appeared with a bigger diamond each time he killed a man, but his taste ran to quantity rather than quality.

Strapped about his hips was a wide yellow cartridge belt, in the holster of which depended a Colt's .45 six-shooter whose butt was well-notched, each notch standing for a life which Diamonds Beck had taken.

A veritable frenzy of hate swept through Andy

as he stood looking at the man. From time to time, the long slim fingers of Beck's left hand went to an inner pocket of his coat to draw out a white silk handkerchief with which he flecked imaginary bits of dust and lint from his clothing.

Andy took one step forward, his eyes burning hotly. Then he got his emotions under control and stopped. "Still got that handkerchief habit, I see," Andy mused.

While he stood there, fighting to master his feelings, Andy caught a slight movement at the far end of the barroom. Sheriff Puffy Baggs rose from a table and came waddling toward the doorway, his face a study in nervous fright.

Andy watched the sheriff negotiate the length of the room. When he came up, Baggs clutched at Andy's arms, whispering hoarsely, "My God, Farlow! Haven't you no better sense than to come here?"

Andy looked cold-eyed at the sheriff. "Why shouldn't I come here?"

"Don't you know, Farlow? Diamonds Beck is going to kill you—"

"So I heard. What are you doing about it, Baggs?"

"My God! What can I do? There'll be a fight. I can't stop it. Turn back, Farlow. Get outside, quick, before Beck sees you."

Andy removed himself from the sheriff's grasp. "You're too late, Baggs," Andy said in a flat, emotionless voice. "He's already seen me."

Drawn by the sound of Baggs' voice, Beck and the two punchers had turned to stare at Andy. Andy disengaged himself again from the sheriff's clutching grasp and strode across the barroom. He stopped a few short paces before reaching Beck.

"Here I am, Beck," Andy said coldly. "I'm Andy Farlow."

Beck didn't say anything for a few minutes. His eyes glittered venomously on Andy's face. He seemed somewhat taken aback by the cowboy's direct approach.

"I understand you've been looking for me," Andy went on.

"Andy Farlow, eh?" Beck's voice was dry, harsh, like the buzzing of a rattler's tail. He forced a short, hard laugh. His left hand went to the inner pocket of his coat and produced the handkerchief. He flicked the end absently across his cuff, put the handkerchief away again. "Farlow, eh?" he repeated.

"The name should mean something to you," Andy said in flat tones.

"Hmm! Maybe it does, Farlow. What you intending to do about it?"

Sheriff Baggs said weakly, "Now, look here, boys, this won't do. Shake hands and be friends—"

"You keep out of this, Puffy," insolently snapped the puncher known as Hannan.

"Go on and sit down, Baggs," Welch snapped.

"This is private business. Mebbe you better get out."

Neither Andy nor Beck had paid the sheriff any attention. He mouthed a few more futile pleas, then slunk outside.

Andy could see Beck was somewhat startled at having the fight carried into his own camp in such manner. Andy decided to pursue his advantage.

Abuptly, Andy laughed. "What am I intending to do about it, Beck? Well, I'm intending to show you up, as the dirty back-shooting coyote you are. The killer brand is written all over you, but you never in your life killed a man in a fair fight. This is your chance to try."

Again, Beck didn't reply at once. His right hand dropped carefully to holster and he patted his gun butt. "You're asking for this, Farlow," he sneered, after a moment. "Do you really want it?"

"I've stated my case," Andy snapped. "The next move is up to you."

Beck held his right hand well away from the holster. He forced a careless laugh and turned toward the crowd in the barroom which by this time had moved well away from the men at the bar and were listening intently.

"You've heard this Farlow hombre, gents," Beck said. "He come here lookin' for trouble. Shall I let him have it?" Without waiting for a reply, Beck drew out the silk handkerchief, idly brushed at an invisible spot on his coat lapel and replaced the handkerchief again.

"I'm waiting, Beck." Andy's tones were like chilled steel.

Beck commenced to back away. His manner changed somewhat. "Look here, Farlow, there's no use you going on the prod against me. I'd like to be friends with you—"

"Liar!" Andy snapped grimly. "Why don't you pull it?"

"Aw, now, Farlow," Beck protested in ingratiating tones, as he continued to back away, "you got me all wrong. I never make a fight unless it's forced on me. Take it easy."

He backed another pace. His right arm was well out from his holster, only slightly crooked at the elbow. His left hand moved toward the handkerchief in his inner coat pocket.

". . . I wouldn't want to pull on you, Farlow," the man was insisting, drawing out his handkerchief.

Andy's right hand flashed down. His gun butt seemed to leap to meet his eager fingers. His six-shooter roared once . . . twice! Twin puffs of dust spurted from the left breast of Beck's coat.

The detonations of the heavy gun shook the building. Powder smoke swirled through the room. A man yelled and dashed frantically toward the swinging doors. Hannan and Welch had leaped to one side, out of gun range.

A look of startled bewilderment had come over Diamonds Beck's features. He swayed uncertainly in the middle of the floor, eyes already glazing.

His right hand closed on the gun in his holster, even as the handkerchief emerged from his inner pocket.

Quite suddenly, the man pitched headlong on the floor, his right arm flung wide, the fingers of his left still clutching the white silken handkerchief. Striving to arise, he succeeded only in rolling on his back. After a moment he became still.

A shocked silence swept through the room. After a moment Andy said dully, "I reckon that's all."

His voice broke the tension. Hannan leaped to one side, gun in hand. "It ain't all, by God!" he snarled. "I got you covered, Farlow!"

"Aw, let him have it," Welch growled.

Andy pivoted, gun still in hand, shooting by instinct rather than aim. He saw Welch stumble and go to the floor. A leaden slug from Hannan's gun whined past his body and thudded into the bar.

Andy whirled, thumbing one quick shot toward Hannan. The shot missed. Hannan fired again—missed. Before he could get set, Andy got his range, and released another slug from his six-shooter barrel. Hannan cursed, the gun went flying from his hand, the impact of Andy's bullet knocking him to the floor.

Andy was thinking fast. He'd fired five shots. If anyone else took up the battle. . . .

"Stick 'em up, Farlow! I got you covered!"

It was the pompous voice of Sheriff Puffy Baggs, approaching Andy's rear. The next instant, the sheriff's gun was boring into Andy's back. Andy shrugged his shoulders, thrust his empty gun into holster. For the first time in his life, he wished it hadn't been his habit to carry his gun hammer on an empty shell. Slowly, his arms came into the air.

"I got you this time," Baggs was saying triumphantly. "One move and you're a dead man! I'm arresting you for murder."

"Murder?" Andy laughed coolly, speaking over his right shoulder. "Sheriff, you're a fool. It was a fair fight. If you figure how Hannan and Welch cut in, I was outnumbered—"

"I ain't talkin' about Hannan and Welch. You murdered Diamonds Beck. I was peeking in through the front entrance. I saw it all. Beck was saying he didn't want to fight. His hand wasn't anywhere near his gun when you drew and plugged him—"

"That's right! That's right," a dozen voices put in.

"I saw it!"

"Beck never had a chance!"

"Farlow never give Beck no chance to draw!"

A low growl ascended from the throats of the assembled men, most of them Rudabaugh sympathizers. The angry voices grew in volume. Somebody yelled something about a lynching.

Somebody else called for a rope. The crowd commenced to close in on Baggs and his prisoner.

Andy was trying to explain the fight, but the crowd refused to listen. Sheriff Baggs' forehead was covered with perspiration. He commenced to back away.

"Now, boys, now, boys," he pleaded, voice shaking with fear. "You got to let the law take its course. Farlow is my prisoner. Just quiet down now, boys—"

"Go on, get out of here, Baggs," a rough voice broke in. "We'll take care of your prisoner. We figure to have a necktie party. One man's dead. Two more's wounded by this killer. We'll show you—"

"You'll show nothing, you scuts!" a new voice broke in from the doorway. "Get back before I wipe out every sneakin' son of you!"

"Back, you yeller-livered coyotes before I salivate yore innards!" came a second voice.

The crowd broke and scattered frantically toward the back of the barroom. Andy whirled around, jerking from Baggs' grasp, to see Ethan Vaughn and Spareribs Pryor standing just inside the swinging doors. A forty-five six-shooter was grasped in Vaughn's fist. Spareribs held a double-barreled shotgun.

"Back you scourin's of hell," Spareribs was shouting angrily, "before I spray yore dirty carcasses with this scatter-gun."

"Vaughn!" Andy yelled.

"It's me, son," Vaughn said angrily. "My cook, here—Spareribs Pryor—sort of convinced me I might be wrong about you. I reckon I was. We followed your trail, saw where it turned toward town—"

"I'll shake yore mitt, Farlow," Spareribs cut in, "when it's safe to put down this scatter-weepon."

"My God!" Vaughn was looking around the room. "You sure cut loose with a vengeance, Andy. You got Beck—and Welch and Hannan! Cripes a'mighty! I'll say I was wrong about you. You got an apology comin' and—"

"Forget it," Andy laughed. "You've squared everything."

The crowd was cowering at the back of the room. Hannan and Welch were sprawled on the floor, groaning. Andy quickly crossed the room, examined Hannan and Welch. Welch had a bullet in his hip. Hannan's shoulder was broken.

Andy returned to face Sheriff Baggs. "You'd better take Welch and Hannan to the doctor's," he said. "There's nothing you can do—or anybody can do—for Diamonds Beck."

"Exactly what I'm arresting you for," Baggs said importantly. "I won't say anythin' about them other two. They threw down on you. But Beck is different. You never give him a chance. You pulled on him while he was trying to avoid fight—"

"Cripes! What a fool you are, Baggs," Andy said contemptuously. "Beck started his draw before I did. You were looking for him to pull that gun in his holster. He never does use that gun for his killings—"

"What do you mean?" Vaughn frowned.

Andy crossed the floor in quick strides, knelt at the side of the dead Beck. The man's forty-five six-shooter was still in its holster. Beck's left hand was flung wide, still clutching the white silk handkerchief. Andy bent back the stiffening fingers while the others in the room looked on. He lifted the white handkerchief, which proved to be wrapped about some bulky object, and laid back the silken folds.

A murmur of surprise went up from the others. Exposed on the handkerchief, in Andy's hand, was a short-barreled, ugly-looking derringer!

"Here's the gun," Andy said grimly, "that Beck did his killings with. That holstered forty-five was only a decoy to draw the victim's attention away from this hide-out derringer. Beck shot with the derringer, through this handkerchief, or one like it. In the confusion and black smoke from the explosion, he'd jerk out the forty-five, then shove it back in holster, creating the impression the forty-five was the one that did the work. At the same moment he was replacing this handkerchief-wrapped derringer in his pocket. He's worked the trick time after time. I know."

The men in the saloon were too startled to speak. Andy tossed the derringer and handkerchief on the floor, beside Beck's motionless form, then he again knelt down and threw back the right side of Beck's coat.

"Two pockets, like I suspected," Andy said. "One to hold only a handkerchief which he drew out continually, thus getting his prospective victims accustomed to the movement. The other pocket held the handkerchief and derringer— which it was necessary to draw out only once."

A man stepped forward from the crowd at the end of the room. "I reckon we went sort of haywire, Farlow. I'm sorry. Beck got what he deserved."

A chorus of voices took up similar words. Men crowded around Andy, some wanting to shake his hand. Andy swung back to face Puffy Baggs.

"Still want to arrest me, Baggs?"

"I—I reckon not, Farlow." Baggs' tones were shaky. "Do—do you want me to put Hannan and Welch under arrest?"

"It probably wouldn't do any good," Andy said contemptuously. "Rudabaugh would make you let them go. I don't care what you do with 'em. Better see they get a doctor's care. Once they've recovered, they can look me up and finish what they started—if they're able to. And, Baggs—"

"Yes, Mister Farlow?"

"You tell Rudabaugh I won't be crowded. I

182

know damn well he hired Beck to get me—I feel it in my bones. You tell Rudabaugh there's a reckoning coming, and it's headed his way if he don't move careful from now on. And that goes for anybody that throws in with Rudabaugh. I won't be crowded any further."

Without waiting for the sheriff's reply, Andy turned and pushed through the crowd to the street, followed by Vaughn and Spareribs. On the street, the three paused a moment.

"Son," Vaughn smiled grimly, "you sure started things with a bang. And you were the one that wanted to avoid an outbreak of war. I'd hate to see you really want a war, sometime."

"This won't start anything," Andy said, "like it would if I'd come in with friends to make a fight. This was personal between Beck and me. Hannan and Welch just cut in. I've got a hunch Rudabaugh will move careful for a spell now. After the way I exposed his hired gunman, Rudabaugh won't be popular like he was in some quarters. Folks don't go much for that crooked stuff."

"I don't see yet," Spareribs frowned, "how you got wise to that handkerchief and derringer stunt."

"I saw Beck in action, once, a few years back," Andy explained slowly.

"You said he killed a friend of yours?" Vaughn put in.

Andy nodded. "In El Paso. I spotted the stunt at that time, though Beck worked it unbelievably

183

fast. I tried to stop him, after he'd done his killin', but he had friends and horses there and made his escape. I went on his trail. Before I could catch up to him, he'd committed another murder—shot a man in the back. The law got him that time. He was sent to prison."

"This friend of yours that was killed by Beck in El Paso," Vaughn said, "would be mighty glad, Andy, if he could know what you did today."

"I reckon mebbe he would," Andy said quietly. "You see, it was my brother Beck killed. That's what made our ruckus a personal affair."

XIV. TOO EASY-GOING

THE EXCITEMENT FOLLOWING the killing of Diamonds Beck died down, after a time. It was rumored around Winghorse that Rudabaugh had sworn vengeance, but, if so, the big 2-R cattle-raiser appeared to be in no hurry to execute his plans. Andy encountered Rudabaugh on three separate occasions on the streets of Winghorse. Each time, Andy was alone. On two of the occasions, Rudabaugh ignored Andy altogether. The third time a frown of hate crossed his face. Andy nodded coldly. Rudabaugh didn't reply.

Andy was satisfied. Rudabaugh had had his chance to take up the fight, but refused it. At the same time, Andy had proved that he wasn't afraid of the big man, wasn't avoiding him. With that point settled, Andy changed his tactics: he started to remain away from Winghorse as much as possible, not because he feared retaliation on Rudabaugh's part, but because he wished to avoid further friction, or at least postpone it, until he'd had an opportunity to seek for the hidden *pesos*. When it became necessary for someone to visit Winghorse, Andy usually sent Kitten, early in the morning, with orders to return as soon as the business was attended to. Rudabaugh's men hardly ever reached town before noon time.

A month slipped quickly past in such fashion.

Rudabaugh dropped slurring hints more than once, in Winghorse to the effect that he had the Crown crew buffaloed and that it didn't dare come to town, but such reports as reached Andy's ears only brought a smile to his face. Andy was, rather, grateful for the temporary cessation of hostilities, as it provided more time in which to look for the treasure Dan Jenkins had left behind. However, though he devoted every spare moment to the search, clues regarding the whereabouts of the *pesos* failed to materialize. Day after day, sometimes alone, often accompanied by Deborah, Andy pushed his pony through deep ravines and along narrow shelves of rock in the Casa de Leonés Range, always on the alert for signs of a cave where the gold might be cached.

But all in vain. One day was like the next. True, Andy did find three small caves, but in them nothing but bats and rattlesnakes. No *pesos*, nor any sign that would indicate that *pesos* had ever been brought into the vicinity. Felipe, too, riding over other parts of the range, met with failure in his search for a cave in which the gold might be secreted.

Andy suspected his every move was followed by either Quillan or Porter, though he was never able to see any material sign of their presence, beyond a few faint hoof-prints, or similar "sign." It must have been known, by this time, Andy's thoughts ran, that he hadn't found the gold. Until he did, it was likely that Quillan and Porter wouldn't make any belligerent moves.

Which was exactly the way Quillan and Porter figured: there was no use putting Farlow out of the way, until he had attained the object of his search. To this view, the pair had persuaded Rudabaugh. And Rudabaugh, as well as Quillan and Porter, was commencing to believe the story of the Maximilian gold was little more than a myth. Being ambitious, Rudabaugh refused to curb his activities, and while he was willing for a time to ignore the Crown outfit, he had taken to rustling, occasionally, a few head of Rafter-V stock. So far he had not stolen enough animals for Ethan Vaughn to notice.

Gradually, as the weeks slipped past, Andy commenced to recover from his disappointment at not finding the treasure. Despite his efforts to the contrary, he found himself becoming more and more interested in the lovely owner of the Crown Ranch. Whether or not Deborah returned the feeling, Andy didn't dare guess. He simply didn't know, though the girl was always friendly and usually inclined to bend to his judgment in matters pertaining to ranch operation, or the search for the *pesos*.

It had suddenly occurred to Andy that Deborah would be a wealthy woman were the treasure located. That being the case, Andy felt he couldn't offer enough, in his own hardworking person, to compensate for the girl's money.

That he should be entitled to half of the gold, never entered Andy's thoughts. He had promised to do his best toward locating it for Dan Jenkins' daughter; that was all there was to it. And so, though he did work his hardest to keep that promise, Andy half hoped the *pesos* never would be discovered.

"I reckon," Andy speculated, as he sat his pony one afternoon, high in the recesses of the Casa de Leonés, "that Rudabaugh and his coyotes have a long piece of trailing cut out for 'em, if they expect me to lead 'em to that gold. It don't look like it ever will be found. If I don't have some luck before many days are past, I reckon I'll head back to that second cave I ran onto one day. I never did examine that hole as thoroughly as I might have. Maybe, once I've cleaned out the bats and rattlers, I'll find a tunnel branching off some place and leading into another cave. *Quien sabe*?"

And with that thought in mind, Andy once again turned his pony toward home, with nothing but another futile exploration to report.

It did look hopeless and, more than once, Andy was inclined to discontinue the search. His thoughts went back to Rudabaugh. That worthy had been too quiet of late to suit Andy's peace of mind. Probably the inactivity merely presaged the lull before the storm. Eventually, warfare was certain to break out between the Crown and 2-R outfits, and he and Vaughn often discussed the possibility and made such plans as were practical.

The Crown Ranch lay ten miles due west of Winghorse. Straight south from town, a distance of twelve miles, Rudabaugh's 2-R was situated. To the southeast of Winghorse, a two hour ride, was Ethan Vaughn's Rafter-V. Thus the owners of the Crown and the Rafter-V could visit back and forth without ever cutting the 2-R trail to town.

Of late, the 2-R punchers had been trying to pick quarrels with the Rafter-V hands, when the two factions met in town, so Vaughn finally adopted Andy's practice of keeping his men out of Winghorse, except in the early hours of the day. With both outfits avoiding him, Rudabaugh commenced to think he had the whole country bullied. His men grew more bold in their depredations on Rafter-V range.

The inevitable happened: one of Vaughn's cowboys, Cal Laramie by name, spied a 2-R puncher driving off a pair of Rafter-V steers. Rudabaugh's man was too far away to be recognized; he broke and ran for it, riding hard, the instant he saw Laramie coming. Laramie dug in his spurs and gave chase, but the 2-R man was mounted on a fresher pony and rapidly drew away. Doggedly, Cal Laramie stuck to the trail which led him to Winghorse.

By the time Laramie reached town, there was no

sign to be seen of the 2-R puncher whom Laramie was only faintly sure of recognizing. Louie Quillan was in town that day. The 2-R puncher had reported to Quillan, whom he met on the street.

"You're a damn fool, Ketcham," Quillan had said. "Why didn't you throw a slug through the Rafter-V waddie's guts? Then you wouldn't have had to run. You could have taken your time and brought the cows with you."

"I ain't no killer," Ketcham had returned sullenly. "I don't mind pickin' up a cow now and then, but I don't hold with shootin'—"

"You're yellow, that's what," Quillan had sneered.

"That's whatever. That Rafter-V hand is coming close on my tail. He might have recognized me. What am I to do?"

Quillan had cursed angrily. "Get down to the Winghorse Bar. You'll find Rudabaugh there. Draw your pay and get out of town as fast as your horse will carry you. Tell Reece I said you were yellow. He'll be glad to let you go." Quillan added, "I'll take care of that Rafter-V cowhand when he rides in.

Quillan was as good as his word. When Laramie pounded his dust-covered pony into Winghorse, Quillan was on hand to meet him. Laramie made certain accusations, mentioning that he suspected the 2-R. That was the sort of opening Quillan wanted. He denied the accusation and added a good many abusive remarks. There are certain words no man will absorb. One word led to another. Quillan goaded Laramie to the drawing point, then, being faster in getting his gun into action, killed the Rafter-V man. With only Sheriff Puffy Baggs to enforce the law, the killing was termed as one brought about in a fair fight. True, Laramie had gone for his gun. Baggs exonerated Quillan almost before the gun-smoke had drifted away, and then sent a rider to break the news to Vaughn.

It was late that night when the grim-faced Vaughn brought word of the killing to the Crown. Andy and Deborah listened in silence while Vaughn repeated such details of the tragedy as he'd been able to gather. They were seated in the main room of the ranch house. A lamp burned on the table. The once-crackling mesquite knots in the fire-place had burned down to dully-glowing embers.

". . . and I don't know," Vaughn was saying sadly, "whatever made that boy go to town. The crew's had my orders. They know they're to avoid the 2-R whenever possible. There was never a finer boy lived than Cal Laramie. He wasn't a gunfighter. I can't see what made him stack up against Quillan, or why he should pick a quarrel with him. . . . Oh, sure, he pulled his gun. There's no doubt about it. Witnesses saw the whole thing.

But I don't understand it. I'm going in for the body tomorrow. Cal once said he wanted to be buried on my holdings if he stayed here long enough. He liked the place. But he never reckoned to die young like this."

"And you couldn't learn what he and Quillan fought about?" Andy asked, frowning.

"One feller in Winghorse," Vaughn said, "told me he heard Cal accuse the 2-R of rustling my stock, but that can't be so. I haven't missed any animals."

Deborah looked thoughtful. "Sometimes you don't miss 'em, Ethan, until quite a number are gone. Perhaps the 2-R has just started on your herds."

"Maybe so," Vaughn agreed somewhat dubiously, "but in that case I think Cal would have come to me first—not go rarin' into Winghorse, pullin' his gun on a man he knew could out-shoot him."

"Look here," Andy said suddenly, "suppose Laramie saw one of Rudabaugh's hands running off a couple of your head. We'll say the rustler made a run for it and Laramie followed him. The rustler might have figured he could lose himself in Winghorse, which would be better than leading Laramie to the 2-R—"

"You figuring," Vaughn broke in, "that Quillan was that rustler?"

Andy shook his head. "Quillan wasn't the

rustler, but he might have agreed to take the fight off the rustler's hands. Quillan was on hand, apparently, when Laramie rode into town. Laramie made his accusation to the first 2-R man he sees. Quillan works him into a fight. The boy loses his temper and starts for his gun—which is exactly what Quillan wanted. Maybe I'm wrong, but that's how it looks to me."

"By Cripes!" Vaughn exclaimed. "I believe you're right, Andy."

"It sounds plausible," Deborah nodded. "I hardly knew Cal Laramie, but from what I know he was never the man to pick a fight unless it was forced on him. Oh, that Quillan's a—" She broke off, unable to find a word that would properly designate her opinion of the murderer of Cal Laramie. "It was murder," Deborah insisted. "I don't care if Cal did reach for his gun."

No one denied that. Vaughn had risen from his chair and was pacing back and forth across the room, his indignation growing with every step. Finally he came to a stop in front of Andy. His voice shook with emotion: "What I want to know," he demanded, "is what you intend to do now. My boys are rarin' to go. I've told 'em how you felt about starting a range war. I've tried to make 'em see reason. But I can't hold 'em down much longer. Only for Spareribs helpin' to hold 'em in check, they'd been out after Rudabaugh's scalp the minute they heard the news."

"Which is exactly what Rudabaugh wants," Andy said shrewdly.

"All right. Let's give him what he wants," Vaughn flared.

"Just a minute," Andy said slowly. "I'll lay dollars to doughnuts that Rudabaugh and Quillan and maybe some others are waiting in Winghorse, right this minute, hoping you'll come raring in, hoping that you'll start the war, so their actions will be held blameless."

Vaughn stopped. "Now that you mention it," he said, "I remember hearing that Quillan and Rudabaugh were staying in town tonight, in case Sheriff Baggs wanted to question Quillan further about the shooting."

"Sheriff Baggs. Paugh!" Deborah said contemptuously. "You know how much questioning he'll do."

"And we know," Andy pursued his point, "that Quillan and Rudabaugh aren't staying in town for that purpose."

"The question is," Vaughn insisted, "what are we going to do about it?"

"If Quillan and Rudabaugh are in town tonight, they'll be there tomorrow, more'n likely," Andy said quietly.

"What are we going to do about it?" Vaughn repeated.

"What do you want to do?" Andy countered.

"The only sensible thing I can see," Vaughn

said, "is for the Crown and Rafter-V to join forces—Oh, I know the idea doesn't appeal to you, Andy, but we can't stand being trampled on forever. There's a showdown due. It's Rudabaugh's finish, or ours."

"I think Ethan is right," Deborah said soberly. "Oh, I hate the thought of killing and bloodshed, but I see no other way, Andy. Sheriff Baggs won't enforce the law. We'll have to take things into our own hands—and I hate the thought. But I can't turn Ethan down now. Long before he'd had trouble with Rudabaugh, he was willing to join us in making a fight. Now, we can't turn him down when he comes to us for help."

Andy's voice was weary when he finally replied, "I know how you both feel. I feel that way myself. Ethan, I asked you once to leave things in my hands. My way worked out, didn't it?"

"I reckon it did," Vaughn nodded reluctantly. "I apologized that time. I'm willing to do it again, if you prove I'm wrong. I don't like the idea of starting a range war, no more than you, but it's forced on us. Rudabaugh is waiting in Winghorse, hoping we'll come riding. I'd like to show him I can give as good as I can take. Are we going to sit here— backing water—until hell freezes over? We'll be the laughing stock of the country if we don't start fighting back sometime. I say, now is the time."

"It isn't," Andy said firmly. "I can't go into explanations, now, Ethan, but I'd like to stall things off as long as possible. Can't you just leave things to me?"

"Oh, Andy!" Deborah turned to Ethan. "He's hoping to find the gold, so we'll be better equipped to fight—"

"Gold?" Vaughn said blankly.

"My father buried some gold money, some place around here, years ago. We've been trying to find it for weeks. Andy hopes to discover it—"

"So long as Deborah has spilled the beans," Andy broke in, "you might as well know, Ethan."

". . . and I've given up hope of ever finding it," Deborah rushed on. "But Andy keeps trying. He says if we fight Rudabaugh we'll have to have money to hire gun-fighters."

"That's true," Vaughn nodded, "if an outbreak is allowed to spread into a regular war. I've got to admit that's what will likely happen, but I'd sooner go down fighting than get wiped out without firing a shot." His interest in the gold overwhelmed his anger, "But this gold—what about it?"

Andy gave brief details, concluding, "I'll tell you the whole story, some time, when things are different. Right now, we've got this Rudabaugh matter to face."

Vaughn had cooled down considerably while Andy talked. He said, "I'm commencing to get your slant, now, son. I think maybe you're wise."

"And you'll leave me handle things a spell—go on as we've been doing?" Andy asked quickly.

"I won't do anything right to once," Vaughn conceded. "I'll hold my boys in check, too—at least until after we've buried Cal Laramie."

Deborah didn't say anything, but there were angry lights in her eyes. A few minutes later, Vaughn prepared to depart. Andy accompanied him down to the corral and waited while he mounted. Vaughn didn't say a great deal. He put down his hand and gripped Andy's as he turned the pony.

"It's all right, son," he said slowly. "You gave your promise to Deb's father. I can see how you feel, how you'd like to stall off a warfare until you can get heeled. Maybe you're wise. S'long. You'll come to Cal's burial, won't you?"

"I'll be there," Andy said soberly. "S'long."

He walked slowly back to the ranch house, while Vaughn's horse's hoofs drummed off across the range. In a few minutes he was back in the main room. Deborah sat as before. She didn't look up as he entered. Andy said dryly, "All right—open up."

"What do you mean—open up?" The girl continued to gaze moodily into the dying-embered fireplace, her face averted.

"Deb, I knew when Ethan left that you were unsheathing your claws for me. Something I've said doesn't set right. What is it?"

The girl stiffened. Suddenly she turned toward Andy, eyes blazing angrily. "You should know," she flashed.

"I probably do," Andy nodded quietly. "You want to do as Ethan said—join forces and move on Rudabaugh. Can't you see that will result in unnecessary killings? We'll have to employ gunfighters. Innocent men will be drawn into the fight—"

"You've said all that before—a hundred times," Deb said hotly. "I'm tired of hearing that story. I don't want trouble any more than you, but what are we to do? Wait until we find the gold, I suppose, so we'll be so well prepared, and Rudabaugh won't dare make war on us. Well, I've thought it over. We don't have to wait. I'll put a mortgage on the Crown and get the money we need—"

"That would be playing into Rudabaugh's hands. He'd like to see you with a mortgage. That's whatever, though. I promised your father," Andy resumed patiently, "that I'd do my best to—"

"I've heard that too," the girl cut him short. "Do you think I care about those damn *pesos*—yes," defiantly, "I said damn *pesos*! I've run this outfit like a man for a long time—long before you came here. I guess I'm entitled to a man's cuss word, now and then. You needn't look at me thataway."

Andy grinned suddenly. "I've got a hunch you've *thought* a lot of damns, from time to time. I don't blame you, Deb."

"You won't even argue back against that," the

girl half sobbed. "You're too easy-going. You wouldn't even fight that Beck killer, until he forced you to it—"

"Wait a minute." Andy looked queerly at the girl. "Say, you don't think I'm showing yellow, do you?"

"I didn't say that."

"You meant it, didn't you?" Andy looked a bit white about the mouth. He swallowed hard.

"Andy! You know I didn't." The girl's voice was a wail. "Oh, Andy! It's not that at all. You just don't—*won't*—understand, it seems. All you think of is that gold. Oh, I know you don't expect anything for yourself. But that's the only idea you have. You gave your word to my father and you can't think of anything else, it looks like—"

"I gave my word," Andy said doggedly. "I intend to carry it out."

"Yes, you would," Deborah flashed suddenly. "You're stubborn! You won't listen to reason—"

"The sort of reason Vaughn puts out, I suppose, about opening up on Rudabaugh. That would be plain suicide, Deb. I'm doing my best to save lives and money. Besides, Vaughn is commencing to think my way—"

"Yes, when he heard about the gold. Do you think I care more for that gold than I do my self-respect? When he came here, asking help, you turned him down. You didn't even ask my advice."

"I'm supposed to be your foreman," Andy reminded the girl. His tones sounded bitter. "If you had other ideas, you should have said so. I'm trying to do as I think best. It's the only way I know."

"Do you think Vaughn will quit now? No, he'll go on in his own way. He'll show me he doesn't need our help—"

"You're all wrong there. Vaughn won't make a move—not for a few days, at least. He as much as told me he wouldn't."

"The fact remains," Deb said stubbornly, "we turned him down when he asked for help—at least, you did. I felt downright ashamed. I've never yet refused help to a neighbor—"

"Maybe you'd better make your own decisions from now on then," Andy flared out suddenly.

"I can do that too," Deb snapped.

"All right, go ahead." Andy was thoroughly angry, now, at his wits' ends. "Kick me off your payroll, if you want. Get another foreman. I'm through!"

"Andy!"

"I'm through, I tell you! But you can't make me leave the country until I've done my best to keep my promise to your father. And whether you like it or not, I'm sticking around, watching over you, taking care of you every minute I know. I—I—I—" He paused suddenly.

Deborah was laughing. After a minute the hot

color faded from Andy's face and he grinned. "I reckon I've been talking like a fool," he confessed.

"Oh, Andy, if you haven't a one-trail mind, I never saw one. You get so mad you could—well, I don't know what you'd like to do to me—and yet, it never enters your mind to ride away and leave me flat. You made a promise to my father. That settles it. If you talked like a fool, it was I who drove you to it. I guess we both talked like fools. I'm sorry, Andy."

"So am I," Andy said sheepishly. "We both sort of lost our heads for a minute. I don't blame you. You've been under a strain and now this other thing comes up, with Cal Laramie being killed and all. . . . You'd better turn in. I'm going down to the bunk-house."

He said "good-night" and turned abruptly away. If Deborah answered him, he didn't hear her. His mind was too full of other thoughts. He didn't see the girl's eyes, full of tears.

The others were in their bunks, when Andy arrived. The lights had been put out. Andy drew off his clothing and rolled in. Sometime during the night he awakened suddenly. "Say, I wonder if she does think I got a yellow streak," he mused. "Maybe it's time I proved otherwise." He grinned in the darkness, "I'd sort of like to find out myself. But I wish I did know exactly what that girl thinks about me. One thing's certain—she's shore got a temper when she cuts loose."

XV. SADDLE POUNDERS

ANDY DIDN'T SAY a great deal during breakfast, the following morning. Though Deborah usually ate with her men in the mess-house, she sent down word not to hold breakfast for her. Beanpot Reardon sent a pot of coffee and some food up to the girl. With the meal out of the way, the men looked to Andy for orders concerning the day's work.

Andy's words came half absent-mindedly. "Felipe, you'd better see that that chuck wagon is in shape. Come round-up, we'll be needing it."

"No riding this morneeng?" Felipe asked.

Andy shook his head. "I figure to keep you hombres out of the saddle for a day or so. Kitten, you and Denny might just as well start sinking the posts for that new corral. That's got to be put up sometime. It might as well be now."

Kitten nodded, without speaking, and hoisted his big frame from the long bench that flanked the breakfast table. He strode out of the mess-shanty, rolling a cigarette, his eyes thoughtful.

Beanpot commenced gathering dishes from the table and carrying them through the doorway to his kitchen. Felipe rose from the table and followed Kitten outside. Denny Devers was still lingering over his cup of coffee. He rolled a cigarette and, rather self-consciously, spilled flakes of tobacco down the front of his shirt. The match scratched loudly as he put flame to the cigarette.

Andy eyed the young puncher quizzically. "What's on your mind, Denny?"

"Huh! My mind?" Denny assumed a look of surprise.

"Yes, if that's what you call it."

"What makes you think I got anything on my mind?"

Andy smiled. "I can read it in your face. You never will make a good poker player, youngster."

"I learned that quite some years ago," Denny drawled.

Andy continued, "What's up? Don't you like the idea of working on that new corral with Kitten?"

"Did you ever see a cowhand that likes to work off'n a horse?" Denny evaded.

Andy chuckled. "That's however. The corral has to be built. What would you sooner do? Not that I'd let you do it, only I'm curious."

Denny toyed with his coffee cup. He didn't look at Andy. "I was just wondering," he said carelessly, "if you were figuring to ride to town. Figured you might take me with you, if you were."

"Why should I go to town? Why should I take you with me?"

"I'll get down to cases, Andy." Denny looked directly at his foreman now. "Cal Laramie was shot to death yesterday. Last night you had a long talk of some kind with Ethan Vaughn. I don't know what decision was arrived at, but it's sort of seemed to me that it was time those 2-R hombres needed a mite of kicking around—"

"You, too, eh?" Andy said ruefully.

"What do you mean—me, too?"

"It doesn't matter. So you think we've stood enough from Rudabaugh and his outfit?"

"Don't you?" Denny paused. "Now, wait, I didn't say that—"

"You're thinking it, though, Denny."

"All right, I'm thinking it, then," the young puncher said bluntly. "What I'm getting at, if you're going to town, I want to go with you. Don't you understand, Andy, that I'd like to be there, if trouble breaks? Here, you went and had that ruckus with Diamonds Beck, and it was all over before I even heard about it. I'd have given ten years of my life to have seen you wipe him out. Gosh! Don't you think a feller's entitled to some enjoyment out of life?"

Andy laughed silently. "Forget it, Denny. If I do go to town, I won't be looking for trouble. I'm still avoiding an open break. Vaughn won't be making any war-medicine—at least for a couple of days. So you can work on those corral posts with a light heart and willing muscles."

"Aw, cripes! Ain't we never going to have any excitement?"

"I hope not, youngster. Gun-fighting isn't as

pleasurable as it may sound to you. You've never had any experience."

"I've got to learn sometime, ain't I?"

"Not if I can prevent it," Andy said firmly. He settled the discussion by rising from the table and heading toward the bunkhouse. Denny went outside, muttering disappointedly, and headed for the barn to locate the post-hole digger. In a few minutes he joined Kitten in the business of starting the erection of new corral posts.

For some time, Andy worked steadily at his desk in the bunkhouse, adding up accounts, making notations of the money spent in operating expenses, cash paid out for supplies and so on. Finally he heaved a sigh of relief and rose from the desk. The ranch affairs were now in order. Andy buckled on his belt and gun, donned his sombrero and stepped through the bunkhouse doorway.

A short time later, Deborah, starting for the bunkhouse to talk to Andy, saw the object of her search near the saddlers' corral, throwing his rig on a pony. Deborah turned abruptly and headed toward the corral.

She walked swiftly up to Andy's side. Andy said, "Morning, boss."

"It's a nice morning, Andy."

Remembering their heated conversation of the previous evening, both smiled a trifle sheepishly.

"You riding someplace?" the girl asked.

Andy said, "Uh-huh," in a nonchalant voice, as he pulled smooth one corner of his saddle blanket. He wasn't looking at the girl now.

Deborah said, "Where's everybody?"

"'Round some place. I suppose Beanpot's working in his kitchen. Felipe is making some repairs to the chuck-wagon. I started Denny and Kitten on that new corral that's needed."

Deborah shifted her gaze across the ranch yard, bright under the mid-morning sun, to a point some seventy-five yards away. "I can see the new corral posts," she said, "but I don't see anything of Kitten and Denny."

"They're around," Andy replied, still not looking at the girl. He appeared to be having trouble getting his saddle blanket arranged to his liking. "Maybe Felipe needed a few minutes' help with that wagon. He might have called them off the job to help him a mite."

"Andy, did you send Kitten and Denny riding— someplace?"

"Why, no." Andy turned from the horse and listened a minute, then said, "They're in the blacksmith shop. I can hear their voices. Probably had to sharpen some tools, or something. Now, you satisfied?"

Deborah nodded. At the same time she sensed Andy was concealing something from her. She asked bluntly, "Where are you heading?"

Andy evaded direct answer. "Don't you think

it's about time I really got to work and tried to find those *pesos*, Deb? Go on laugh at me. I know it's the same old story."

But the girl refused to laugh. "You're not riding toward the Casa de Leonés," she accused. "You said, only yesterday, that you were going to take today off and see if you couldn't think out some place, nearby, where Dad might have concealed that gold."

"I can change my mind, can't I?" Andy grinned, tightening his saddle cinch, one booted foot against his pony's ribs. Again he was refusing to meet the girl's eyes. "You know, it isn't just women who are allowed to change their minds."

Deborah eyed him suspiciously. "Are you figuring to take Felipe with you?"

"Why should I?"

The girl breathed a trifle easier. "If you and Felipe were to ride off, together, I'd know you were heading for Winghorse, and trouble."

"Meaning," Andy asked easily, "just what?" He let the horse from the corral and closed the gate. He was still avoiding the girl's gaze. A proper adjustment of his bridle seemed to be occupying him more than was usually necessary.

"Look here, Andy, suppose I ride up to the Casa de Leonés with you? You can be saddling my pony while I change this dress for some riding things."

Andy stiffened, then relaxed. "Why, sure, if you

want to go. But it'll be plumb tiresome, riding over the same old ground we've already covered. It'll be sort of rough riding, in spots, too. Some of that thorny brush will be mighty tough on clothing. But if you want to go, why—"

"Andy Farlow! Look at me."

Andy turned from his horse and faced the girl.

Deborah continued, "You don't fool me for a minute. You were intending to ride, looking for Rudabaugh. Now, weren't you?"

Andy laughed uneasily. "Why, no, ma'am, not exactly. To tell the truth, I just sort of figured to ride into Winghorse to talk to Doctor Griffin. I wanted to see how Zach Watson was getting along—"

"Fiddlesticks! And don't you 'no ma'am' me. You know as well as I do that we heard from Doctor Griffin, just day before yesterday. Zach is getting along fine and will be out in a few more weeks."

"Sure enough. I'd forgotten that." Andy stumbled over his words. "We-ell, you see, Deb, now that Zach is getting all right, again, and can have visitors, I sort of figured to ask him where he kept the tally book. I've never been able to find it, since I took over his job, and now—"

"Oh, it's the tally book you want. Well, I'll save you a ride to town. Come up to the house, Andy, and I'll give it to you. I always keep the tally book up there."

Andy looked uneasily away. "I'll look at the tally book later, Deb."

"Andy Farlow, *do* you know what you want? You're not fooling me for one minute. Just what are you intending to do?"

Andy fiddled with his pony's reins. He didn't speak for a few moments. Suddenly he faced the girl squarely. "Look here, Deb, I've been thinking things over. We can't avoid trouble forever. I am intending to head for town—"

"I knew it!"

"You see, plans have got to be made—"

"Rudabaugh will—" Deborah commenced.

"I don't know what Rudabaugh will or will not do, but I intend to avoid him—if possible. I'd like to stall off trouble, until we've found that gold—"

"Oh, that gold—"

"I know how you feel," Andy nodded. "Trouble can't be stalled off, if the 2-R gets to riding the Crown and the Rafter-V too hard. We'll have to face it. But if I could only locate those *pesos*— well, if anything happened to me, you'll be able to carry on with Vaughn's help—"

"If anything happens to you?" Deborah looked startled. "What do you mean?"

Andy changed the subject. "What I mean," he said quickly, "is that I want to talk to Vaughn. He and I might as well get together and commence laying plans."

"If you want to see Ethan Vaughn, why do you

209

have to ride through Winghorse? You're taking a mighty long trail to get to the Rafter-V—"

"Wait a minute, Deb. I expect to find Vaughn in town. You know, he was going to Winghorse this morning, to bring back Laramie's body, after the undertaker had finished—"

"I remember, now," Deb cut in, "but why can't you wait until Ethan gets back home, then I'll ride over with you?"

"I'd rather go now," Andy said, somewhat stubbornly.

Remembering the argument of the previous evening, Deborah had no wish to start another discussion of the same sort. She surrendered suddenly, "All right, I suppose you know what you want to do."

"I hope so."

"And you'll avoid trouble?"

"If possible. I won't start trouble, if that's what you mean. You know me well enough for that." There was a certain concern in the girl's eyes that Andy wasn't missing. He was about to add something else, but checked the words that were in his heart. "I'm not even taking Felipe with me. You seem to feel we're a bad combination for hunting trouble."

"You've been a good combination for me—for the Crown," Deborah corrected herself hurriedly.

That was the moment when Andy should have followed up his advantage, before the girl had turned abruptly away from him, but being unversed in women's ways he lacked proper understanding. Andy thought Deborah was irritated because of his proposed trip.

The girl faced him after a moment. "You're really not taking Felipe with you?" she persisted.

"Cross my heart," Andy smiled. "I told you he was busy on the chuck wagon—bending a tire on one of the wheels, if you must know. Honestly, Deb, I'll do everything I can to keep out of Rudabaugh's way," he added earnestly, so earnestly that she overlooked all thought of Louie Quillan—as Andy had intended she should.

The girl's anxiety lessened. "I still don't like the idea of you going to Winghorse alone. Won't you take someone with you?"

"I'll take Denny Devers, if you insist."

"Good grief, no!" Deborah exclaimed. "Then you *would* get into trouble—Denny would get you into trouble, rather. He's too much of a wildcat to keep out of a fuss, or use his head."

"That takes care of Felipe and Denny," Andy said dryly. "There's only Kitten and Beanpot left. Which do you want me to take?"

The girl's smile was as forced as her levity: "Well, you know, the Crown simply couldn't get along without its cook."

"That puts it up to Kitten," Andy laughed. "All right, if you insist."

"I do insist. I know there isn't a troublesome

211

bone in Kitten's big frame. If anybody can avoid trouble, it's Kitten—"

"You sending a nurse along with me?" Andy was suddenly nettled.

"Andy!" Indignation filled Deborah's tones. "You know I don't—" She broke off suddenly and turned away that he might not see the tears welling in her eyes. Starting toward the house, she called back over her shoulder, "I'll see you tonight."

"Tonight it is," Andy returned crisply. He felt angry with himself, without half realizing why, as he swung up into his saddle and rode, at a walk, toward the blacksmith shop. Reaching the building, he saw Kitten just emerging from the doorway.

"Get your bronc, Kitten," Andy addressed the man shortly. "We're pounding saddles for Winghorse. I'll wait for you here."

"Right," Kitten nodded, and turned his big body, in lumbering strides, toward the saddlers' corral.

Andy settled in his saddle to wait for Kitten's return, his gaze following the huge fellow as he headed around the corner of the blacksmith shop. It wasn't a bad idea, at that, Andy mused, this taking Kitten with him. Kitten was an unknown quantity, so far as concerned fighting ability. It might be sensible to learn early how good a hand he'd make in a ruckus.

". . . and," Andy concluded thoughtfully, "in

spite of what Deb says about him not being a trouble-maker, I'd stake my poke that he's a hound-dawg for battle once he gets mad. I've seen these slow, good-natured hombres in action before, and never yet have I seen one that couldn't whip his weight in puma-cats, once he was riled proper."

Felipe and Denny had popped from the blacksmith shop. Felipe had heard Andy's words, and intended to go to Winghorse, too, if it could be managed.

"*Seguro*, Andee, I'll be right weeth you. My *caballo* grows—how you say heem?—hoggish-fat?—weeth no saddle on the back for t'ree-four days, now—"

"Huh? Where are you going?" Andy gazed down from his saddle at the smiling *mestizo*.

"To Winghorse, *amigo*," Felipe replied innocently. "Did you not say to saddle my *caballo*, and prepare to go weeth—?"

"You know dang well I didn't," Andy smiled suddenly. "Nope, you ain't going. You and I always get into trouble—"

"And out again," the *mestizo* returned pleadingly. "Look you, Andee, I'm always obey the orders like the tin-soldier. When you say I am stay here, I am stay here. Not once have I been to Weenghorse, since the night we arriv'. I would like to see theese Rudabaugh hombre an' wring hees neck. Nevair, do I even yet lay the eye on

213

theese man. Maybee so, it is, you will be force' to make the introduction—no?"

"Not to Rudabaugh," Andy chuckled. "You can introduce yourself, Felipe, when you see Rudabaugh—preferably with one of Mister Sam Colt's lead slugs—when the time comes."

"Is good," Felipe nodded. "But, now, I ride to town with you—no?"

"No," Andy replied. "Kitten and I are making this trip alone—and we're not hunting trouble. This is to be a peaceful journey."

"As you say," Felipe sighed in resignation.

"Yeah, I'll bet it's going to be a peaceful journey," Denny Devers said ironically. "You got blood in your eye, right now, Andy. You'd better let me go along. Now, wait, don't get me wrong. I won't start anything. I just wanted to get a sack of Bull. I'm plum out and cravin' a smoke—"

"Saving empty sacks, eh?" Andy eyed the Durham tag dangling from Denny's shirt pocket. "Nope, you're out too, Denny. Kitten and I are headed on a peace mission and you don't fit in."

By this time, Kitten was mounted and moving toward the blacksmith shop. Andy touched spur to his pony's ribs and joined the big puncher. Side by side, they loped out of the ranch yard and turned on the trail that led toward Winghorse. Once away from the ranch, they plunged in their spurs and lined out their mounts in swift, ground-devouring strides that soon left the Crown far behind.

Felipe and Denny watched sadly from the door of the blacksmith shop until the two riders had passed from view. Then, disgruntedly, they returned to the job of overhauling the chuck wagon.

"Damn such luck!" Denny exclaimed fervently, slamming a bolt-and-nut down on the floor. "I never do get to see any excitement."

"Don't make the worry," Felipe advised. "The excitement, she is come pret' soon. Maybee not this day—but she is come pret' queeck now. Eet is like you say, Andy has the bloody in hees eye. When that happens always there is hell to pay wages."

"Speaking of money," Denny said suddenly, "didn't I hear you ask Andy, a few days back, if he'd found some cached *pesos*, or something of the kind?"

To date, the Crown crew hadn't been let in on the secret of the treasure. Felipe immediately emulated a clam.

"*Pesos*?" he said blankly. "You mus' be mistake. No doubt eet was *pistols* you overhear us make the *habla* concerning. For the pistols, I'm think, soon there will be plenty to do!"

XVI. WAR TALK

FOR AN HOUR, Andy and Kitten pounded their horses steadily along the trail. The animals were flecked with foam, their hides streaked with sweat and dust. No conversation had passed between the two men. Kitten hadn't once hinted that he would like to know the reason for the journey. Andy looked at the big man racing at his stirrup and wondered if Kitten realized what he might be getting into. Finally, Andy signaled to pull to a walk.

"Kitten," he said soberly, "we're right likely to meet trouble in Winghorse."

Kitten grinned slowly. "Do you think that thought was original with you, Andy?" he drawled.

Andy didn't say anything for a few minutes. Kitten showed no sign of continuing the conversation. The horses walked on, side by side, hoofs kicking up slow dust along the trail. Winghorse was only a short mile distant, now.

Andy spoke again, not quite sure that the big puncher realized the form trouble might take. "It's this way, Kitten, I'm going to try for a plain talk with Rudabaugh, make it clear to him that we don't want a fracas, but that we won't be crowded none, either."

"That ain't a bad idea," Kitten replied calmly.

"What I'm trying to make clear," Andy went on, "Rudabaugh may resent what I say."

"I hope he does," Kitten grunted.

"Lead may get to flying," Andy spoke more plainly. "Rudabaugh may take a shot at you, or me. What then?"

"What then, Andy?" Kitten repeated gently. "We-ell, if Rudabaugh ever takes a shot at me, and I find it out, I'm right li'ble to fill him so full of lead that his carcass won't hold liquor—though he might assay right high in mineral value."

"That's fine, as far as it goes," Andy said, "but you're paid wages on the Crown to work cow critters—not to make gun fights. Miss Deborah didn't hire you for your gun-work."

"Miss Deborah," Kitten said a trifle stiffly, "pays me wages—Damn good wages—to protect her interests. I can't think of any better way to earn said wages than by throwin' lead in Rudabaugh's direction." The big man seemed to sense what was passing through Andy's mind, and added, "Don't you worry, Andy. I won't sprout myself any wings, even if hot lead does start flyin' around. Me, I've smelt powder smoke in a heap o' places, before this. Lately, I've even got so I crave to smell it some more."

"I'm glad to hear it," Andy nodded soberly. "You're plumb likely to have your cravin's fulfilled."

He knew now that Kitten was no quitter and if

worse came to worse, he could count on Kitten backing him to the last ditch.

The two kicked their ponies in the ribs and swung swiftly past a huge upthrust of granite outcropping that marked the last curve in the trail before Winghorse was sighted. The next instant, the buildings of the town came into view, and then Andy and Kitten were trotting their ponies, side by side, along the street that entered Winghorse.

Suddenly Andy stiffened. Ahead of him, in front of the Brown Jug Saloon, a crowd of men was gathered in the road. Andy immediately sensed that some sort of trouble, connected with his own interests, or Vaughn's, was taking place. Loud voices reached his ears as he and Kitten drew nearer. In a few minutes, they were at the very edge of the crowd, gazing over the heads of the assembled men. Andy took one look; he swore suddenly under his breath. So great was the crowd's interest in what was taking place, that it didn't notice the two riders who had drawn rein on its fringe.

In the center of the circle of men stood Vaughn and Herb Kimball. Kimball's gun was out. Vaughn's hands hung helpless at his sides.

". . . and you go get yoreself a gun—damn *pronto*!" Kimball was snarling. "We've seen just about enough of you yellow bastards, around this neck of the range, you measly . . . !"

Kimball spat out a word that made Vaughn clench his fists and step forward, his face suddenly ashen.

Kimball's six-shooter jerked up to cover Vaughn's body. Vaughn struggled with his temper and came to a reluctant halt.

"C'mon and get it, Vaughn," Kimball sneered, "if you don't like what I called you. C'mon, if yo're so anxious to square up for that name. I'm wishing you'd get a gun, but suit yourself. Come a-rarin' any time."

Andy heard Kimball's gun-hammer click back; he caught the killer gleam in Kimball's bloodshot eyes, as Kimball taunted the unarmed Vaughn.

Andy's six-shooter came out. "You, Kimball," Andy snapped, "put that gun away. If anybody here is yellow, his name is Herb Kimball. I don't see any gun on Vaughn. Dammit! Put that gun away, I said!"

The crowd noticed Andy and Kitten for the first time. Kimball spun around, stark fear suddenly washing across his ugly features. He looked nervously back at Vaughn, then toward Andy again. The gun in his hand was slowly lowered, as he opened his mouth to speak, but no words came forth.

In that instant, Vaughn leaped forward, his grizzled features crimson with righteous anger. His clenched fist crashed against Kimball's jaw, spinning the larger man off balance. Only the nearness of the crowd saved Kimball from falling. Someone pushed him back toward Vaughn.

Fists doubled, Vaughn closed in again. "Come on, you dirty scut," he raged, "let's see how good you are without your gun."

"Hold it, Ethan," Andy cut in sternly. "I don't blame you for socking Kimball, after what he called you, but once is enough. You squared the account."

Reluctantly, Vaughn relaxed, though his eyes still gleamed belligerently. Kimball righted himself, holstered his forty-five and commenced to back away through the crowd, his face a contorted mask of hate.

"You'll hear from me again, Farlow," he threatened, "before the day's over. You stay in Winghorse and you'll hear plenty."

"If that's a challenge," Andy spoke sternly from his saddle, "I'm willing to take it up any time you say, Kimball. Right now, suits me."

Kimball cursed, still backing through the crowd. He was on the outside of the circle of men now, directly opposite Andy and Kitten.

"Yeah," Kimball rasped, "you would be willing to take it up now—'specially when you got one of yore hands with you. But you wait. I'll be back. We'll even the score."

The man jerked angrily around and walked swiftly off, along the street. The crowd commenced to break up.

Andy and Kitten guided their ponies over to the Brown Jug tie-rail and dismounted. Vaughn was talking excitedly. Andy turned to him.

"Look here, Ethan," Andy said quietly, "you calm down. The fracas is over. You squared your account—"

"But—but—but—!" Vaughn sputtered.

"Might's well take it easy, Ethan," Kitten spoke easily. "The way you're carryin' on ain't good for blood-pressure. It don't ever pay to get excited."

"C'mon, we'll go in and get a drink," Andy continued, taking Vaughn's arm. "You can tell me what happened inside."

The three men entered the Brown Jug. Toby Byers was behind the bar. He greeted his customers with a nervous smile.

"Good thing you and Kitten happened along, Andy," he said.

"I'll tell a man," Vaughn said fervently. "Kimball had me plumb riled. Gun or no gun, I'd a rushed him, and he'd have plugged me."

"Exactly what he was working you into," Andy said grimly. "You should have held your temper, Ethan."

"There's times when a man can't," Vaughn growled.

"How about a drink, Toby?" Andy cut in.

"What'll it be, gents? You're the first customers I've had today."

The men gave their orders. Toby placed a bottle

and tumblers on the bar. By the time the drinks were consumed, Vaughn had calmed down.

"Now," Andy suggested, "let's have the story, Ethan. Just what happened?"

Nervously, Vaughn pushed back the gray hair that drooped on his forehead, below his sombrero brim. "There isn't much to tell, Andy. I'm still stating that it's a good thing you arrived. Gun or no gun, I'd come to the end of my rope. I—"

"So you said before," Andy smiled, "a dozen times, anyway. But where was your gun?"

"I left it home," Vaughn explained. "I figured I might avoid an argument thataway, in case I run counter to any of the Rudabaugh crowd. You see, I come in for Cal's body—drove my buckboard in. But before I went to the undertaker's, I figured to see Rudabaugh and talk peaceful with him, if possible—just try to make it clear to him that I won't be pushed clean off'n the earth. But I didn't intend makin' any war talk—"

"I rode in with something the same intentions," Andy said. "Likewise, I figured I might see Quillan—"

"The murderin' buzzard," Vaughn spat. "Only for him, Cal Laramie would still be alive—"

"I figure Quillan should be brought to trial," Andy cut in. "I thought there was just a chance that Rudabaugh might be persuaded to see things our way—not that I counted on it very much, though. But I interrupted you—did you see Rudabaugh?"

Vaughn shook his head. "He's in town, some place, though. Two or three people told me they'd seen him. When I couldn't find Rudabaugh, I went to Sheriff Baggs and demanded that he arrest Quillan. Baggs wouldn't, of course. That swollen fathead won't do a thing without Rudabaugh puts his approval on it."

"What did Baggs say?" Andy asked.

"The cowardly son!" Vaughn spat. "About what you'd expect him to say. He claims there's nothing he can do. Says Cal was killed in a fair fight. And besides, he claims he doesn't know where Quillan is, either, though I talked to a feller that said he saw Quillan hanging around town, earlier in the day. He's probably keepin' out of sight, some place. Trouble is, Puffy Baggs is plumb afeared of Rudabaugh. So long as he holds office, we never will get justice."

"Baggs is a mess—no doubt about that," Andy said grimly. "I reckon I'll have to talk turkey to that big windbag, when I get a chance. . . . But what brought on the trouble with Kimball?"

"I'd got back on the seat of my wagon and was headin' for the undertaker's. Then, when I was passin' here, I felt the need of a drink. I was so plumb disgusted at not findin' Rudabaugh and the way Puffy Baggs acted that nothin' would relieve my feelin's but a slug of red-eye—"

"I don't blame you," Kitten grunted.

"I pulled my wagon to a stop, out front,"

Vaughn went on. "Just as I was crossin' the sidewalk, headin' in here, Kimball comes along. I tried to pretend I didn't see him, but he grabbed my arm and told me I'd better do my drinkin' at the Winghorse Bar, if I knew what was good for me. He sort of shoved me out in the road, when he said it. I tells him I drink where I choose. One thing led to another and we got to callin' names. Finally, Kimball challenges me to jerk my iron. The dirty son had seen I didn't have a gun in my holster. Why, I left my six-shooter home, on purpose, thinkin' it might help me avoid trouble—"

"Better pack it next time," Andy advised. "There's some skunks that keep askin' for trouble."

"Then Kimball commenced to lay me out for fair," Vaughn continued. "A crowd gathered around, but nobody attempted to interfere. Just about that time, you and Kitten rode up. Mebbe I shouldn't have hit Kimball while you was holding a gun on him, but I was mighty mad and hot inside. Some of the names he laid tongue to would make a sage hen tackle a mountain lion—"

"Look here, Farlow," Sheriff Puffy Baggs' querulous whine broke in on Vaughn's words, "you've been making trouble again."

Baggs came stamping pompously through the swinging doors of the Brown Jug, his right fist clenched on the butt of his holstered gun.

Andy glanced over his shoulder, then swung

slowly around. "Yeah?" Andy queried softly. There was a dangerous gleam in his eyes. "What have I done now?"

"Plenty," the sheriff puffed. "You've overstepped the law this time. You done plenty—"

"Cripes!" Andy swore impatiently. "Put a name to it, Baggs."

"You," the sheriff's eyes dropped before Andy's steely gaze, "you held a gun on Herb Kimball while Vaughn beat him up. Herb's face is all blood—the skin's broken. He's bruised bad—"

An explosive oath from Vaughn interrupted the words.

Andy held up one protesting hand. "You let me handle this, Ethan."

Vaughn fell silent. Andy turned back to Baggs.

"So I've been making trouble, have I, Baggs?" Andy said softly. "Well, now, that's just too damn bad, sheriff. Sure, I held a gun on Kimball. Vaughn admits he struck Kimball—once."

Baggs' eyes bulged a trifle. "You two confessin' to it?"

"Confessin' hell!" Andy snapped. "We're boastin' of it. We'll do it again, if the same situation comes up. You're too thick-headed to realize it, Sheriff, but my action saved Kimball from murderin' Ethan Vaughn. You should be glad that somebody in this town tries to keep the law. And what Kimball got, he deserved—"

"Here, here, here, Farlow!" Baggs said

wrathfully, "You can't talk that way to me. I won't have it."

Andy's soft laugh should have warned the sheriff. "You won't have it?" Andy asked. "Just what are you aiming to do about it, Sheriff Baggs?"

"I'm arrestin' you, that's what," Baggs stated importantly. "Now, you come quiet, or it will be the worse for you. You can't come into my town making trouble." The sheriff drew his gun.

"Making trouble, eh?" Andy's tones were almost gentle. "Well, Puffy, I'm not through making trouble for you, yet."

Moving swiftly, Andy closed in on the startled sheriff. His left hand batted Baggs' six-shooter to one side; his right open palm swung with stinging force across Baggs' face. The sheriff's gun clattered to the floor. Again Andy slapped him with his open hand and again.

Puffy Baggs wiggled and squirmed and sputtered. Both of Andy's open palms were at work now. Slap! Slap! Slap! The smacking blows landed with swift, monotonous regularity, as Baggs backed away and Andy followed closely.

"So I'm making trouble for you, am I?" Andy laughed grimly.

Slap! Slap! Slap! The blows smothered the frightened words that rose to the sheriff's open mouth. Finally, Andy ceased. The sheriff's face was as red as tomato catsup. He wheezed and grunted and gurgled, still backing away, trying to reach the swinging doors.

"Baggs," Andy snapped, "you're just about the poorest excuse for a peace officer I've ever seen. Now, you drag your fat carcass out of here and go find Rudabaugh and tell him you're not taking orders from him any more—"

"I—I—can't do that," Baggs gasped, his eyes bulging. "I—I wouldn't dare—"

"If you don't," Andy's words crackled, "I'll run you out of Winghorse, Baggs."

"I—I—I" the crimson-faced sheriff stammered. "You got me—got me all wrong, Farlow. I do my best to keep law and order—and this is all the thanks—I get for it. I—I ain't never took any orders from Rudabaugh—"

"Don't lie to me," Andy said sternly. "You've still got one chance to make good. Do your part like a man. If you don't—well, I'll not only run you out of Winghorse, but I'll fix it so you won't dare show your face in the whole state. I'll drop a letter to the governor of this state and when he takes action—"

"The governor!" Baggs' face turned swiftly from red to white. "My Gawd, Farlow, that would ruin my political career—"

"Oh, my God," Andy groaned in disgust, turning away. "Get out of here, Baggs. You smell bad. Horrible, in fact. Go see if you can find Rudabaugh. Tell him if he doesn't look me up

227

right soon, I'm aiming to start looking for him. Vaughn says he isn't to be found in town, but I'm going to stick around for a spell and see for myself. Go on, get going. And don't forget your gun. If you had the brains of a louse, you'd use it to blow the top off your empty head. Now, drift! Hit the breeze *pronto*! Scatter! If you don't I'm plumb likely to get a notion to gun-whip you."

Kitten gave the sheriff's six-shooter a shove with his foot, sent the weapon spinning across the floor. Whimpering with fright, Baggs stooped and retrieved the gun, then turned and sped like a clumsy rabbit toward the door, nearly tripping over his own feet in his haste to depart from the Brown Jug. The white marks of Andy's fingers still showed plainly on his usually florid countenance.

There was a few moments' silence after the sheriff had departed. Without a word, the grinning Toby Byers set out drinks.

Vaughn heaved a long satisfied sigh. "Andy," he chuckled, "congrats on that little act. Baggs has been needin' that sort of treatment for a long spell. I feel better already. Things are opening up. Hell is due to break loose, I'm thinking. I'm going to get me a gun. You and me have been peaceful as long as possible—and nobody can be peaceful long, with sidewinders rattlin' all around. I'm goin' to get me a gun."

"I got a gun I'll loan you," Toby Byers said.

"Got to thinking I should have one. Bought it two weeks ago. It's never been fired though." He dived under his bar and came up with a Colt's single-action six-shooter in his hand, which he passed across to Vaughn.

Vaughn said "Thanks" and accepted the gun, looking it over. Then, "Got any loads for this? She's a mite longer in the bar'l than I like to use, but it'll do."

Toby reached to his back-bar and got a box of .45 cartridges. Vaughn broke open the box, loaded the six-shooter, and shoved a handful of empty shells in his pocket. He shoved the box back across the bar. "Now, I feel heeled."

"I don't want to seem touchy, fellows," Toby said embarrassedly, "but I don't feel like having my barroom all shot up."

Andy nodded. "We'll keep watch. If we see any 2-R skunks headed this way, we'll move outside to meet 'em."

"Thanks." Toby's voice showed considerable relief.

Kitten moved over near the door.

An hour drifted past, with nothing untoward taking place.

"Looks like we threw a scare into Rudabaugh," Vaughn said.

Andy shrugged his shoulders. "I doubt it. It may be that he isn't in town, after all."

"I'm bettin' a mess of fried rattler's puppies he

is—leastwise, I'm almost sure he was this morning."

"He and Kimball and Quillan may have gone back to their ranch," Andy said. "Maybe Baggs hasn't had a chance yet to tell them what happened." He looked at his watch. "Cripes! It's one o'clock—dinner time. I thought my stomach felt like it was hinting at something. Let's go eat."

Three-quarters of an hour more drifted past, while the three men ate at a restaurant. When they were once more on the street:

"Looks like the excitement was all over for the day," Andy commented a bit disappointedly.

All was peaceful along the sun-bathed street. Men went about their business as usual.

Andy continued, "Ethan, you drove in to get Cal Laramie's body. It don't look like we'll see any further action, today. Mebbe tonight, Rudabaugh will send his guns on the prod. Meanwhile, you might as well drift down to the undertaker's and get Cal's body and drive it out to the Rafter-V."

Vaughn nodded. "I've been thinking the same thing myself. But I'll be back—and I'll bring my men with me. What you and Kitten aim to do?"

"We'll stick around town—until after supper time, anyway."

"Good. I'll be back—and I'll have my own gun, this time, too. And my hands will be heeled. We'll see what's what."

A short time later, Vaughn drove out of

Winghorse. On his buckboard was a long pine box in which lay the remains of Cal Laramie.

"C'mon," Andy said to Kitten, "we might as well drift back to the Brown Jug and kill some more time. I'm commencing to think Rudabaugh and his 2-R snakes aren't in town."

"Which same is plumb disappointing," the big puncher said slowly.

The two men headed toward the Brown Jug, to await Vaughn's return, though by now, Andy felt the stay in Winghorse was just a waste of time.

"I reckon," he said to Kitten, "if I want to see Rudabaugh, I'll have to make a ride to the 2-R."

"Looks thataway," Kitten agreed.

XVII. ROARING FORTY-FIVES!

BUT REECE RUDABAUGH had only been biding his time. In the back room of the Winghorse Bar he sat closeted with Louie Quillan, Tom Porter and Herb Kimball, talking in low tones and drinking steadily from the bottle that stood on the table before them.

Sheriff Puffy Baggs had come, shaken and desperate, to tell of the slapping he'd received at Andy Farlow's hands, and had been thoroughly cursed by Rudabaugh and the others for his pains. What is more, Baggs had been practically kicked out of the Winghorse Bar when he'd tried to warn Rudabaugh it might not be wise to crowd Farlow any farther.

"I tell you I'm cravin' action," Louie Quillan growled, tossing off a glass of whisky and throwing the tumbler to the table.

"What we should do," Tom Porter rasped, "is get our whole crew, Reece, and raid the Rafter-V and then the Crown."

"Now, look here, boys," Rudabaugh said quietly, "what's the use of bringing my crew into this, unless it's necessary. They ain't gun-fighters. You men know that sort of business. They don't. If you'll just listen to me and stay here, Farlow will begin to think we're not in town. I know that Vaughn came in to get Laramie's body. If we keep him waiting long enough, he'll get impatient and start for his ranch. Then, there'll be you three against Farlow and that big, clumsy hand that rode in with him."

"But why should we wait?" Porter wanted to know.

"Common-sense should tell you that," Rudabaugh snapped. "With Vaughn out of town, you'd only have two guns to face—it'll be three against two. That makes it more certain. I'm trying to give you boys the advantage. That's the only sure way."

"So you say," Quillan said meaningly, "but if you want us to have the advantage, Reece, why don't you come along with us? You used to be right good with a gun, if I remember correct. Then we'd be four against three, and we wouldn't have to wait for Vaughn to pull out of Winghorse."

Rudabaugh shook his head. "That's not my idea on the matter," he said.

"You afraid of Farlow's gun?" Quillan asked.

"You know I ain't, Louie. But I'm beyond that now. I hire you hombres to sling lead. I'll get into a fight any time it becomes necessary—but not while I can hire men to fight for me. That's only using my brains, as you'll admit."

"I reckon," Quillan said sullenly. "One way or the other, though, I'd like to see some action. This waiting around is getting on my nerves—"

A knock sounded on the door leading into the back room.

"See what it is," Rudabaugh ordered.

Herb Kimball, his face darkly bruised in the vicinity of the jaw, rose and unbolted the door. Rudabaugh's bartender stuck his head through the opening.

"Boss," he said, speaking to Rudabaugh, "that fellow you paid to watch Vaughn has just reported."

"What's he got to say?" Rudabaugh snapped.

"He says Vaughn drove out of town with Laramie's body, about half an hour ago."

"Why in hell didn't that hombre let us know sooner?"

"That's what I ask him. He claims he was stalling around to see what Farlow and his pard would do."

"Well, out with it."

"Farlow and that big puncher stood talking on the street, a few minutes, then went to the Brown Jug. They're in the Brown Jug now."

"Good. Tell that spy I'm much obliged. Give him a bottle and tell him to clear out of town for a few days."

"Okay, boss."

The bartender withdrew. This time, Kimball didn't rebolt the door. He stood waiting. Rudabaugh got to his feet. Porter and Quillan rose, both moving their holstered guns a trifle nearer the front. Kimball reached for a shotgun in the corner.

"You know what to do, boys," Rudabaugh was saying. "I'll wait here until I hear the shots, then I'll come—no, I'd better stay here until you bring me word. I wouldn't want anybody to think I planned this."

"Reece," Quillan said in ugly tones, "you've gone too far to fool folks regarding your part in this scrap."

Rudabaugh laughed. "Mebbe. It don't bother me any. Once we've put Farlow out of the way, I'll have this town—this whole range—jumping every time I crack the whip. Get going, now, boys—and shoot straight. There's nothing to be afraid of. Three against two—and it'll take mighty fast shooting to match the kind of lead-slinging I know you'll do."

The men passed through the barroom, with never a side glance at the customers lined along the bar. Hard-faced and determined, Quillan, Porter and Kimball pushed out through the swinging doors of the Winghorse Bar. Behind them came further advice from Reece Rudabaugh, though Rudabaugh didn't step outside.

Quillan snarled a short-voiced reply over his shoulder. Porter and Kimball merely nodded. None of the three hesitated in his stride, as he stepped to the sidewalk and started toward the Brown Jug.

The men walked three abreast when they moved out to the dusty road. Kimball strode in the center, carrying a double-barreled shotgun, loaded with buckshot. On his right and left were Porter and Quillan, fingertips brushing gun-butts as they walked.

Eyes straight ahead, looking neither to right nor left, the three advanced steadily toward the Brown Jug. Pedestrians along the street shrank back from the line of march. Whispers ran the length of the thoroughfare. There'd been rumors about town for the past couple of hours of something of this kind. Sidewalks were cleared as though by magic, but from every doorway and window peered curious, fearful eyes, noting the killer masks that served as features on the three men.

"It's the end of Andy Farlow," a man whispered hoarsely to a companion. "Rudabaugh's sending his executioners to finish Farlow."

The other nodded. "Farlow's crowded Big Reece too far this time."

The three killers strode on, speaking no words to any man. Each had had his plans made for him by Rudabaugh; each knew what he was to do. Rudabaugh didn't intend to face Andy Farlow, if it could be avoided.

Quillan, Porter and Kimball were half way to the Brown Jug, when Sheriff Puffy Baggs stepped out from a shelter between two buildings where he had been cowering, trying to bolster his courage to the point of interfering in the prospective fight. Baggs' features were white; his lips moved loosely. He stumbled out to the road, one shaking hand raised in a futile protest.

"Look here, fellers," he commenced in quavering tones, "don't you go for making trouble. I can't stand for anything of that sort. I got my hands full now—" He came to a stop before the advancing three, his knees shaking, his voice refusing further utterance. He looked haggard and old and desperate.

"Out of the way, nit-wit," Porter rasped. "We got a job to do. Get out of our way!"

Baggs moved from their path with some alacrity. "But I told Rudabaugh—" Again he choked on his words.

"We heard what you told Rudabaugh," Kimball spat. "We heard the message Farlow sent to Reece. Reece has given us our orders, and all hell can't stop us now. Farlow has been asking for this. We aim to blast him wide open!"

The three executioners pounded on, with Baggs, like a frightened cur, scrambling along at their heels, begging, protesting, pleading. "Now, now, boys," Baggs whined, trying to hold his voice steady, "you know this ain't right. 'Tain't lawful. Don't lose yore tempers. This will all blow over, if you'll just sit tight. If anything happens and the governor hears of it, it'll mean my job. Please, boys, turn back. I got to keep the peace."

Quillan cursed the sheriff in cold jerky accents, without removing his gaze from the Brown Jug building on the opposite side of the street, farther on. Baggs panted at his heels.

"But I tell you, Louie," Baggs persisted, "this will make bad trouble. Farlow's on the prod." Frightenedly, the sheriff clutched at Quillan's sleeve. "Farlow's bad when he gets started. You don't know him like I do. He's really ready for a fight."

Quillan exploded with an oath. His arm swung savagely back, knocking the sheriff to the road, sending him sprawling.

"Ready for a fight, is he?" Quillan cursed. "Where in hell do you think we're going, Baggs— out to pick daisies?"

Baggs picked himself from the road and scurried for shelter into a nearby harness shop. Here, through the glass of a closed door, he peered out with bulging eyes at that which was to follow.

"I done my best," he moaned to the proprietor of the shop, "I done my best to stop 'em."

The three killers kept steadily on, walking shoulder to shoulder. Another block drifted swiftly to their rear. Suddenly a sharp ejaculation broke from Louie Quillan's lips:

"There's Farlow now! Hold your fire. Get close enough to make every shot count."

Dust puffed up from the road beneath the steady, determined strides of the three, as they slowed pace only a trifle.

Andy and Kitten had just emerged from the

Brown Jug, with the intention of going to the Winghorse Bar to see if they could learn anything regarding Rudabaugh's whereabouts, having grown impatient at waiting longer without word, or sign, from the 2-R owner. Andy was a little in advance of his companion, nearly to the hitch-rack, when he happened to glance across the street.

As his gaze fell on the three killers, they scattered for shelter behind a group of three ponies tethered on their side of the road. Andy and Kitten were in the open, their own mounts a few yards to the left.

"Watch yourself, Kitten!" Andy exclaimed.

He leaped swiftly to one side, right hand darting to hip. A leaden slug whined past his body. A gun sounded unbelievably loud along the street.

Andy's movement brought Herb Kimball into plain view. Kimball was just bringing the buckshot-loaded shotgun to his shoulder.

Andy's six-shooter roared once. He saw Kimball stagger back. To Andy's right and behind him, Kitten's forty-five made a heavy, crashing sound. Andy fired again, this time missing Porter, who replied with two shots from under a pony's belly.

Quillan's six-shooter was thundering savagely. Dust spurted up in tiny clouds at Andy's feet. He and Kitten started at a run across the street, to close in.

He heard Kitten swear, hear the big puncher's forty-five crash out once more. Porter screamed and rolled into plain view, hands tearing at a wound in his stomach.

Kimball had regained his feet by this time, and was reaching for the shotgun he'd dropped. He was having difficulty raising it to his shoulder.

A slug cut the bandanna at Andy's throat, and whined harmlessly on. But Quillan, shielded behind a pony, was getting Andy's range. Andy thumbed one quick shot, furrowing the ear of the pony behind which Quillan was sheltered.

The beast snorted, jerked back, but was brought up short by its tethered reins. In an instant the ponies on both sides had taken fright and were plunging and jerking on their reins, fighting frantically to break loose from the tie-rail that held them. The tie-rail was old. Abruptly, the rail splintered and came loose from the posts!

The three ponies leaped to one side, the tie-rail swinging and lurching from their reins. But Quillan was in plain sight, now. Andy laughed grimly and fired once.

Quillan stopped in mid-stride, his body stretched to tiptoe, before he crashed, full-length, in the dust.

In front of Kimball, still struggling to get his shotgun into action, the three ponies were snorting frantically, plunging this way and that. The tie-rail lashed through the air, one end striking Kimball's head and sending him sprawling, just as he got the shotgun raised to his shoulder.

Kitten was closing in on the run, white fire blazing from his right hand. Kimball groaned and fell back. This time he didn't try to get up.

XVIII. "I'LL SMOKE HIM OUT!"

THREE MEN LAY stretched on the road. Powder smoke floated lazily in the air and drifted off on the breeze to become invisible. An abrupt silence descended on the street as the shattering explosions ceased.

Kitten and Andy gazed at the three bodies sprawled in the dust, bodies which now looked like old dirty heaps of clothing someone had thrown carelessly down. There wasn't any movement to be seen. A few yards off, a shotgun that hadn't even been fired once, lay near the edge of the road.

After a moment, Andy spoke. "It's all over, Kitten," he said, as though with an effort.

The big man nodded silently and commenced to reload his six-shooter. Andy followed suit. The guns were holstered.

Kitten said, "The lead was sure flyin' hot for a minute. Me, I was plumb scared. Them ponies gettin' loose, helped us a heap. They were sure spooky."

"I nicked one of 'em. Quillan was hiding behind it."

"You were thinking fast, Andy."

Andy smiled thinly. "I had to think fast."

Kitten said again, "Me, I was plumb scared."

"I know how you felt. Nasty business all around. I certain thought it was the end."

"It was," Kitten said slowly, "for those three. We're lucky Kimball didn't get that scatter-gun to working."

"I never felt luckier in my life," Andy said grimly. He noticed suddenly that Kitten's fingers were dripping blood. "You're hit, Kitten," he said in some alarm.

Kitten shook his head. "Not to speak of. A slug just glanced off'n the back of my hand. Took some skin off'n my left knuckles. It'll stop bleeding in a minute."

Shouts along the street increased in volume. A crowd commenced to gather as men emerged from stores and houses. The three ponies were still rearing and plunging, half a block down the street, by this time. Several men finally got ropes and subdued them.

Men were talking to Andy and Kitten. Neither paid any particular attention to what was said. Toby Byers emerged from the Brown Jug, bearing a bottle. Andy was examining Kitten's left hand. It proved to be slightly wounded. Andy wrapped it in a bandanna.

Groups of men gathered around the three bodies in the road. A man left the crowd and came over to Andy and Kitten. "You fellers got two of 'em, Farlow—Quillan and Porter. They're stiffening fast. One of them ponies kicked Porter's head in, looks like, but his wound would have finished him, anyhow."

Andy said, "What about Kimball?"

"Hit twice. Neither time serious. Skin off'n his right ribs. One arm broken. He's nigh scart to death—been lyin' doggo, not makin' a movement. Afeared you might finish it up if you knowed he was still alive."

Andy said wearily, "Oh, hell."

Men gathered around, asking questions. Andy and Kitten replied briefly, and started to push through the crowd. Kimball was on his feet, now, braced up by two men. His eyes were nearly closed, his mouth hung open; his face was ashen. One arm dangled helplessly at his side. His shirt was stained crimson. He shrank back as Andy and Kitten approached.

"Don't—don't blame me for this, Farlow," he whined. "I didn't want to do it, but—but Rudabaugh made us. It's all his fault—"

"Don't whine, Kimball," Andy interrupted sternly. "C'mon, I'm taking you to the jail."

"Oh, my Gawd, Farlow! I'm dyin'. I got to have a doctor."

"You'll get a doctor," Andy said coldly, "but you can make to walk to the jail first. You're not hurt bad—not as bad as you should be. We'll see about that doctor, later."

Andy took one arm and with Kitten walking on Kimball's other side, they started off down the street, followed by a crowd. Twice the man almost fainted and Andy and Kitten had to half carry him, but it was from fright, rather than a weakness induced by injuries.

The door to the sheriff's office was closed, when they arrived. Andy put out one foot and kicked it open. The door swung back. They entered and closed the door again.

Andy said sternly, "I figured we'd find you here."

Puffy Baggs was cowering in a chair back of his desk. He tried to speak as Andy appeared, but fear choked his words. Finally, he managed in a quavering tone, "I told 'em you was on the prod, Mister Farlow. I warned 'em what would happen. They wouldn't listen to me. Quillan knocked me down—"

"It's too bad he didn't knock you clean out of the county," Andy snapped. "You started your warnings too late. Maybe now you'll take a brace. Here, get up on your legs and put Kimball in a cell, then get a doctor to fix him up. And be sure you get a good doctor. I don't want the coyote to die. He's due to serve a long sentence."

"Yessir, Mister Farlow, I'll take care of it."

The sheriff came hastily out from behind his desk and roughly seized Kimball's arm. "Come along, you dirty killer," he growled, "I got a cell—"

"Take it easy, Baggs," Andy snapped. "The man's wounded. After all, he did have the nerve to put up a fight—which is more than can be said for you."

"Yessir, Mister Farlow—"

"And when you get through with Kimball, Baggs, you'd better see about those two bodies in the road, in front of the Brown Jug. And move *pronto*! I'm giving you your opportunity to be a man. Try and take advantage of it."

"Yessir, Mister Farlow," Baggs said meekly.

"C'mon, Kitten," Andy said disgustedly, "let's get out of here."

Kitten opened the sheriff's door and the two strode out to the street. Here, they paused a moment. Most of the crowd had evaporated by this time.

Kitten said, "Where next?" while he and Andy were rolling cigarettes.

Andy said tersely, "Rudabaugh."

"I figured as much," Kitten nodded. He struck and held a light for Andy, then the two strode off along the street.

By the time they'd reached the Winghorse Bar, the big saloon was empty, except for one scared-looking bartender standing behind his counter. There had, apparently, been a hurried exit of Rudabaugh sympathizers.

The barkeep looked at Kitten and Andy, white-faced, and gulped, "What'll you have, gents?"

"Rudabaugh," Andy snapped. "I want Ruda-baugh."

The barkeep swallowed noisily. "Sorry, gents, but Big Reece ain't here."

"Don't lie to me," Andy spoke grimly.

"S'help me Hanner, I don't know where he is—" the man commenced.

"You'll need help if I find you're lying," Andy said.

He started toward the closed door at the end of the barroom, then spoke over his shoulder to Kitten, "Keep your eye on that drink-slinger, Kitten. He might have something up his sleeve."

Kitten nodded. "Don't worry. He won't start anything."

Andy tried the door at the end of the room. It wasn't locked. He shoved it open and found himself looking into Rudabaugh's office. The place looked empty, but to make sure, Andy looked under a big desk at one side, and opened the door of a closet at the rear. Some clothing hung on hooks in the closet; there was no sign of Rudabaugh. A wide-brimmed hat also hung there, and a belt with two holstered guns.

Andy turned and came back to the barroom. He said to the bartender, "Where's Rudabaugh?"

"S'help me God, mister, I don't know. There was some shooting down the street a short time back. Maybe you gents heard that shooting too—"

"Just faintly," Kitten drawled.

"Cut it, hombre," Andy said sternly. "You know who we are. I'm asking for the truth."

"Well, I'm trying to tell you," the barkeep

247

said, nervously. "When the shooting started, Rudabaugh went outside."

"That's the truth?"

"S'help me."

"His guns are hanging back there," Andy pointed out.

"He don't always wear 'em," the bartender said.

"Seems to me he would at a time like this," Andy snapped.

The barkeep shrugged his shoulders. "I don't happen to know what he had in mind when he left. He left. That's all I know."

"His hat's still back there," Andy said.

The bartender shrugged again. "That don't mean nothin'. He's got three or four hats around."

Andy said, "Oh hell," and drew his six-shooter. He leveled it at the bartender. "I'm through talking," Andy said, "you'll tell me where Rudabaugh is, or else. . . ."

The barkeep turned ghostly white. His teeth commenced to chatter. "S'help me God, mister, I don't know."

"That's the truth?"

"God's truth."

Andy put his gun away, deciding that his bluff hadn't been worth while. He eyed the barkeep narrowly, trying to decide whether or not the man was speaking the truth. He had a hunch the fellow was lying; at the same time, Andy decided to give him the benefit of the doubt. The fellow might not know were Rudabaugh had gone.

"All right," Andy nodded more quietly. "Sorry if I've misjudged you."

The barkeep appeared considerably relieved. "I'll tell Big Reece you were here."

"You do that," Andy said shortly, adding, "If I don't see him first. If I do, it won't be necessary for you to say anything. I know Rudabaugh's around town some place. His game is up. He's got to face me, now. I'm through palaverin' around. If you see Reece Rudabaugh before I do, you tell him I'm waiting for him at the Brown Jug—"

"Yessir," the barkeep nodded.

Kitten laughed suddenly. "Seems like," he drawled, "there's a lot of gents sayin' 'yessir' to you, of late, Andy."

"They'll say 'uncle' before I get through with 'em," Andy said grimly. He again turned to the barkeep, "Rudabaugh will be returning here, all right. When he does, you tell him to light out *pronto* for the Brown Jug. Tell him to come with his guns a-smoking—or ready to surrender to the law. But make it clear that he's to come. I'll be waiting for him. If he doesn't show up, I'll round up a crew of gun-slingers and smoke him out of the 2-R—or any other place he hides out. You got that straight, hombre?"

"I got it straight—yessir."

Andy nodded, softening a little. "You tell Rudabaugh I'll be expecting him by nightfall—at latest. Vaughn will be back in town by then. Vaughn has got business with Rudabaugh too. And Vaughn will be bringing Rafter-V hands with him when he comes—men that crave to know just why Cal Laramie had to die. Rudabaugh's in for a showdown. Understand?"

"Yessir, I understand. I'll tell him, if I see him."

Andy nodded shortly. Without another word, he and Kitten left the Winghorse Bar and headed for the street.

On the sidewalk, heading toward the Brown Jug, Kitten looked curiously at his foreman. "Damned if you don't really cut loose," he drawled admiringly, "once you get started. To tell the truth, Andy, I'm plumb surprised."

"I figure you won't be the only one," Andy smiled thinly, "Rudabaugh's going to learn he made a mistake of judgment too."

XIX. DYNAMITE!

FOR A FULL FIVE minutes after Andy and Kitten left the Winghorse Bar, the bartender didn't move. Sweat stood out in tiny beads on his forehead; his lips were pallid. Finally, he gave a long sigh of relief and moved on quaking legs around the end of the bar. He moved cautiously to the swinging doors and, shoving one open, peered nervously outside and along the street. Some of the color had returned to his face as he came back and took his position behind the bar once more.

"They're gone, boss," he said, and his voice shook a little. "Gone to the Brown Jug, I guess, like Farlow said."

Slowly, his features crimson with anger, Big Reece Rudabaugh crawled up from beneath the bar where he had been hiding from Andy's wrath. The barkeep eyed him somewhat resentfully.

Rudabaugh didn't look at his bartender. "I won't forget this, Curly," and Rudabaugh smiled nervously. "You stuck by me like a pal. For a minute or so I was afraid you'd tell Farlow where I was—"

"Fat chance there was of me doing that," the barkeep said bitterly, "with you holding your underarm gun against my belly. You knew damn well I wouldn't dare speak. I don't take that kindly, boss. There wasn't any call to shove that gun into my guts. I'd have stuck by you—"

"Maybe you would and maybe you wouldn't," Rudabaugh cut in. "I was just playing safe."

"Well, I don't want to help play any more such games. The way Farlow looked at me, I expected to feel hot lead, any instant. With you holding one gun on me and him pulling another, geez! I damn near passed out—"

"Aw," Rudabaugh blustered, "you don't want to let Farlow get your nerve that way."

"No?" The barkeep's words were coldly questioning. "I didn't see you showing any great amount of nerve."

Rudabaugh's face went scarlet and he cursed the bartender. The bartender fell silent and, from force of habit, automatically commenced to polish glasses. Rudabaugh jerked a bottle from the back bar, pulled the cork and took a stiff drink, the liquor spilling down his chin and across his shirt-front. Then he moved slowly around to the other side of the bar, carrying the bottle with him. After a minute he put down the bottle and lighted a cigar; his hand, holding the match, had difficulty contacting the tobacco.

"Farlow says," the bartender said after a few minutes, "that he'll be waiting for you in the Brown Jug."

Rudabaugh glared at his employee, then opened up with a torrent of abuse. "You fool," Rudabaugh concluded angrily, "don't you suppose I heard what that damn Farlow said?"

"I reckon you did," the bartender said quietly, "but I promised Farlow I'd tell you, and I'm doing it. If anybody else gets in wrong with that shootin' son, it ain't going to be me."

"Shut your trap," Rudabaugh bellowed hotly. "If I feel like going to the Brown Jug, I'll do it."

"It don't look to me like you got much choice in the matter," the barkeep replied sullenly. "What else can you do?"

"I can go out to my ranch and gather my crew. They'll obey orders. Then, I'll come back and I'll visit the Brown Jug in a way Farlow won't like!"

The barkeep looked dubious. "Sure, you could try that. But how do you know Farlow hasn't posted somebody to cut you off? You can't lick Farlow and that big puncher both. You know what that feller told us—Porter, Quillan and Kimball, all down. And Kimball totin' a shot-gun, too. You got to hand it to Farlow and that big cowhand. They're hell on wheels. You can't buck a combination like that, Reece. Why, that feller that brought the news says that Quillan and the others didn't have a chance and that Farlow and—"

"God damn it!" Rudabaugh snarled. "I got ears. You don't need to tell me—"

"You can't count too strong on that crew of yours, neither," the bartender continued. "They're tough in a bunch, but I'd bet they're not real scrappers with their backs against a wall and the odds all even."

Rudabaugh cut the man short with an oath. The polishing of glasses continued in a sullen silence. Rudabaugh made his way to his back room and buckled on his guns. Then he came back and stood near the entrance, undecided what to do next. Five minutes passed while he stood there, peering cautiously over the tops of the swinging doors.

By this time the town had again become normal. Business continued as usual. Men passed along the sidewalk, but none offered to enter the Winghorse Bar. Rudabaugh cursed silently. A shooting affair usually brought increased business to his bar. Now, it looked as though the town was finished with the Winghorse Bar.

Rudabaugh turned and asked querulously, "Where's everybody? Why don't nobody come in?"

"I'm no fortune-teller, but I might make a guess."

"What's your guess?"

The bartender replied, "I figure the Brown Jug is getting the trade. It's probably all over town that Farlow is waiting there for you to show up. And folks is scary about coming here, for fear Farlow will come here to get you, and stray bullets might be flying. Either that, or they're avoiding you, to show Farlow which side they're on. That Farlow cuts a lot of ice right now, boss."

Rudabaugh swore at the man to make him shut up.

The barkeep nodded. "All right, I won't say any more. You know your business."

Rudabaugh calmed down somewhat. "But what'll I do?"

He received a careless shrugging of shoulders for his reply, then, "I can't tell you. I'm just a drink slinger. It's your problem—not mine."

Rudabaugh said wrathfully. "You'd better do some thinking on my problems too. I can get along without you, Curly."

"I already decided that, boss. I drew my wages in advance, or I'd get out right now. But I'll be through at the end of the week."

Rudabaugh started cursing again. The barkeep said nothing. After a time, Rudabaugh fell silent, and returned to his peering over the swinging doors. Rudabaugh swallowed hard. Apparently his star was setting. He stood in a quandary, trying to summon sufficient nerve to face Andy Farlow. There were no two ways about it. He'd have to face Farlow and beat him in fair combat.

"Beat him some way, leastwise," Rudabaugh muttered.

That was the only solution. Wipe out Farlow. Once that was accomplished, Rudabaugh could resume his position in Winghorse. Customers would again flock to his bar. Quillan, Porter and Kimball were gone, but another crew of gunfighters could be built up. That was just a matter of money. Of course, Kimball was still living, it was said. No telling what Kimball might tell. Rudabaugh frowned. He'd have to find some way of stopping Kimball's mouth. Perhaps, a shot through the bars of Kimball's cell, some night. . . .

The sounds of hammering a few doors away, fell on Rudabaugh's ears. His new dance hall under construction. The workmen were going on with their building as though nothing had happened.

"How do they know I'll be here when it's finished?" Rudabaugh speculated. "No, I mustn't even think that. I've hired that job done. I'll go through with it. Those men are earning their wages."

Another wave of fear swept through Rudabaugh. Blood rushed to his face as he grew angry. Could it be that the new dance hall would never open? After all the money he'd spent on labor and materials? He remembered the rock the workmen had been forced to blast out before a foundation could be laid. That had taken a lot of dynamite— all but a few sticks of the supply he had ordered. Was all that money to be wasted? Had he gone to a huge expense for nothing?

At that moment a rider passed Rudabaugh's vision. The rider had slowed to a walk and seemed undetermined whether to proceed or come to a halt. Rudabaugh frowned. He'd seen that man before, somewhere. Memory's fingers traced certain happenings in Rudabaugh's mind. In a country where Mexicans and 'breeds are numerous, one looked like another to Rudabaugh, but somehow the rider looked familiar to Big Reece.

The name Pico is a common one among those of Spanish blood, and if Rudabaugh had ever heard it mentioned in connection with Andy Farlow, he had forgotten the instance. Furthermore, it so chanced that Rudabaugh had never laid eyes on Andy's pardner, since his arrival in Winghorse. All this being the case, it is not strange that Rudabaugh jumped to certain conclusions, upon seeing Felipe Pico ride within his range of vision. Without pausing to consider the matter, Rudabaugh acted. He opened his mouth and called,

"Hey, Pico!"

Felipe had been sent in to find Andy. Deborah had been considerably worried after Andy had departed from the Crown, and after some speculation, the girl had ordered Felipe to ride to Winghorse. Felipe had straddled his pony to a lather in his haste to get to town, but noticing that the town seemed quiet upon his arrival, he had reined his pony to a walk. He pulled up short, upon hearing his name called.

"Hey, Pico!"

Felipe reined his pony toward the hitch-rack, eyes squinting to place the face he saw framed above the swinging doors of the saloon.

"Pico by all that's holy!" Rudabaugh exclaimed. It never occurred to the man to connect Pico with the *mestizo* whom Quillan had been trying to place as Andy's companion on the night Andy and Felipe arrived in Winghorse. Rudabaugh's brain was working too fast in another direction now to think of that. Here was help—the sort of help, Rudabaugh felt, that would pull him out of the hole in which he found himself.

Felipe slipped from his saddle and approached the swinging doors warily. On the Crown Ranch he was known as Felipe, and by no other name. No one, there, excepting Andy, knew that Pico was his surname.

"Come inside here," Rudabaugh ordered gruffly. "I'm glad to find an old friend again, Pico." He held open one of the swinging doors.

Felipe hesitated. "Who are you?" he asked cautiously.

"Don't you remember me, Pico, old friend?"

Rudabaugh stepped back. Felipe entered. The door swung at his back as he followed Rudabaugh into the barroom.

"Have you forgot me, Pico?" Rudabaugh asked genially.

Felipe looked closely at Rudabaugh, then grunted somewhat sourly, "Oh, Race Runyon, eh? I am theenk sure you are string up by necktie party, by theese time, Runyon—"

"Hush, Pico. Forget that name. My name's

Rudabaugh, in this town—Reece Rudabaugh."

"So?" No trace of emotion crossed Felipe's face. He wondered what was up, but decided to keep his mouth shut until he could find out. So this was Reece Rudabaugh. "Is it, *Mister Rudabaugh,*" he asked, smiling, "that you no longer rustle the cows an' steal the horseflesh?"

Rudabaugh shook his head hastily and frowned. "You forget that, Pico. That's old history. I'm a big man in Winghorse. I got a ranch and a big business. This is my saloon."

Felipe looked around the big room, empty except for himself, Rudabaugh and the bartender. "You are saying big business?" he asked ironically.

Rudabaugh flushed. "There'll be a crowd in later," he said. "Take my word for it. The place is jammed every night. But, look here, I think I've got a job for you. You're in luck. I was just thinking of something when you showed up. You're just the man I need. Come back to my office and we'll talk it over."

Without giving Felipe time to refuse, Rudabaugh went to the bar and secured a bottle and glasses. At the same time he whispered a few words to the bartender. The barkeep frowned, shook his head. Rudabaugh talked a few moments longer and put some money on the bar. After a minute the barkeep nodded and put the money in his hip-pocket.

259

Carrying the bottle and glasses, Rudabaugh escorted Felipe to his office at the back of the room, and closed the door after they had entered. Felipe took a chair near the desk. Rudabaugh poured two drinks and found another seat.

"Well, Pico," he said jovially, after drinks had been consumed, "it's good to see you again. They never caught you after that little affair in Rayecco, eh?"

Felipe frowned. "What affair is theese that you mention?" assuming an appearance of nervousness.

"You know, Pico," Rudabaugh laughed. "You can't stall me. It's that knife-sticking I'm talking about."

"That affair—eet was a fair fight," Felipe protested. "If I am kill that man, it was hees own fault—"

"Yaah!" Rudabaugh sneered. "Try and convince the authorities in Rayecco on that point. They were hot on your trail, Pico. I'm surprised you gave 'em the slip. They were mighty disappointed when they came back to Rayecco, empty-handed. Where did you escape to?"

"Maybe it is bes' if we do not talk about that. I'm feel as you do about the horse stealing you once operate' with so moch of success."

Rudabaugh nodded. "All right, we'll forget ancient history, and come up to date. Who you getting away from this time, Pico? I noticed yore horse was plenty lathered. You been riding fast."

Felipe shrugged his lean shoulders. "Me, I was jus' in leetle hurry—"

"Don't lie to me, Pico. It wouldn't surprise me none to see a sheriff's posse on yore trail, today or tomorrow. Now, don't get mad. I want to be your friend. Look, I think I can hide you. Luck sort of threw you in my hands—"

"You mention' somezing about a job," Felipe reminded. He wondered what Rudabaugh was getting at.

Rudabaugh got down to cases: It's this way, Pico. I got an enemy in town that needs rubbing out. He and another crook leaded three of my friends a spell back. I want to square that account."

"*Socorro*!" Felipe exclaimed. "Three shootings in one day? Who are theese dead hombre?"

"You don't know 'em. Quillan and Porter is the names of the two that was killed. My foreman, Kimball, was bad wounded. Three fine pards— and laid low by a dirty, back-shooting killer called Farlow—him and another coyote named Kittenger."

Felipe's heart leaped, but he maintained his stolid appearance. "Ho! Theese Winghorse, she's tough like a burg—no?"

Rudabaugh nodded. "There's some bad hombres, here, Pico, trying to make a tough town of it. They're out to get my scalp—Hey! Where you going?"

Felipe was half out of his chair. "I'm theenk I'm

better move on," he said nervously. "I'm don't like these toff town, where is scalping and shooting of the guns—"

"Sit down," Rudabaugh said, pushing Felipe back in the chair. "Don't be in a hurry. You can move on after you've done a little job for me."

"What is theese job?"

"This Farlow hombre, I mentioned, is waiting for me in a place called the Brown Jug—him and Kittenger—"

"The Brown Jog?"

"It's down the street a spell. You ain't ever been in Winghorse, before, eh?"

"Me, I'm just come to theese part of the country—recent. Nevair have I seen theese state ontil a month or so backward."

"You'll be able to find the Brown Jug, all right."

"For why am I go to theese Brown Jog?"

"To kill Farlow."

"*Por Dios*!" Felipe was half way to the door, when Rudabaugh caught him and pulled him back. "Leesten, Señor Race Runyon—Rud'baugh—I have no grodge for theese Farlow hombre. Besides, today, he hav' already shoot three men. One more would make no difference to him, if I try to cooking his goose. Me, Felipe Pico, I am not so good of aim weeth the six-shootaire. Maybee another day would be better—"

"Now, take it easy, Pico," Rudabaugh soothed. "You're getting all in a sweat about nothing."

"Is true. I am sweat." Felipe looked worried and pretended to mop perspiration from his brow, while he kept casting uneasy glances toward the door.

"You see," Rudabaugh went on, "you won't have to face Farlow's gun. It'll be simple. And you'll be doing it to help me—an old friend."

"That time in Rayecco," Felipe reminded, "you deed not act like the friend, Señor Rud'baugh."

Rudabaugh spread his hands wide in an appealing gesture. "What could I do, Felipe? I wanted to help you, but I didn't dare. But forget that. . . . I'll pay you well for the job—"

A knock on the door interrupted. The barkeep entered, placed a newspaper-wrapped package on Rudabaugh's desk, and went out, closing the door behind him.

Felipe remained silent, curious to know what Rudabaugh was planning. Rudabaugh unwrapped the package to disclose a stick of dynamite, coiled fuse and detonating cap.

"*Diantre!*" Felipe yelled, jerking back in his chair. "Dynamite!"

"Yes, dynamite!" Rudabaugh replied harshly. "Pico, Farlow's waiting in the Brown Jug. I want you to take this dynamite down there and blast that hombre plumb to hell!"

XX. A JOB FOR PICO

FELIPE'S EYES SEEMED about to pop from his head. "What is theese you say?" he gasped.

Rudabaugh repeated, "I want you to take this dynamite down to the Brown Jug and blow Farlow straight to hell!"

Felipe arose abruptly and headed straight for the door. "I'm jus' remember—I'm promise a man to be in the next state by tonight. I would like to make the accommodation for you, Señor Runyon—Rud'baugh—but my time is short—"

"Hold it, Pico!" Rudabaugh snapped, jerking out one gun. "You come back here and sit down. You're going to do what I say."

Reluctantly, Felipe returned to his chair. Rudabaugh re-holstered his gun. He tried to make his tones sound friendly, "Look here, Pico, there's no use you getting all excited. You might as well realize that—"

"But, Señor Rud'baugh," Felipe protested weakly, "you hav' pick the wrong man for theese job. I'm know nothing of theese blow-to-hell sticks."

Rudabaugh laughed. "Why, it's a cinch. I'll tell you just what to do. Look, I'll fix the stick of dynamite for you."

Felipe looked on, aghast, as Rudabaugh affixed a cap and length of fuse to the stick of explosive.

When he had completed the job, he placed the dynamite warily on the table, then continued his talk, chuckling fiendishly.

"Pico, it will all be down-right simple. All you've got to do is go to the Brown Jug, light this fuse—it's good for three minutes—and when it's nearly burned down, just sort of toss it in the back door of the saloon—"

"Een the back door?" Felipe queried innocently. "Ees there some objection eef I go in by the front?"

"You damn fool! Somebody would be sure to see you."

"Oh, it is that nobody must see me?"

Rudabaugh growled disgustedly, but concealed his impatience long enough to explain the working of the dynamite. Felipe listened intently, though he was already well acquainted with the explosive, its sometimes freaky action and so on. But of this he said nothing.

He shook his head dubiously. "Somebody may get injure'."

Rudabaugh cursed. "Exactly. That's what I want. I'm figurin' this explosive will put an end to Farlow and Kittenger."

"But there may be othairs in the Brown Jog—"

"T'hell with them. It'll teach folks in this town better than to go there for their drinks. Now, I don't want to hear any more objections. There's the dynamite. I've told you what to do. The sooner you get started the better."

"Eet is too dangerous," Felipe shook his head. "I do not want theese job, Señor Rud'baugh."

"I'm paying you a hundred bucks for it. Didn't I tell you that before—"

Felipe laughed scornfully. "Not for two hundred!"

"Three hundred!"

"Nozzing is doing. I am no fool." Felipe wanted to know just how high Rudabaugh would go.

"Don't be a damn fool, Pico," Rudabaugh said roughly. "This job has got to be done. It's Farlow's life or mine."

"Why do you not do eet your ownself?"

"I got other plans. Look, Pico, I'll give you five hundred dollars for the job. That's my final figure."

"I can not see eet at any figure. Suppose I'm get caught—?"

Rudabaugh laughed confidently. "You won't. You'll be out back of the Brown Jug. Folks will be too excited to notice you. If you did get caught— well, the sheriff, here, is a friend of mine. I'll get you off."

Felipe pretended to consider the matter. Finally, he shook his head. "Theese job is not for me."

Black rage flooded Rudabaugh's features. He threw aside all pretence. "By God!" he rasped. "It *is* a job for you. I'm paying you five hundred dollars—"

"The money is nozzing—"

"—and I won't raise my price. I can't afford more, anyway—"

"But, Señor Rud'baugh—"

"You listen to me, Pico. You were wanted bad, in Rayecco, for that knifing—"

"*Madre de Dios*!" Felipe assumed a look of fright. "But that was all made squared up—"

"Don't lie to me, Pico. I don't figure it was. Now, you listen to me—either you blow up the Brown Jug, or I'll turn you over to the sheriff. I'll send you back to Rayecco. And I'll bet there's a posse on your trail, right now. Make up your mind, you knife-slingin' greaser. Do you take my job, or do I send you back to Rayecco?"

"I can not do eet—"

"By Cripes, you will!"

Felipe continued to refuse, but his arguments grew weaker and weaker, in the face of Rudabaugh's threats. Finally, he capitulated.

"But," he added, "suppose theese Farlow hombre what you mention, is leave the Brown Jog before the dynamite makes the blow-up?"

"He won't leave," Rudabaugh grinned nastily. "He's waitin' there for me. He'll wait until dark, anyhow—unless something unexpected happens. Hell, yes, Pico. I'll chance his leaving."

"Is not so good," Felipe frowned, shaking his head, "but I'm try it. Geeve me theese five 'ondred dollar."

"I'll pay you when the job is done, Pico."

"No. I mus' have my pay in the hand—now."

"But, Pico, can't you see—?"

"The cash in the hand—now," Felipe said firmly, "is bettair than two stitches in the time-bush—"

"What in hell you talkin' about?"

Felipe said with some dignity. "I'm speak plain English. The money. I want heem now."

The two wrangled for some time, but in the end, Felipe won his point. Rudabaugh had planned not to pay for the job, once it was done, but now he considered that five hundred dollars was a reasonable figure for disposing of Farlow and the Brown Jug at the same time. At one fell swoop he'd be rid of an enemy and competition in the liquor business.

Rudabaugh nodded at last, rose from his chair and went out to the bar. In a few minutes he returned with five hundred dollars in gold, silver and bills. This money, Felipe distributed about his person. He arose to leave, wrapping the dynamite with its fuse and cap in the newspaper and tucking it under one arm.

"Theese job," he announced confidently, "ees as good as finish'."

Rudabaugh caught him by the arm. "Don't you double-cross me, greaser," he snarled. "If you don't blow up the Brown Jug and everything in it, I'll cut out your heart and eat it for breakfast."

"Roasted or fried?" Felipe queried innocently.

"You'll find out," Rudabaugh growled. "Cut out that joshin'. I don't like it. I've paid you good money. I don't aim to have any greaser double-cross me—"

"Enough!" Felipe drew himself up stiffly. "I hav' pass my word. Me, Felipe Pico, I don' break my word, once she hav' got pass'."

"See that you don't. Get goin', now."

Rudabaugh followed Felipe to the swinging doors and watched while the *mestizo* headed up the street.

"Great Jumpin' Christopher!" Rudabaugh mused, his gaze on Felipe's broad back. "It was a lucky break for me to have that knifing greaser come riding through Winghorse. He'll blow Farlow sky-high. Him not knowing anything about dynamite, he'll pro'bly blow himself to hell, too. Me, I sure got brains."

"Who's your oiler friend?" the bartender asked, seeing that his employer appeared to be in a vastly better humor than had been the case before Felipe arrived.

"Him?" Rudabaugh replied. "Oh, he's just an old acquaintance that I got the deadwood on. I've sent him on a little job to end Farlow."

"With that dynamite?"

"Certain. I told you that's what I wanted it for."

"You didn't say how you were going to work it."

"The Winghorse Bar has got too much competition," Rudabaugh chuckled. "Pico will cut it down considerably. Just you wait. Something big is due to come up to catch our attention." He laughed harshly.

The barkeep paled. "You're not telling me you sent that oiler to blow up the Brown Jug—just so you would get Farlow?"

"And Kittenger."

"I know, but—but, geez! boss—"

"What's eating you, now?"

"There'll be other hombres there, too. Have you forgot that? Innocent men that have never done anything to you?"

"That," Rudabaugh said coldly, "is just too bad for them. It'll teach folks to bring their trade here."

"Reece, you're a devil."

"You're in this as much as I am!"

The bartender looked startled. "How do you figure that?"

"You went and got that dynamite for me. You knew I was going to kill Farlow with it—"

"I know—but, my God, Reece, I didn't know you intended to blow up the whole Brown Jug with everybody in it—" The barkeep's voice faltered.

"Well, you know it now," Rudabaugh returned brutally. "And just remember you got a hand in it, so, if anything comes up, you keep your mouth shut."

"My God, oh, my God," the barkeep muttered

over and over. He slumped weakly back against the back-bar.

Rudabaugh laughed at the man and reached for a bottle and glass on the bar. Lounging over his drink, Rudabaugh waited at the long counter.

The barkeep half-stumbled down toward the end of the bar.

"Where you going?" Rudabaugh snapped.

"I—I feel sort of sick," the man said weakly.

"You stay where you are," Rudabaugh ordered, "or you're li'ble to feel a heap sicker."

The man returned to his former position, a few feet from Rudabaugh. His face was a sickly green color, dotted with beads of perspiration. He was trembling all over.

The minutes passed. Once or twice the barkeep started to say something, but his voice failed. Gradually, the confident smile faded from Rudabaugh's face, and was replaced by an expression of worry.

"By Judas!" he growled, "if that greaser has crossed me up I'll fill him full of lead."

"I hope he has," the barkeep said with sullen defiance.

"You shut your mouth, Curly, or I'll fill you—"

The windows in the Winghorse Bar shook violently. From some distance down the street came the sound of a deafening explosion.

The strain of waiting had passed. Rudabaugh burst into an uncontrolled yell of triumph.

"By God! Pico done it!"

The barkeep was making retching sounds back of the bar. Rudabaugh walked swiftly toward the swinging doors, stepped boldly outside and started at a rapid walk toward the Brown Jug. Men passed him on the run, yelling wildly. Rudabaugh increased his pace. From somewhere a woman's frightened screams carried shrilly along the street. Rudabaugh hurried on.

XXI. FELIPE KEEPS HIS WORD

WHEN FELIPE DEPARTED from the Winghorse Bar, with the newspaper-wrapped dynamite under his arm Rudabaugh's admonitions ringing in his ears, the sun was swinging low toward the western horizon. He left his pony at the hitch-rack and started at a walk toward the Brown Jug.

There was a large number of customers in the Brown Jug when the *mestizo* arrived. Men were waiting to see if Rudabaugh would accept Andy's challenge. More men were gathered about the front of the saloon, on the sidewalk.

Andy spotted Felipe, almost as soon as Felipe entered the saloon. He and Kitten were standing at the bar, with the other customers. Toby Byers was doing a rushing business.

"Felipe!" Andy exclaimed. "What are you doing here?"

"The Señorita Deborah hav' ordair me to ride in," Felipe explained. "Evair since you hav' left she has worry about you. Finally, she say to me, 'Felipe, maybee Andee need the help. You bettair go see.' So, I'm come. That ees all."

"Deborah, eh?" Andy's face lighted. "Gosh! She does think something—" He broke off, flushing, in some confusion, and changed the subject, "What you got in that parcel under your arm?"

"Dynamite," Felipe said simply, "all fix' to go."

"T'hell you say!"

"Dynamite!" Kitten exclaimed.

"Is fact," Felipe replied. He took the prepared stick of dynamite from its wrapping and displayed it. Some of the customers in the saloon commenced to back away.

Andy frowned. "What you aimin' to do with it? What's the idea?"

Felipe grinned. "Me, I'm just take pay—five 'ondred dollar—for bloweeng the Brown Jog skyhigh to hell."

Andy and some of the others laughed, as though at a joke. Then Andy sobered. "You say you were paid five hundred dollars to blow up the Brown Jug?"

"Is fact," Felipe said. "Is cheap at half the price—no?"

"Look here, Felipe," Andy said, "let's have it straight."

"By cripes!" Toby Byers looked pale. "Is this a joke?"

"Is no joke," Felipe returned. He faced Andy again, "I'm speak truth, Andee." Quickly he told Andy of Rudabaugh's mistake in hiring him for the dynamiting job.

Kitten swore softly and started for the doorway before Felipe had finished. Andy caught his arm.

"Wait a minute, Kitten," he said. "I want to get all this story."

Kitten came back to the bar. Customers,

forgetting their fear of the dynamite, crowded close to hear the story. Andy's face grew black as he listened. An angry muttering ran through the saloon. Several men went out to break the news to those waiting outside.

"And look you, Andee," Felipe concluded, "I'm think Rud'baugh have play ball right in our hands. Eet was the bad mistake he made. Now, we have him on the dogwood, eh? We can take up Rud'baugh to prison—or shoot heem—and ron his crew out from theese country. Theese Rud'baugh is one damn fool. Once, in Rayecco—I hav' already told you I'm have the misfortune to put a knife through a man. Rud'baugh knows of theese. He threaten to turn me back to Rayecco—"

"The low-lifed, lousy son of a sin-twisted buzzard!" Andy broke in hotly. "Yep, he's played right into our hands, hiring *you* for this job—" Andy interrupted himself to say, "Wait here. I'm going to the Winghorse and call Rudabaugh out. If he won't come out, I'm going in after him."

Andy started swiftly to the door. Kitten started to follow. Andy whirled back, "You stay here, Kitten. You too, Felipe. Rudabaugh's my meat. I'm going after him alone. Stay here. I don't want anybody to go with me."

His eyes threw back hard, grim reflections from the light over the bar. He nodded once and passed through the swinging doors, calling back over his shoulder, "I'll be right back."

There was a moment's silence, then a buzz of conversation rose in the Brown Jug.

Kitten said, "Have a drink, Felipe?"

Felipe was still holding the stick of dynamite. He started to accept the invitation, when Toby Byers broke in irritatedly to say, "For cripes sake, greaser, put that dynamite in some safe place. You might drop it and—"

"Greaser?" Felipe stiffened, a trifle angrily. "You do not have to worry about me. I'm know all about this blow-'em-high stick. I'm spend long time, mining, one day. I can make leetle explosion, or beeg—"

"C'mon, Mex," a customer said nervously, "put that explosive away, some place. Hell, you'd be first to run if somebody else held it."

"Ees that so?" Felipe's eyes narrowed dangerously. For a moment he was angry, then he cooled down. After all, Byers and the Brown Jug's customers knew very little about him. Felipe resented names such as 'Mex' and 'greaser', but decided for the moment to let it pass, and have some fun instead.

"I asked you to have a drink," Kitten said.

Felipe suddenly grinned, motioning to the stick of dynamite in his hand. "*Muchas gracias*, Kitten, but I hav' not the time for enjoy the drink, now. Theese is serious business."

"Yeah?" Kitten laughed as though at a huge joke. He wondered at the same time about Andy, but Andy had said to remain in the Brown Jug. Kitten laughed again, "Felipe, you're going ahead and earn Rudabaugh's money, eh?"

"Sure. Felipe Pico always keeps his word."

There was some nervous laughter among the customers in the saloon, and more requests for Felipe to put the dynamite away. Several men passed quickly out to the street, muttering something to the effect that they wanted to see if Farlow had found Rudabaugh yet.

The laughter and voices quickly ceased as Felipe scratched a match and held it near the fuse. There came a sudden wild rush for the doorway as men struggled to get out. Cries of "The Mex has gone crazy!" lifted on the air. In a moment the Brown Jug was empty, save for Felipe and a much-alarmed Kitten and Toby Byers.

"Come on, Mex," Toby pleaded in a shaky voice. "Cut the funny business. You don't know how to handle dynamite like a white man does. There'll be an accident—"

Felipe allowed the match to go out. "*White* man?" he said coldly. "You think I'm not—" He broke off again, holding his temper. "You think I am not got as much nerve as you, Señor Byers?"

Byers didn't reply. He kept looking at the stick of dynamite.

"Look here, Felipe," Kitten said soberly, "a joke is a joke, but holdin' that match so near the fuse, like you did a moment ago, is carrying the joke too far. It's plumb dangerous, in fact. You'd better let me have that stick."

Felipe backed away grinning. He'd teach these doubters a lesson. "Eet is no joke—except on Rudabaugh. I am intend to blow theese Brown Jog sky-high from hell to breakfas'." He scratched another match.

"Hey," Toby Byers wailed, "put out that match. You might blow us up. I got quite a bit of money tied up in liquor. You aiming to put me out of business?"

Felipe laughed softly and dropped the lighted match on the floor, stepped on it. He approached the bar and emptied his pockets of money. "See, Señor Byers, I offer to buy your so valuable stock. For theese stock I'm pay five 'ondred dollar which Rud'baugh pay me. Take theese money and get out. In one more moment—pouf!—these Brown Jog gets his handle blowed off." He scratched a third match.

"By cripes!" Kitten whispered in awe. "Felipe has gone insane, I do believe. He's blowed his top. He's gone stark, ravin' mad! . . . Here, Felipe, let me have that dynamite, before your match gets too close to the fuse."

It was all a huge joke to Felipe now. He chuckled and for answer touched the lighted match to the fuse. "In three minutes—pouf!" he grinned.

Kitten backed swiftly toward the swinging doors. Toby Byers' hands moved frantically over the bar as he scooped up the five hundred dollars Felipe had placed there.

"Maybe you're crazy, Mex," Toby muttered, as he crammed the money into his pockets, "but I'm not. Five hundred is a right nice price for my stock and fittings. Do your damndest!"

Byers valuted over the bar and sped past Kitten who was still backing away. He gave a scared yelp as he dashed outside.

Kitten was retreating, step by step. The fuse was hissing and sputtering by this time. Felipe carried the death-dealing object at arm's length and started toward Kitten, who had turned suddenly pale.

"Aw, that ain't real dynamite," Kitten said. "You're just fool-in', Felipe."

The crackling of the fuse carried through Felipe's words: "Is real, Kitten. I'm know what I am doing. But maybee you better make the quick run for outdoors."

Kitten didn't stop to argue longer, but turned and fled outside, heading for the opposite side of the street, to join the big crowd that had gathered there. By this time, Kitten was thoroughly convinced that Felipe had gone insane.

With the lighted dynamite still held at arm's length, Felipe sauntered carelessly through the swinging doors and stopped on the plank porch that fronted the entrance to the saloon. A roar of laughter from the crowd across the street greeted his appearance. Nearly everyone, by this time, believed Felipe was just playing a joke and that which he held in his hand was only a dummy stick of some sort, and not genuine dynamite.

Felipe stood grinning under the wooden awning that shadowed the entrance to the Brown Jug. All eyes were on him—that is, on Felipe as well as on the glowing fuse-end—a third of which was already consumed.

Felipe strutted back and forth on the porch. It was his big moment. He would show these *Americanos* how much nerve and courage a *mestizo* really possessed. Tucking the stick carelessly under one arm, he rolled a cigarette and lighted it from the sputtering fuse-end—two-thirds consumed by this time!

Now, the crowd across the street, having talked to Kitten, commenced to back away and scatter to points of safety. There were wild yells from frightened citizens. Other men wanted to run, but stood as though hypnotized to learn what Felipe would do, and if it would all turn out to be a huge joke, after all.

Felipe laughed loudly. "This should be the lesson to everyone," he cried. "Nevair again allow such skonks as Rud'baugh to enter Winghorse. Let it be the lesson to you!"

He drew deeply on his cigarette and eyed the

sputtering, swiftly traveling fire running up the fuse. Abruptly, the grin faded from Felipe's face. He had waited an instant too long, before pinching out the spark!

"*Socorro*!" he yelled wildly. "I'm theenk this is lesson to me, too!"

Swiftly, he flung the hissing stick of dynamite over his shoulder and through an open window of the Brown Jug, as he leaped for the dubious safety of the street and started to run.

For the barest fraction of an instant all air seemed drawn from the street. A sort of hot quivering silence pervaded the vicinity.

Abruptly the dynamite let go! There came an eardrum-shattering roar that shook Winghorse from end to end!

Felipe stumbled, felt the wind from the concussion whip around and past him, and hurl him violently on his face.

In an instant he was up again, shaky and weak-kneed, a frightened grin illuminating his usually swarthy features. He turned and walked uncertainly back toward the Brown Jug.

A few windows had been shattered in nearby buildings, but none except the Brown Jug had been damaged to any extent. Gray smoke rolled from the doorway of the saloon and one corner of the structure was crumbled and sagging weakly. Men were approaching at a run, now, to surround Felipe.

"You see," he smiled, white teeth flashing, "what would have 'appen, if Rud'baugh had hees way? As it is, no one is injure'. Me, Felipe Pico, I have see to that!"

XXII. GUN SMOKE!

ANDY HAD nearly reached the Winghorse Bar when the noise of the explosion struck his ears. He felt a sudden breath of air sucked down the street. Andy stopped short.

"Oh, hell!" he groaned. "Felipe has had an accident with that dynamite."

It never for an instant entered Andy's head that the *mestizo* had purposely exploded the dynamite. He started to turn back toward the Brown Jug, then stopped again. Men were running past him, mouthing unintelligible, excited words.

Abruptly, Andy again turned toward the Winghorse Bar. "I started for Rudabaugh," he muttered doggedly. "If Felipe's hurt, there'll be plenty to take care of him. If he isn't, and I went back, Rudabaugh might escape. In either event, there's nothing I can do for Felipe now, that others won't do. Kitten's there. He'll handle things."

Andy strode determinedly on, pushing past groups of running men headed in the opposite direction. One man stopped, seized Andy by the sleeve, and yelled something unintelligible while he gestured frantically toward the Brown Jug. Andy shook him off and kept grimly to his course, walking in the center of the road, now.

Suddenly, he caught sight of Rudabaugh, hastening toward him At the same instant, the big man spied Andy. Rudabaugh's face went livid with rage and disappointment. He stopped short, made as though to turn back, and again hesitated.

Andy walked deliberately toward the man, right finger-tips brushing the walnut butt of his six-shooter.

"I want you, Rudabaugh!" Andy called clearly. "Your game's finished. You picked the wrong man for your dynamiting."

Rudabaugh cursed. One hand commenced to edge toward the gun at his right hip; his left was closing on the other gun-butt. Pedestrians halted to listen, then recognizing the two men, commenced to back away.

"What are you crabbin' about now, Farlow?" Rudabaugh's voice was hard with burning rage. "What dynamiting you talking about—?"

"Felipe slings a straight loop, Rudabaugh," Andy said grimly. "He doesn't double-cross his friends." Then sharply, "Don't try it!"

Rudabaugh's hands had closed about gun-butts. His left gun came out, even as Andy drew. Two shots sounded almost as one. Rudabaugh's bullet missed. Andy's slug, aimed for the body, went wide, striking the gun in Rudabaugh's left hand. The gun went spinning through the air.

Andy fired again, as Rudabaugh brought his right gun into action. Andy saw a puff of dust raise from Rudabaugh's vest, near the shoulder. At the same instant he felt the sombrero jerk on his head. Rudabaugh was shooting too high.

Even as that thought crossed Andy's mind, he saw Rudabaugh right himself, cursing. White fire and smoke lanced from Rudabaugh's gun-barrel. Andy swayed back, one boot-heel caught on an imbedded rock in the road. Something struck his shoulder a tremendous smash as he tipped and went down. Abruptly, he found himself seated on the earth, thumbing a shot from his gun.

Even as he fell, Andy saw Rudabaugh crashing down. Smoke drifted between the two men. Sweat stood out on Andy's forehead, trickled down into his eyes. There was a loud roaring in his ears. He brushed his vision clear just in time to see Rudabaugh reaching for the gun he'd dropped.

Both men were on the ground now. Andy laughed grimly. Through a sort of crimson fog he saw Rudabaugh, sprawled like a great frog, fighting to raise his weapon for a final try. Andy waited for his own head to clear. No use tryin' to shoot straight when a feller's nerves are upset this way.

He watched through that swirling crimson fog and saw Rudabaugh's gun raise deliberately toward him. The weapon jerked in Rudabaugh's hand. Living flame spurted from the barrel. Again, Andy gave that grim dogged laugh. He'd heard the leaden missile whine high overhead. Andy's brain was clearing slowly.

With a tremendous effort, Rudabaugh clambered to his knees. Once more his gun came up. He was holding it with both hands. The man was fighting desperately to steady himself.

Andy's head was clear now. Slowly, deliberately, he lifted his six-shooter, taking careful aim. He followed his first shot with a quick second one. A look of agony crossed Rudabaugh's face. He stiffened and pulled trigger. But his bullet ripped into the earth this time. Clawing frantically at his breast, he fell forward and lay still.

A grim smile curved Andy's lips. He *knew* the end had come to Reece Rudabaugh. Andy was still seated on the earth. Methodically, he punched out his empty shells and reloaded the cylinder of his six-shooter. Then, he arose—slowly, but under his own power.

A group of men swept up and engulfed him, all talking at once. Andy's shoulder didn't hurt now, he just felt numb. A loud excited yelling carried swiftly along the length of the street. A man pushed through the crowd, placed his lips close to Andy's ear and fairly yelled the news that Rudabaugh was dead. Andy nodded and turned away. He already had that information.

"Goddlemighty!" a new voice broke in. "That was great stuff, Mister Farlow. Can I help you to—?"

Andy turned his head and saw Sheriff Puffy Baggs. "Was it?" Andy said coldly.

"Damn' right! Rudabaugh has run things too long. I should have come to my senses long ago, but—"

The sheriff didn't finish. His eyes dropped before Andy's contemptuous gaze. Suddenly Andy felt sorry for the man.

"That's all right, Baggs," Andy said quietly. "We all make mistakes. Forget it. There's work ahead for you."

"What's that, Mister Farlow?" Baggs asked eagerly.

"I want you to raise a posse and ride to the 2-R. Discharge Rudabaugh's crew. Tell 'em Rudabaugh's dead. Tell 'em to get out of the country. We don't want 'em. If they show fight—"

"They won't," Baggs said quickly. "I know that gang. Their nerve will plumb evaporate when they learn how you finished Rudabaugh—hey! you're wounded!"

Andy glanced down. A touch of crimson was seeping through his shirt, high near the left arm. "I don't reckon it's much," Andy dismissed the matter. "One of Rudabaugh's slugs scraped flesh, near the underarm."

"We'll fix that up *pronto*," Baggs said cheerfully.

Before Andy could protest, the sheriff had cut open his shirt to disclose a clean red furrow, just below the arm-pit. While they were examining the wound, a man came running from a store, carrying a clean bed sheet, which he was tearing into strips.

Andy said "Much obliged, pardner." Baggs took the bandages from the man's hands.

Kitten came pushing through the crowd. An expression of relief crossed the big puncher's leathery features when he saw Andy standing.

"Heard you'd gone down, Andy, when I was headin' here," he explained.

"I did," Andy replied. "Tripped and stumbled on something in the road, just as one of Rudabaugh's slugs hit me. The combination had me groggy for a couple of seconds—"

"If you were groggy," a man in the crowd grinned, "I'd like to see you shoot when you're normal."

"I'm hoping," Andy answered, "that all shooting is finished for a long time."

Sheriff Baggs was busily engaged in bandaging Andy's shoulder, while Kitten talked. Kitten occasionally lent a hand in wrapping the wound, but the sheriff was accomplishing a deft, workmanlike job.

". . . I heard that dynamite let go," Andy was saying. "Just what happened? Was Felipe bad hurt? How did it happen, anyway?"

"Damned if it's all clear in my mind," Kitten shook his head. "To me, it looked like Felipe went haywire, all of a sudden. Either he went crazy, or he was just showing off. I don't know which."

"Is he hurt bad?" Andy insisted anxiously.

Kitten shook his head, laughing a little. "I don't

think that 'breed can be hurt. No, he ain't hurt a-tall. The shock of the explosion knocked him down, pounded the breath out of his body. Beyond being a little shaky, when I left to come here, he was all right. I told him to get a drink, while I come running to see what had happened to you. By the same token, I reckon you could use a drink."

A dozen flasks were thrust toward Andy by men in the crowd. Andy accepted a sip from the nearest one, thanked its owner, and handed it back.

The sheriff gave a final delicate pat to the bandage and arranged Andy's shirt. "There you are, Mister Farlow. Doc Griffin couldn't have done a neater job."

"Thanks, Sheriff—and you can forget that 'mister'." He turned again to Kitten: "Come on, we'll get back to the Brown Jug—what's left of it. I want to see Felipe."

"The building ain't hurt to any great extent," Kitten said. "One corner's damaged some—but these old adobe buildings will take a lot of punishment. It would take more than one explosion, like the one Felipe staged, to knock down those thick walls."

Andy nodded and turned back to the sheriff, "Baggs, you'd better see to having Rudabaugh's body removed. Then, gather that posse I mentioned and head for the 2-R."

"I'll do that, Andy, plumb *pronto*," the sheriff

replied, and hurried away to carry out Andy's orders.

Except for a slight throbbing in the region of his left shoulder, Andy was feeling normal again. Someone offered him a horse, but Andy refused with thanks. He and Kitten set out for the Brown Jug on foot, with three-quarters of the citizens of Winghorse strung out at their rear.

But the crowd gradually commenced to drop behind as Andy and Kitten drew near the Brown Jug. It was still cautious about coming close to that "crazy, dynamitin' Mex," as one man expressed it. Very few, apparently, had any desire to approach the building while Felipe was still standing near.

Andy gave a short exclamation of relief when he saw Felipe standing before the damaged building, talking to Toby Byers and two or three other men. Felipe grinned sheepishly as Andy and Kitten came up, and advanced to meet them.

"Thanks to the *buen Dios*! You are unharm'. I was just about to go to you, when someone said you were coming—"

"Suffering rattlers, Felipe! How did the explosion happen? Did you have an accident?"

"Andee!" Sudden concern showed in the *mestizo*'s swarthy features. "You are wounded—"

"I'm all right. It's just a scratch. I asked you a question. How did it happen?"

The sheepish grin returned to Felipe's face. "Eet

290

was all my fault, Andee. I'm make the one beeg fool out of myself. You see, I'm try to show othair men I can be so brave, too. I'm light the fuse, thinking I'm pinch out the fire at the last few seconds. I am nozzing but the show-off. I'm wait too long. There is jus' time to throw that stick of dynamit. Poof! She's go up with the bang! But there ees no great damage done, I'm theenk. Come, we shall see."

XXIII. CASA DE LEONÉS

THE DESCENDING SUN was just dropping below the rolling hills of the *Casa de Leonés* Range, when Andy and Felipe entered the Brown Jug through the swinging doors which had remained in place. Kitten and Toby Byers were close on their heels. No one else chose to enter, though some of the crowd did come a trifle nearer. Winghorse was still distrustful of "that crazy Mex" as they called Felipe, and half expected, any minute, to see him produce another stick of dynamite and light another fuse.

As they passed through the entrance of the Brown Jug, Andy and Felipe looked curiously around.

Toby Byers sighed, "There's a lot of good liquor been wasted, but that ain't no skin off'n my teeth. I got well paid for the stock."

" 'Tain't smashed up like you might expect," Kitten commented.

Broken glass cluttered the floor of the barroom. The bar, itself, had been knocked over. One roof rafter sagged loosely. The odor of spilt liquor was heavy in the acrid, smoky air.

Felipe was asking for details of the fight with Rudabaugh, but Andy was more interested in the extent of the damage to the building. He gave Felipe brief details while he continued his examination.

"Shucks," Andy said at last. "This place can be

292

repaired easily. There's a lot of good liquor been spilt—"

Byers laughed. "It's Felipe's liquor. He bought it off'n me with that five hundred dollars Rudabaugh gave him. I got money enough for that stock to start a bigger place. Maybe I could get the Winghorse Bar—"

"That's not a bad idea," Andy nodded. He glanced around. "These old three-foot walls sure can stand a heap of abuse—"

He stopped suddenly, looking intently at one corner where the wall sagged a trifle. A large section of adobe and rock had crumbled away. Beyond was a dark, irregular-shaped hole forming an opening in the wall.

Andy crossed the floor in quick strides, stooped down, peered into the dark interior, then thrust an arm through the two-foot ragged opening in the damaged wall.

"Andee! What is it?" Felipe exclaimed, sensing the excitement in Andy's quick movements.

"Looks like," and Andy's voice wasn't steady when he spoke, "I was wrong on my guess regarding the *Casa de Leonés* Range, Felipe—"

"What do you mean, Andee?"

"I think we've found the real Home of the Lions," Andy said quickly.

"Andee! Are you sure?"

"Hey," Kitten frowned, "what are you two talking about?"

"Gold, Kitten!" Andy said exultingly. *"Gold pesos!"*

Byers said, "Felipe isn't the only one that's gone crazy."

"Somebody strike a match," Andy said. "It's getting too dark to see."

Kitten, still frowning with perplexity, struck a match.

Byers picked a short length of candle from the floor and held it for Kitten's match. Felipe jerked the candle from Byers' hand and knelt at Andy's side.

Andy was tugging and heaving excitedly at something within the opening in the adobe wall. His wound was entirely forgotten now. Sweat stood out on his forehead as he tugged and panted. Felipe was swearing soft oaths in Spanish. Byers and Kitten had crowded near, now. They were talking too, but no one answered them.

Andy rose and stood to one side. "No can do," he panted. "Opening's too small. Kitten, put your foot against the edge of that hole."

"I don't know what it's all about," Kitten said, "but I'll do it."

Andy explained tersely. "Dan Jenkins buried some treasure here, between these walls, when he built the building, years ago."

Toby Byers gave a groan of dismay. "And me crabbin' about business bein' bad. I knew I should have tried to buy this building."

Nobody heard him.

Kitten raised one powerful foot and jammed it at the edge of the opening. The adobe commenced to crumble. He gave a second powerful kick. A section of wall showed a sudden crack.

"That's enough!" Andy cried. He dropped on his knees again, tugging at the edge of the opening with both hands. Rock and crumbling adobe and dust piled on the floor. Again, Andy thrust his arms through the hole. He was tugging feverishly at something inside.

Then, with a final grunt, he moved back and dragged into view a huge bundle of something wrapped in a section of cowhide and tied with rawhide thongs.

His fingers trembled as he found his knife and cut the rawhide. Dust rose thickly from the movements.

"You are right, Andee!" Felipe exclaimed. "You have found the hiding place."

"It took you to uncover it, *amigo*," Andy grunted, feverishly tugging at the wrappings. Suddenly he jerked back a corner of cowhide to reveal a pile of gold coins gleaming dully in the candle light.

"We've found it!" Andy yelled. He moved from the bundle on the floor, back to the hole in the wall. Again, he thrust his arm through the opening. His voice shook with excitement, "There's—there's m-m-more—two more bundles—n-no, three! G-great guns!"

Outside the Brown Jug, horses pounded to a stop. Andy paused. That was surely Deborah's voice he heard coming from near the hitch-rack. He started toward the door, just as the girl burst into the room, followed by Denny Devers.

"Andy!" Deborah cried. "Thank God, you're safe! I just had to come in and see what was happening. On our way here, we heard an explosion. It seemed we'd never arrive. Then, we heard people on the street saying—"

"Dang nigh killed the horses getting here," Denny grinned. "Somebody said you killed Rudabaugh and there was an explosion— sa-a-ay!" catching sight of the gold *pesos*, "what the hell!"

"The gold, Deb," Andy yelled. "The Spanish *pesos*! We found your dad's hiding place—"

"What's that?" The girl's eyes swept from Andy to the coins on the floor, then back to Andy again. "Andy!" she wailed. "There's blood on your shirt. You've been wounded. Oh-h-h, Andy-y-y-y—!"

"It's nothing, Deb. Just a scratch. Honest. But, look, we found your gold—"

"I-It's far better," and Deborah was smiling through tears of relief, "to have found you safe, Andy honey. You're sure your wound isn't— Andy, tell me—"

Her voice broke. For the moment, all others in the room were forgotten. Thoughts of the gold vanished from Andy's mind. It was as though he and the girl stood alone, facing each other, drawing closer and closer together. And then, suddenly, their bodies touched. Andy's arms whipped about the girl's shoulders with a hungry ferocity that wouldn't longer be denied.

Kitten's jaw dropped, then abruptly, he turned back to the hole in the wall and commenced tugging at the second bundle of coins. Denny Devers came to assist him, shooting questions with machine-gun-like rapidity. Byers found an unbroken bottle of liquor among the débris on the floor, which he and Felipe had considerable difficulty in opening, even though the cork had once been withdrawn.

It was Kitten who brought Deborah and Andy back to consciousness of their surroundings.

"Here's the second one, folks," the big puncher rumbled.

Somewhat self-consciously, Andy and Deborah drew apart. Now, Andy remembered something. He said, and his voice wasn't quite steady, "You're a mighty rich girl, Deb."

"It's half yours, Andy."

Andy shook his head. "I can't take it, girl."

Deborah smiled. "Not even if I throw myself in to boot? Andy, you've got to take it—and me too."

Speechless, Andy shook his head. The girl seized him by the arm, "Come on out back. I want to know all that has happened." Her face crimsoned happily. "You see," turning to the others, "Andy and I have to go out back and learn if any further damage was done to my building— *our* building—"

Andy was blushing furiously. "Felipe, Denny, Kitten—watch this gold. Deb and I have to go out back and see if much damage was done out there—you know, if the back of the building was smashed up—"

"It looks all right from the inside," Toby Byers said dumbly, "you don't need to go out—"

A sudden kick in the shins from Felipe's boot stopped him.

"Anyway, I'd like to see for myself," Andy said, his face hot and red, "I sort of feel responsible."

He took Deborah's arm. The back door of the Brown Jug opened easily. He and the girl disappeared. The door closed again.

Kitten chuckled, "Responsibility sure comes easy to that hombre."

Felipe grinned. "Andee, he is jus' commence to learn what responsibility is. But, *Diantre*! soch easy lessons. We envy him—no?"

Outside there was a staccato pounding of horses' hoofs, then voices. The swinging doors of the Brown Jug banged open. Vaughn and Spareribs Pryor, followed by two Rafter-V punchers came barging in, armed to the teeth.

Vaughn glanced around. "I hear the excitement's all over. That Rudabaugh's finished. That we've arrived too late."

"Too late?" Felipe chuckled. He extended the bottle of liquor he and Byers had opened. "No *señores*, you are jus' in time to drink to the good things that hav' happen. *Salud, amigos!*"

Vaughn accepted the bottle. "Where's Andy?"

Kitten drawled. "Go ahead and drink. Don't wait for Andy to come back. Lord only knows how long he'll be gone—him and Deborah. They're holdin' an important conference—"

"What do you mean?" Vaughn demanded, puzzled. "Where are they?"

"I haven't the least idea how far she's got with him by this time," Kitten chuckled. "And I sure misdoubt that they know themselves. They looked like they were floatin' on air when they left. Meanwhile, Ethan, drink hearty. I know they'd want it that way."

(Allan) William Colt MacDonald was born in Detroit, Michigan in 1891. His formal education concluded after his first three months of high school when he went to work as a lathe operator for Dodge Brothers' Motor Company. His first commercial writing consisted of advertising copy and articles for trade publications. While working in the advertising industry, MacDonald began contributing stories of varying lengths to pulp magazines and his first novel, a Western story, was published by Clayton House in *Ace-high Magazine* in 1925. MacDonald later commented that when this first novel appeared in book form as *Restless Guns* in 1929, 'I quit my job cold.' From the time of that decision on, MacDonald's career became a long string of successes in pulp magazines, hardcover books, films, and eventually original and reprint paperback editions. The Three Mesquiteers, MacDonald's most famous characters, were introduced in 1933 in *Law of the Forty-fives*. His other most famous character creation was Gregory Quist, a railroad detective. Some of MacDonald's finest work occurs outside his series, especially the well researched *Stir Up The Dust* which was published first in a British edition in 1950 and *The Mad Marshal* in 1958. MacDonald's only son, Wallace, recalled how much fun his father had writing Western fiction. It is an apt observation since countless readers have enjoyed his stories now for nearly three quarters of a century.